Queens of Romance

*A collection...
the world's ...*

**Two novels ...
bestselling author**

HELEN
BIANCHIN

"Fans of Helen Bianchin will enjoy this
fast-paced read with deeply emotional
characters and sexy scenes."
—*Romantic Times* on
The Wedding Ultimatum

"Helen Bianchin's latest is packed with
drama, angst and passion."
—*Romantic Times* on
The Pregnancy Proposal

100 Reasons to Celebrate

We invite you to join us in celebrating
Mills & Boon's centenary. Gerald Mills and
Charles Boon founded Mills & Boon Limited
in 1908 and opened offices in London's Covent
Garden. Since then, Mills & Boon has become
a hallmark for romantic fiction, recognised
around the world.

We're proud of our 100 years of publishing
excellence, which wouldn't have been achieved
without the loyalty and enthusiasm of our
authors and readers.

Thank you!

Each month throughout the year there will
be something new and exciting to mark the
centenary, so watch for your favourite authors,
captivating new stories, special limited
edition collections…and more!

HELEN BIANCHIN

Their Wedding Deal

Containing

**The Wedding Ultimatum
& The Pregnancy Proposal**

The Wedding Ultimatum

HELEN BIANCHIN

The
Queens of Romance
Collection

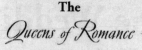

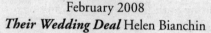

Dear Reader,

I'm delighted to be starting the Queens of Romance collection in the year Mills & Boon celebrates its 100th birthday.

I read my first Mills & Boon® romance when I was twelve, becoming spellbound by the characters, the romance, and even then I made up stories in my head…always romance, of course!

A budding author? Well, that didn't occur until I was married and housebound with three very young children! But there was never any doubt Mills & Boon would be the publisher to whom I'd submit!

My first book was published by Mills & Boon in 1975, and I value being part of their publishing history.

I adore the process of creating characters, exploring a theme, and bringing the story to life. Each book becomes a fascinating voyage of discovery as the characters' personalities develop, and their emotional reaction to each other evolves into everlasting love.

The Wedding Ultimatum and *The Pregnancy Proposal* are brought together for you today in this special centenary collection. I hope you enjoy them.

Regards to all readers of romance in this very special Mills & Boon centenary year,

Helen Bianchin

Helen Bianchin was born in New Zealand and travelled to Australia before marrying her Italian-born husband. After three years they moved, returned to New Zealand with their daughter, had two sons, then resettled in Australia. Encouraged by friends to recount anecdotes of her years as a tobacco sharefarmer's wife living in an Italian community, Helen began setting words on paper and her first novel was published in 1975. An animal lover, she says her terrier and Persian cat regard her study as as much theirs as hers.

Look for *The Martinez Marriage Revenge* by Helen Bianchin in March 2008 from Mills & Boon® Modern™.

CHAPTER ONE

WHAT did one wear to a date with the devil?

Danielle cast a practised eye over the clothes in her wardrobe, made a considered decision, and began dressing with care.

The penthouse suite she shared with her mother in Melbourne's exclusive Brighton suburb had been *home* for as long as she could remember. Luxurious, spacious, it represented the epitome of moneyed class.

But not for much longer. The writing, she reflected grimly, was on the wall. Valued paintings had been sold, secondhand pieces replaced priceless antique furniture. Items of jewellery pawned and auctioned. A standard sedan replaced the stylish Bentley, and creditors circled with shark-like anticipation for the moment bankruptcy was declared and the ultimate mortgaged-to-the-hilt penthouse went on the auction block.

Her mother's collection of credit cards had long reached their ceiling limit, and the La Femme lingerie boutique she jointly owned with Ariane could at best be described as floundering, Danielle admitted wryly as she fixed a diamond stud in each ear. An heirloom that had once belonged to her maternal grandmother, and the only jewellery Danielle had kept.

In less than a week they'd have to walk out of the penthouse, take what personal belongings the bankruptcy court would allow them, seek mediocre rental accommodation, close La Femme, and find employment.

She was twenty-seven, and destitute. It wasn't a good feeling, she reflected as she caught up her evening purse and made her way out to the lift.

It was almost a year since they'd entertained at home, and social occasions were limited to gratis invitations from a few remaining friends loyal to the widow of a man linked to a revered Spanish dynasty.

This evening's meeting was a last-ditch effort to appeal for some form of clemency from the man who owned their apartment building and the shopping complex which housed their boutique. That he also owned a considerable slice of prime city and industrial real estate was immaterial.

In the city's social echelon, Rafe Valdez represented *new money*, Danielle reflected as she reached the basement car park.

An almost obscene fortune accumulated from means, it was rumoured, that didn't bear too close scrutiny.

In his late thirties, he was known to gift large sums to worthy charities, and had, some waspish tongues snidely wagged, used his generous beneficence as an entrée into the élite social circle of the city's rich and famous.

An élite circle to which Danielle and Ariane no longer held access.

Yet she couldn't fail to be aware of his existence. His photo graced the business section of the country's newspapers on occasion, and was reproduced among

the social pages at one function or another...
inevitably accompanied by the latest beautiful young
thing clinging to his arm, a known society matron
anxious to receive media coverage, or any one of several attractive young women who fought for his attention.

Danielle had met him once, almost a year ago, at
a dinner hosted by a so-called friend who, as Ariane's
financial position became known, no longer chose to
extend her hospitality.

Then, she'd taken one look at him and retreated
behind a slight smile and polite but distant social conversation. Self-preservation, she'd qualified at the
time, for to have anything to do with a man of Rafe
Valdez's calibre would be akin to dancing with the
devil.

Now, she had no option. It had taken weeks to
arrange an appointment with him, and it was *he* who
insisted they meet over dinner.

The restaurant he'd nominated was situated in the
inner city, down a one-way narrow lane housing no
fewer than five boutique eating houses. *No parking*
signs were posted on both sides of the lane, and she
circled the block in the slim hope of finding a vacant
space.

Consequently she was ten minutes late...a forgiv-
able time-lag, but not one Rafe Valdez would view
favourably.

She saw him at once, leaning against the small
semicircular bar, and, even as she gave her name to
the *maître d'*, he straightened and made his way towards her.

Tall, dark and dangerous, he bore the chiselled bone structure of his Andalusian ancestors. Eyes as black as sin locked with hers...electric, mesmerising.

An involuntary shiver feathered the length of her spine, and her heart quickened to a thudding beat.

There was something about him that brought all her protective defences to the fore. An intrinsic quality that went beyond the physical impact of the man.

'I hope you haven't been waiting long.'

One dark eyebrow rose slightly. 'Is that an apology?'

His voice was a deep drawl, and held a faint American-accented inflexion.

There was a hint of leashed savagery beneath the sophisticated veneer, an elemental ruthlessness that lent credence to the rumour he'd spent his youth on the Chicago back-streets where only the tough survived.

'Yes.' She met his gaze without flinching. 'If you require an explanation as to *why*...parking was a bitch.'

'You could have taken a taxi.'

'No,' she said evenly. 'I couldn't.' Her budget didn't stretch to taxi fares, and a woman alone didn't choose to use the public-transport system at night.

He lifted a hand and signalled the *maître d'*, whose attentiveness almost bordered on the obsequious as he led them to their table and summoned the drinks steward with an imperious click of his fingers.

Danielle declined wine, ordered a light starter, settled on a main and declined dessert.

'I imagine you're aware why I initiated this meeting?'

He studied her carefully, seeing the pride, the courage...as well as the degree of desperation. 'Why not relax a little, enjoy some food and conversation before we discuss business?'

She held his gaze. 'My sole reason for conversing with you *is* business.'

His faint smile was devoid of humour. 'It's as well I don't possess a fragile ego.'

'I doubt there's anything *fragile* about you.' He was granite, with a heart of stone. What hope did she have of persuading him not to foreclose? Yet she had to try.

'Honesty,' Rafe concluded, 'is an admirable trait.'

The waiter delivered their starter, and she forked a few morsels without appetite, careful not to destroy the chef's artistry as she ate.

All she had to do was get through the next hour...or two. When she left here he would have given her an answer, and her mother's fate as well as her own would be sealed.

She was sure the food was delectable, but her taste-buds appeared to have gone on strike, and she toyed with the main course when it was served, and sipped sparkling mineral water.

He ate with evident enjoyment, his hand movements economical as he utilised cutlery. He looked what he had become, Danielle mused idly...a man among men, attired in impeccable clothes, his suit fashioned by a master tailor. Armani? His deep blue shirt was of the finest cotton, his knotted tie pure silk. The watch adorning his wrist was expensive.

But what of the man beneath the fine clothes? He had a reputation for ruthlessness in the business arena, a power that was utterly merciless on occasion.

Would he be equally inflexible when she voiced her request?

Danielle schooled her nervous system and waited only as long as it took for the waiter to remove their plates before launching into well-rehearsed words.

'Would you be willing to grant us an extension?'

'To what purpose?'

He was going to refuse. Her stomach clenched with tangible pain. 'Ariane can manage the boutique on her own,' she offered. 'While I go to work for someone else.'

'For a wage that will barely cover week-to-week living expenses?' He leaned back in his chair, and indicated the drinks waiter could refill his wine glass. 'It isn't a viable proposition.'

Their debt amounted to a fortune, and one she could never hope to recoup. She met his gaze. 'Does it give you satisfaction to have me beg?'

One eyebrow rose. 'Is that what you are doing?'

Danielle got to her feet and caught up her evening purse. 'Tonight was a mistake.' She turned, only to have her wrist caught in a firm grip.

'Sit down.'

'Why? So you can continue to watch me squirm?' Pink coloured her cheeks, and her brown eyes held a gleam of anger. 'Thanks, but no, thanks.'

He applied pressure and saw her eyes widen with

pain. 'Sit down,' he reiterated with deadly softness. 'We're far from done.'

She looked at her water glass, and for one wild moment she considered flinging its contents in his face.

'Don't.' A silky warning that held immeasurable threat.

'Let go of my wrist.'

'When you resume your seat.'

It was a battle of wills, *his—hers*, and one she didn't want to relinquish. Except there was something prevalent in his dark gaze that warned she could never win against him, and after several tense seconds she sank back into her chair, unconsciously soothing her wrist.

A faint shiver slid over the surface of her skin at the knowledge he could easily have snapped her fragile bones.

'What do you want?' The words slipped out before she could heed them.

Rafe picked up his glass and took a sip of wine, then replaced it on the table as he studied her. 'Let us first discuss what it is that *you* want.'

Wariness curled inside her stomach to mesh with apprehension.

'A wish-list which features a freehold apartment with antique furniture restored, art works, jewellery, all debts cleared.' He waited a beat. 'Ariane's boutique relocated to Toorak Road with an advantageous lease.'

It was impossible to guess his motives, and she

didn't even try. 'That amounts to a considerable sum,' she ventured slowly.

'A million and a half dollars, give or take a few thousand.'

'What did you do?' Her anger simmered beneath the surface, and she held onto it with difficulty. 'Conduct a running inventory?'

'Yes.'

Her fingers clenched until the knuckles showed white. *'Why?'*

'You want me to spell it out?'

He'd sat on the fringes of her life and watched as Ariane's treasured belongings were sold off, one by one? To what purpose?

'I instructed an agent to buy every item you and your mother have been forced to sell.'

What manner of man was he?

One who was prepared to do anything to achieve his objective.

Something which chilled her to the bone.

Danielle examined his chiselled features and felt her nerves stretch to breaking point. *'Why?'*

His gaze was unwavering, and his lips curved slightly in a faint smile that was totally lacking in humour. 'A whim, perhaps?'

A man of Rafe Valdez's ilk hadn't built his life by indulging in a *whim*. Her eyes flashed with barely hidden anger. 'Please. Don't insult my intelligence.'

He lifted the goblet and took a measured sip of wine, then held the stemmed glass and slowly swirled the contents, studying the texture and colour for several seemingly long seconds before shifting his gaze to fuse with her own. 'You intrigue me.'

Something jolted deep inside, and raced through her nervous system with alarming speed. Only a naïve fool would mistake his meaning, and she was neither.

Pride, and sheer courage, enabled her to query with icy calm, 'With almost the entire city's female population, eligible and otherwise—' She paused deliberately, then added with polite sarcasm, 'I fail to see the fascination.'

The waiter served coffee, his smile fixed as he sensed tension thick enough to slice with a knife, then he retreated with polite speed.

Danielle banked down the desire to do the same.

Only the certainty that Rafe Valdez would ignore any histrionics kept her in her seat.

'My father and his father before him laboured in the d'Alboa family vineyards, and considered it an honour to serve such a wealthy landowner.' His gaze never left hers. 'Ironic, wouldn't you agree, that the son of an immigrant peasant has the power to rescue the granddaughter of the revered Joaquin d'Alboa?'

A cold fist closed around her heart. 'This is about *revenge*?'

He smiled, but there was little warmth evident. 'I was merely explaining the connection.'

Danielle watched as he spooned sugar into his black coffee, then lifted the cup to take a measured sip.

His gaze speared hers, his expression enigmatic. 'Everything has a price, don't you agree?'

Why did she get the feeling this was manipulation

at its worst? Yet she had to ask. 'What is it you want?'

'A child of my own to whom I can bequeath my fortune. A child born in wedlock. Who better to conceive and gift me that child than a descendent of the d'Alboa aristocracy?' He watched her features, saw the comprehension, the doubt, then the anger.

'Are you insane?' she demanded in a voice she didn't recognise as her own. 'There are plenty of needy children in the world. Adopt one.'

'No.'

She cast him a look of total incredulity.

'It's a question of needs,' Rafe offered with damnable imperturbability. 'Yours and mine.'

'The hell it is!'

His gaze narrowed, and his expression assumed an implacability that was frightening. 'That's the deal. Take it, or leave it.'

Dear heaven. It was unconscionable. *Wasn't it?*

'Let me get this straight,' she said tightly. 'You're advocating I marry you, and act as a surrogate mother to your child…then walk away?'

He didn't pretend to misunderstand her. 'Not until the child enters the scholastic system.'

She wanted to *hit* him, and nearly did. 'Are we talking kindergarten level, pre-school, or *school*?'

His eyes narrowed fractionally. 'School.'

'Almost seven years, given I should be sufficiently fortunate to fall pregnant immediately?'

'Yes.'

'For which I'll be recompensed to the tune of approximately two hundred thousand dollars for each year?' She paused to bank down the anger and take a fresh breath. 'Paid up front in the manner that freeholds the apartment, clears all debts, restores all Ariane's prized possessions, and resettles the boutique?'

'Yes.'

'And what of the years I spend as your wife?'

'You get to enjoy all the fringe benefits of living in my home, acting as my social hostess, a generous allowance.' He waited a beat. 'And sharing my bed.'

She forced herself to conduct a raking appraisal of his features. 'Forgive me, but I don't see having sex with you as a bonus.'

His expression didn't change. 'That's a foolish statement,' Rafe drawled with a tinge of humour. 'For someone who has no experience of me as her lover.'

She banked down wild images of that powerful body engaged in intimacy, and held his gaze. 'Really? Is that knowledge gleaned from superb feminine acting and countless ''you were *wonderful*, darling'' compliments?'

'Do you require recommendations as to my sexual prowess?'

Why did she have the feeling she was fast moving out of her depth? 'And when I've fulfilled my side of this diabolical scheme you've devised...what then?'

'Elaborate.'

'After the divorce,' she said succinctly.

'That is something for negotiation.'

'I want all the facts now. Do I get to have visiting rights to my child? Or am I to be cast aside after my use-by date?'

'A suitable arrangement will be made.'

'How *suitable*?' she persisted.

'It is not my intention to banish you from the child's life.'

'But you'll legally limit it to minimum time during the holidays and the occasional weekend.' He'd employ the best legal brains in the country to ensure his influence over the child was total.

'And naturally a pre-nuptial agreement will ensure I walk away after the divorce with nothing.'

'You'll be settled in a suitable residence and maintained with a generous allowance until the child comes of age.'

'I imagine you're prepared to put all this in writing?'

'I already have.' He slid a hand into his jacket pocket and withdrew a folded legal document. 'It's signed and notarised.' He placed it on the table in front of her. 'Take it with you, read it carefully, and give me your answer within twenty-four hours.'

It was unbelievable she was still sitting here. Pride had caused her to attempt to walk out on him once. She knew with certainty the next time he would make no move to stop her.

'What you ask is impossible.'

'You're in no position to bargain with me.'

'Is that a veiled threat to withdraw your offer?'

'Your words. Not mine.' He regarded her steadily. 'This is business. Nothing more, nothing less. I have spelt out the terms. It is for you to accept or decline.'

He was that heartless? She felt sickened as she rose to her feet and collected her purse. If she remained much longer in his company she'd say or do something regrettable.

'Thank you for dinner.' Politely spoken words that lacked sincerity.

Rafe lifted a hand and summoned the waiter. 'I'll see you to your car.'

'That's totally unnecessary,' she responded stiffly, and began making her way towards the entrance.

She acknowledged the *maitre d'*, then stepped out onto the pavement, and she had only managed a few steps when a tall male frame drew level.

'In such a hurry to escape?' Rafe drawled, watching the play of street-lighting on her expressive features.

'You got it in one.'

She reached the corner, turned, and walked as quickly as stiletto heels would allow.

Another block and a half, then she'd be free of him, and she almost counted off the seconds until her car was in sight.

'Goodnight.'

He ignored the obvious dismissal and accompanied her to the small sedan, then stood waiting as she unlocked the door and slid in behind the wheel.

The ignition fired and she attempted to pull the door closed, only to have him hold it open as he leaned towards her.

'Twenty-four hours, Danielle,' Rafe reminded silkily. 'Think carefully. You have much to gain, and everything to lose.'

Then he stood back, and she eased the car out of its parking space and into the flow of traffic.

Damn him. Who did he think he was, for heaven's sake?

Don't answer that, an inner voice prompted as she attempted to focus her attention on negotiating her way out of the inner city.

A marriage arranged to the mutual benefit of both partners wasn't unheard of in this day and age.

The question was whether she could enter into such a business agreement with a man she professed to dislike.

A child. Her stomach muscles twisted into a painful knot at the thought of surrogacy. Rafe Valdez had given his verbal assurance she'd retain an active part in the child's life after the divorce.

Was it too high a price to pay?

First, Danielle determined, she'd have a lawyer peruse Rafe's written agreement.

Then she'd make a decision.

CHAPTER TWO

SEVERAL days later Danielle stood at Rafe Valdez's side in an ornate gazebo situated in the gardens of his beautiful Toorak home and exchanged marriage vows directed by a celebrant in the presence of Ariane and Rafe's lawyer, who acted as witnesses.

The previous week had passed in a blur, each day seemingly more hectic than the last as legal documents were signed and Ariane's affairs brought to order pending the wedding itself.

Soon after signing the marriage certificate, Rafe Valdez would attach his signature to an affidavit authorising payment of all Ariane's debts and the restoration of her previously sold assets.

Wealth was equated with power, and he'd used it ruthlessly to achieve his objective.

Danielle extended her hand for him to slip the wedding ring onto her finger, and her own hand shook slightly as she returned the tradition.

'You may kiss the bride.'

She heard the words, experienced momentary panic as the man at her side cupped her face and covered her lips with his own in an evocative open-mouthed kiss that tugged at something deep inside.

Surprise caused her eyes to widen momentarily before she quickly lowered her lashes, forcing a smile as she accepted the celebrant's voiced congratulations, closely duplicated by Ariane and Rafe's lawyer.

Ariane's hug conveyed maternal concern. The words had all been said, and it lent much to Danielle's resolve that she'd managed to convince her mother that her decision to become Rafe Valdez's wife was not born out of capricious insanity!

Now, however, she wasn't so confident.

Bankruptcy had been averted, a considerable debt wiped, and precious d'Alboa possessions restored. All for a price.

One she was about to begin to pay for.

The man who stood at her side was an unknown quantity. Yet before the night was over she'd share her body with his and engage in the most intimate of physical acts.

The knowledge ate at her equilibrium and almost brought her undone.

During the past week she had seen him once, and that had been in his lawyer's office when she'd attached her signature to the pre-nuptial agreement.

One contact had been made by telephone, informing her of the date, time and place their marriage would take place.

This morning her clothes and personal possessions had been transported to his home, and less than an hour ago she'd driven her small sedan through the tall gates guarding his elegant mansion and entered the spacious lobby with Ariane at her side, where they were greeted by Rafe, introduced to his housekeeper, Elena, and then taken upstairs to an elegant suite.

Attired as she was in a classically styled suit of

ivory silk, the only concession towards *bride* was a single ivory rosebud she held in one hand. Her hair was swept up into a smooth twist, and she wore minimum make-up.

Rafe had chosen formal attire, and she'd taken one look at him, noted the impeccable tailoring, the crisp white shirt, and suppressed the momentary urge to flee.

He had the look of an indolent predator, all darkly coiled strength and indomitable power. Enhanced by a tall frame and an impressive breadth of shoulder. Together with an intrinsic quality that was elemental, primitive.

The celebrant handed Rafe the marriage certificate, offered the customary pleasantries, then left.

There was champagne, and Danielle sipped the sparkling liquid, aware of its potential potency, given that she'd eaten a token slice of toast for breakfast and picked at a salad for lunch.

It seemed superfluous, even hypocritical, to have Rafe's lawyer propose a toast to their union, and a proffered tray of hors d'oeuvres did nothing to tempt her appetite.

Rafe's gaze narrowed as he caught a flicker of concern chase across Ariane's features, and he selected a bite-size portion and deliberately fed it to the woman who now bore his name.

He watched as flecks of gold fire sparked in those dark brown eyes, and for a moment he thought she'd refuse. Certain, had they been alone, that she would have.

The lawyer murmured words Danielle didn't catch,

and Rafe placed his champagne flute down on a nearby table. 'If you'll join me in the study for a few minutes?'

An affidavit requiring his signature following the marriage. Their agreement was a done deal. All *she* had to do was deliver…on a very intimate level, and gift him a child.

She felt her stomach twist into a painful knot. There was no room for second thoughts.

Both Ariane and the lawyer took their leave at the same time, and Danielle watched the small sedan ease down the driveway, followed by the lawyer's late-model BMW.

Rafe turned back towards the lobby, and Danielle followed.

'The master bedroom is upstairs overlooking the gardens and pool, if you want to freshen up.' He indicated the wide curving staircase leading to the upper floor. 'Elena will have unpacked your clothes.' He pulled back a cuff. 'Dinner will be served in half an hour.'

She took it as a dismissal, and was relieved when he turned and retraced his steps to the study.

The Spanish influence was much in evidence, Danielle noted as she made her way towards the staircase.

Pale cream marble-tiled floors patterned and edged with a combination of dark grey, black and a heavy forest-green. Mahogany cabinets hugged the wall space, large urns stood atop marble stands, and original artwork graced the cream walls.

High ceilings in the spacious lobby were offset by

an elegant crystal chandelier suspended above an ornate water fountain. A wide balustraded staircase led to the upper floor.

Guest rooms each with an *en suite*, Danielle determined, a comfortable sitting-room, and there was no mistaking the large master bedroom. His-and-her walk-in wardrobes, a large *en suite* containing luxurious fittings and a spa-bath.

Her toiletries and make-up were neatly positioned at one end of the long marble vanity, her clothing and shoes rested in one of the spacious walk-in wardrobes, and the many drawers held her underwear and lingerie.

She let her gaze skim over the room, noting the pleasing neutral colour scheme in cream and ivory, offset by an abundance of low- and high-set mahogany cabinets, a mirrored dressing-table.

It was impossible not to have her gaze linger on the king-size bed with its heavy quilted spread. Equally difficult to ignore the nervous tension curling painfully in the region of her stomach.

Get a grip, she admonished silently. Rafe Valdez is a man like any other.

However, the prospect of having sex with a man she hardly knew, even within the bounds of marriage, wasn't in her comfort zone.

Yet all she had to do was occupy his bed, and allow him to fuse his body with her own. Maybe if she fell pregnant quickly, he'd leave her alone.

She drew a deep breath and averted her attention from the bed. Maybe she should change? Yet it seemed doubtful Rafe would exchange his suit for something less formal, unless, she determined with a quick glance at her watch, he chose to do so within the next few minutes.

'I imagine you've had time to acquaint yourself with the layout,' a deep voice drawled from the doorway, and she turned slowly towards him.

His jacket was hooked over one shoulder, and he'd loosened his tie. He looked dark and dangerous, his breadth of shoulder impressive without the emphasis of superb tailoring.

'You have a beautiful house.' She couldn't for the life of her call it *home*.

'*Gracias.*' His gaze raked her slender curves. 'Dinner is almost ready.'

She made an instant decision. 'I'll only be a few minutes.' With smooth movements she entered her walk-in wardrobe, selected a dress at random, then hastily exchanged the ivory suit for a red shift, cinched a gilt belt at her waist, touched up her lipstick, then emerged into the bedroom.

Rafe was waiting for her, and she met his brooding scrutiny with equanimity, then preceded him from the room.

Calm, poise. She possessed the social skills to employ both, and she slipped into the familiar role as he seated her at the dining-room table.

There was more champagne, and Danielle toyed with the idea of sinking into a pleasant alcoholic haze, only to discard it in favour of alternating the champagne with mineral water sipped slowly between each few mouthfuls of food.

Elena had prepared a veritable feast, and Danielle attempted to do justice to each course.

'Not hungry?'

She met his piercing gaze and held it. 'Not particularly.'

'Relax,' Rafe bade brusquely. 'I'm not about to sweep all this—' he paused to indicate the china, crystal and various serving dishes '—to one side, and ravish you on the table.'

He watched her eyes widen, then become veiled as her lashes lowered. He was adept at reading an expression, skilled in the art of mind-play.

Most women of his acquaintance would have slipped into seduction mode, teasing with the promise of sensual delights beneath the sheets. Sure knowledge of the sexual act and the mutual pleasure each could derive.

Yet the young woman seated opposite him was consumed with nerves. It was evident in the fast-beating pulse at the edge of her throat, the careful way she consumed each mouthful of food.

'I'm relieved to hear it.' She replaced her fork, unable to face another morsel. The image of that broad male frame sweeping the table's contents to the floor, then crushing her beneath his weight...

'Dessert?'

'No.' Was that her voice? It sounded so calm and controlled, when she was anything *but*. 'Thank you,' she declined.

Elena entered the room, gathered their plates, nodded as Rafe relayed they would take dessert and coffee later, then she left.

The need for conversation prompted Danielle to query, 'At what age did you leave Andalusia?'

One eyebrow lifted. 'Question-and-answer time?'

She toyed with the stem of her glass, her gaze level. In this light she could see the tiny lines fanning out from his eyes, the faint groove slashing each cheek. His facial features bore a chiselled look, and his mouth... She could still feel the touch of his lips as he'd claimed her as his wife, sense the slow sweep of his tongue on hers.

'Anything I know of you amounts to hearsay,' Danielle qualified evenly.

'Will the knowing make a difference?' His faint mockery held a cynical edge, and there was a hardness evident she was loath to explore.

'None at all.'

'Yet you'd prefer to delve into my background, discover what shaped and made me the black-hearted devil I am today,' Rafe drawled. 'With what purpose in mind?' A slight smile curved his lips, but didn't reach his eyes. 'To better understand me?'

Two could play at this game, and she didn't hesitate. 'To separate fact from fiction.'

'Fascinating.'

'Yes, isn't it?'

'Don't stop, Danielle.'

She ignored the warning purr in his voice. 'Fiction tags you as having lived on the Chicago streets, a gang member who walked the wrong side of the law.'

'You believe that?' The tone was silk-smooth and dangerous.

She studied him carefully, attempting to see beneath the façade, aware he would permit only a cho-sen few to get close. 'I think you did whatever was necessary to survive.'

'A chequered past, hmm?'

To have acquired great wealth in his lifetime meant risk-taking, and living on the edge.

'Is any of it fact?'

His expression didn't change. 'Some of it.'

A street warrior, shoulder-length hair tied back, dark clothes, with attitude. A leader, rather than a follower.

'Somewhere along the way you cleaned up your act. One assumes crime didn't pay?'

He had a hard-nosed cop to thank for turning his life around. A man who had seen potential beneath the bravado, and fostered it, directing the anger to-wards oriental combat skills in a back-street *dojo*, where discipline was of the mind as well as the body, a spiritualism that channelled energy into something meaningful. That, and one man's faith in his ability to succeed.

He had gone back to school, gained a college schol-arship and worked his butt off, graduating with hon-ours. The cop had pulled in a favour that gave him a chance...and the rest was history.

No one knew he'd arranged a retirement package and heavily supplemented the cop's superannuation plan. Or that he'd organised privately funded assis-tance to provide street kids with sports centres. Centres he personally visited each time he returned to the States.

'Let's just say I made the decision to walk on the

right side of the law,' Rafe declared with thinly veiled mockery.

'That's all you're going to tell me?'

'For now.'

'You didn't answer my original question,' she pursued.

He didn't pretend to misunderstand. 'I was nine years old.' And life, as he knew it, had changed forever. Tension, friction, and a disenchanted father unable to get steady work had eventually split the family. Lack of money had ensured a downhill spiral that fashioned his youth and robbed him of both parents at an early age.

Dusk encroached, and Danielle watched as the day's colours began to fade. There was almost a surreal quality as night descended, an eery stillness before electric lights sprang to life, providing illumination.

'More champagne?'

Danielle met his gaze and was unable to determine anything from his expression. 'No, thanks.'

'We'll move into the sitting-room, and I'll have Elena serve coffee.'

'Does Elena live in the house?'

'No. She comes in Tuesday through to Saturday with her husband, Antonio. Elena looks after the house, prepares and leaves me an evening meal when required, and Antonio takes care of the grounds, the pool, any minor maintenance.'

Danielle took her coffee sweet and black, and she sipped the brew slowly. How long before he would suggest they go to bed? An hour…less?

There was a part of her that wanted the sex over and done with. Another that wished she could slip into an accomplished seduction mode.

'The Toorak boutique is ready for Ariane to move in her stock,' Rafe informed. 'I've organised for transportation tomorrow.'

'I'll ring and arrange to meet her there.'

'Aren't you forgetting something?'

She looked askance at him in silence.

'You're now my wife.'

'Ariane and I are business partners. It wouldn't be fair of me to expect her to set up stock alone in our new premises.'

He examined her features, taking his time before offering comment. 'What if I've made arrangements that preclude you being available to assist your mother?'

'Have you?'

'We're due to attend a tennis party in a private home at two in the afternoon.'

'Which leaves me the morning free to help Ariane,' she responded evenly.

'You have no need to work.'

'You expect me to sit in this house twiddling my thumbs while I wait for you to service me at the end of the day.'

'*Por Dios.*' The oath slipped softly from his tongue. '*Service* you?'

There was a quality evident in his voice that sent apprehension scudding down the length of her spine.

'Given that pregnancy is the main objective, sexual activity should be restricted to my fertile cycle.'

It was impossible to ascertain anything from his expression. As a card player he would be brilliant, she perceived. Yet this was not a game.

'Rather like a brood mare put to stud?'

The softness of his tone was deceptive, and although she was willing to swear he hadn't moved a muscle his posture seemed to have assumed a menacing ruthlessness.

'Why not call it what it is?'

His gaze was unwavering, and it took all her courage not to flinch beneath the silent power emanating from the depths of those dark eyes. Evident was a hard intensity that was almost frightening.

'We occupy the same bed each night,' he said with dangerous softness.

'You intend to enforce conjugal rights?'

'Did you hope that I wouldn't?'

'Yes!'

'Your mistake,' he refuted simply.

'That's—' words temporarily failed her '—barbaric.'

'I doubt you've experienced the true meaning of the word.'

Her chin lifted fractionally, and her eyes blazed with open hostility as she watched his lengthy frame uncoil from the chair.

'You expect me to walk calmly upstairs with you?'

'On your feet, or slung over my shoulder.' He effected a negligible shrug. 'Take your pick.'

'You have the sensitivity of an ox!'

'What did you imagine? Pretty words and romance?'

Danielle stepped ahead of him and made her way towards the elegant staircase. 'I should be so fortunate.'

Careless, foolish words, she chastised silently as she reached the upstairs lobby and turned towards the hallway leading to the master bedroom.

The nerves in her stomach seemed to intensify with every step she took, and she was supremely conscious of the man who walked at her side.

There was no easy way to ignore the large bed, or its significance, as she entered the room.

Did her step falter slightly? She hoped not. Hesitation wasn't on the agenda. Without a word she slipped off her shoes, then she crossed to the set of drawers that held her lingerie. There was a beautiful satin and lace nightgown, a gift from Ariane, which she ignored in favour of a cotton T-shirt, then she moved towards the *en suite*.

A shower might help soothe her soul.

Minutes later she'd shed her clothes, removed her make-up, and pinned up her hair. Then she adjusted the water dial to a comfortable temperature, stepped into the large glassed cubicle, and caught up the soap.

Pride ensured she didn't take overlong, and, towelled dry, she completed the usual ritual, donned the T-shirt, then re-entered the bedroom.

Only to have the breath catch in her throat at the sight of Rafe in the process of pulling the covers from the bed.

A towel was knotted at his hips, highlighting a toned body that displayed an admirable flex of muscle with every move he made.

The olive texture of his skin was offset by a smattering of dark hair at his chest, extending in a single line to his navel. Lean hips and powerful thighs added to a composite that exuded raw strength. Also apparent was a primitive alchemy that fascinated and disturbed in equal measure.

She looked little more than a teenager with her face scrubbed clean of make-up and her hair caught into a careless pony-tail, Rafe mused, his gaze narrowing fractionally as he perceived her hesitation.

CHAPTER THREE

'WHICH side of the bed do you prefer?'

One eyebrow arched. 'Does it matter?'

Oh, *hell*. What could she say? *I'm not very good at this*?

She took the few essential steps to bring her to the edge of the mattress, then she sank down onto it, all too aware of Rafe's actions as he loosened the towel.

She quickly averted her gaze. 'Could you turn out the light?' Was that her voice? It sounded as if she had a constriction in her throat.

'No.'

She was willing to swear she detected a hint of amusement as she felt the faint depression as he sank down onto the bed.

'Let's get rid of this, hmm?'

Danielle felt his hands slide up her thighs as he caught hold of the T-shirt's hem and lifted it over her head. A protest rose and died in her throat, and she crossed her arms across her breasts in an automatic reflex action.

He possessed no such reservations, Danielle observed with resentment, aware of his powerful frame, the sheer size of his arousal.

Dear heaven, how was she going to be able to accommodate him?

A hand closed over her wrist and shifted her arm

away from her breasts, and she lowered her lashes in a protective veil. Only to have him tilt her chin.

'Don't hide.'

The chastisement brought a tinge of colour to her cheeks and her lashes flew wide. 'Maybe you're used to bedding a willing female on short acquaintance,' she vented as he lightly traced the contours of her breast. 'But I'm not comfortable getting intimate with someone I barely know!'

Sensation began deep inside and flared through her body, activating a host of nerve cells in open betrayal. Damn him! Did he know what he was doing to her?

Stupid question! Her jaw clenched, silencing the gasp threatening to escape as he teased one nipple, then rolled it gently between thumb and forefinger.

He lowered his head down to hers and brushed his lips against one temple.

'Please.' There was a catch in her voice as she lifted a hand and indicated a nearby lamp.

'I want to see your reaction to my touch,' Rafe murmured as his mouth trailed down towards her own.

Gentle pressure on her shoulders lowered them down onto the mattress, and she lifted her hands to his chest in an attempt to increase the distance between them. Only to have them freeze as he traced her lower lip with the edge of his tongue, then slipped in to tangle with her own in a slow open-mouthed kiss.

He had the skill to render a woman mindless, and he used it mercilessly in an evocative dance that brought her unbidden response.

She was so caught up with the pleasure of it, she was scarcely aware of the seeking trail of his fingers as they explored her waist, the soft indentation of her navel, then traced a slow path to the juncture between her thighs.

She tensed as he probed the moist cleft, and she was powerless to prevent a protest escaping her throat as he circled the sensitive clitoris, teasing it to such a highly sensitised degree she instinctively pushed against his shoulders.

A hollow groan rose and died in her throat as he eased a finger into the moist orifice, imitating the sexual act itself, and she instinctively arched against the increased pressure of his oral stimulation, alternately exulting in it and hating herself, *him*, for the attack on her emotions.

Danielle almost cried with relief as his mouth left hers and sought a sensitive hollow at the base of her throat.

Not content, he trailed a slow path to her breast, teasing the hardened nipple until she tangled her fingers in his hair and endeavoured to shift his head.

Sensation arrowed through her body as he began to suckle shamelessly before shifting his attention to the other sensitised peak, and she gave an anguished groan as his mouth travelled to her waist, then trailed down over her quivering stomach.

He wouldn't... But he did, holding her flailing hands together with effortless ease as he bestowed the most intimate kiss of all.

She attempted to use her feet, her legs, to buck against him, but he simply adjusted them beneath his weight, locking her into immobility as he took his time gifting a sensual feast that shattered her equilibrium and sent her climbing to heights she hadn't known existed.

Did she cry out? She had no idea of time or place as sensation ruled.

He felt her body quiver, heard the husky sounds emerge from her lips, and he levered himself up over her in one fluid movement, nudging her thighs apart as he eased himself into her.

She was tight, despite his preparation, and he took it slow, feeling her stretch, aware of her momentary panic as she attempted to ease the pressure.

His mouth closed over her own, absorbing her startled cry as he withdrew a little before increasing that initial thrust, repeating the action until she took all of him.

Dear heaven. Danielle swallowed painfully against the feeling of complete enclosure as her muscles contracted around him, causing waves of sensation she was unable to control.

Then he began to move, slowly at first, and she twisted her head from one side to the other as the sensation intensified.

She was conscious of him watching her, and, unbidden, her gaze locked with his as he slowly rocked back and forth, increasing the pace until she was able to accept each long thrust.

It happened again, that powerful, almost excruciating, exquisite spiralling sensation that took her so high she felt as if she was going to fall off the edge of the world.

His climax followed soon after, and she witnessed his attempt at control, watched as he lost it, then marvelled at the extent of his passion.

Nothing she'd experienced came close to the primitive emotion he'd managed to arouse. Raw, spellbinding pleasure meshing with complete fulfilment.

It said much for the man who only hours ago had placed his ring on her finger. Was the seduction deliberate? Or was this his usual *modus operandi* in the bedroom?

If so, she decided shakily, it was little wonder women sought him out.

Seconds later she gasped in shocked surprise as he rolled onto his back, carrying her with him. His eyes were impossibly dark and slumberous with sated desire, and her own widened as his fingers tangled in her hair.

'What are you doing?'

'Removing the band from your hair.'

Free, its length spilled down onto her shoulders, and her eyes widened as he finger-combed the thick mass, then he cupped her face and brought it down to angle his mouth to her own in a kiss that tore at the very foundation of her emotions.

So, he could kiss, part of her brain registered dimly. On a score of one to ten, she'd have to accord him a twenty. And then some. Sensual skill…he had it in spades, aware just which buttons to press to achieve a desired effect.

This is a man you profess to hate, remember? For any number of reasons. Uppermost, the diabolical scheme he'd devised, waiving a considerable debt in exchange for several years of her life...and the gift of a child.

With a muted groan she wrenched her mouth away from his and used her hands to push against his chest.

'I'd like to get some sleep.' She'd had as much of him as she felt she could handle for one night.

Yet even as she voiced the words she felt him swell inside her, his arousal stretching and expanding until he filled her completely.

He couldn't, surely? Not so soon?

'So you shall,' Rafe drawled as his hands moved from her waist to shape her breasts. 'Later.'

He teased the tender peaks, brushing his knuckles back and forth, then he traced a feathery path over her midriff, her stomach, to where they were joined.

Her body jolted as sensation flared, and she clutched his chest as he gently rocked his hips in the first of several undulating movements, each more active than the last until she became lost in an electrifying ride that had her crying out as she reached the brink, then tumbled over the edge in a sensual freefall.

She felt the breath tearing from her throat as she endeavoured to control it, and she had no idea that her skin was flushed with sexual heat, or that her eyes held a dreamy almost witching moistness in the aftermath of passion.

Rafe wanted to roll her over onto her back and take his own pleasure in a series of long hard thrusts that would surely shock. Except he tamped down the desire, equally sure it would leave her hurting.

Unless he was mistaken, she'd had few partners, and unimaginative ones at that.

Or she was a superb actress. Something he very much doubted.

With care he disengaged, then slid to his feet and lifted her from the bed. 'Let's go shower.'

Danielle looked at him blankly for a few seconds, then realisation sank in. 'I'm not sharing a shower with you.'

'Yes,' he drawled softly. 'You are.'

He didn't give her the option to protest further, merely swept an arm beneath her knees and carried her into the adjoining *en suite*.

'Put me down!'

Danielle smote a clenched fist against his shoulder as he reached into the capacious tiled cubicle and adjusted the water-temperature dial.

'Don't you *dare*,' she warned sibilantly as he calmly stepped in beside her and closed the glass door.

He was too close, too intimidating, *too much*. After what they'd just shared she didn't want him in her face, and she particularly didn't want to have him administer to her in any way.

'Isn't anything sacred…even my privacy?' she demanded seconds later as he picked up the soap and began lathering her skin.

'Get used to it,' Rafe drawled as she attempted to twist away from him.

Without success, and she sent him a venomous glare that had no effect whatsoever. 'I hate you!'

Hard fingers closed over her wrist before the fist

she aimed at his ribcage could connect. 'Don't,' he warned. 'You won't win.'

He had the height, the strength, to beat her at any-thing she chose to fling at him. Although she did pos-sess an advantage or two...one she didn't hesitate to use, only to have him block it in an instant.

A cry of outrage escaped her lips as he lifted her high against him and curved her legs around his waist.

Gone was any hint of amusement. In its place was hard implacability, and she felt a moment's instinctive unease.

'You want to play?'

The query held a silent warning she was too angry to heed, and without thought she lowered her mouth to his shoulder...and bit him *hard*.

Danielle heard his angry hiss at the same time she tasted blood, and she cried out as he hauled her high, her scream of pain very real as he rendered a love-bite to the tender underside of her breast.

When he lifted his head her stunned gaze locked with his for seemingly long seconds, then with delib-erate intent he took her mouth with his own in a kiss that was almost savage in its intensity.

Hungry, brazen, he ravaged a primitive assault that lashed at her soul.

Any movement was limited as she was held locked close against him. In desperation she flailed fists against his shoulders, his ribcage, anywhere she could connect...without effect.

How long did it last? Danielle had no idea. It seemed like forever, but could only have been minutes before he released her mouth.

He filled her vision, to the extent there was nothing else, only him. Features harsh in their chiselled perfection, his eyes dark as sin. Compelling, ruthless.

Was this the same man who had indulged her in an evocative journey beyond her experience? A lover who'd fostered her reticence and gifted something so wildly sensuous her body still throbbed from his possession?

She was suddenly conscious of the fine needle-spray of water beating down against his back, her own irregular breathing.

The day, its significance, *Rafe*…it all seemed too much, and she fought against the moisture threatening to well in her eyes.

Oh, for heaven's sake, she silently begged…*don't cry*. Tears, even one, would be a sign of weakness she refused to condone.

Yet she was powerless to still the escape of two lone rivulets that rolled in a warm trail to her chin, and she glimpsed a muscle bunching at the edge of his jaw.

Pride kept her from escaping, and she stood still, fighting the tide of emotion that threatened to fragment any remaining shred of composure.

In seeming slow motion he lifted a hand and smoothed a thumb-pad over one cheek, then the other.

Her mouth felt swollen and slightly numb, and she didn't move as he traced its contours before dropping his hand down to his side.

'Get out of here, *mi mujer*,' he directed huskily.

*   *   *

His voice was the catalyst that set her limbs in motion, and she didn't waste a second stepping out from the shower. Her need to be free of his disturbing presence prompted her to snag a towel and fasten it around her damp form before escaping into the bedroom.

There, towelled dry, the T-shirt in place, she spared the large bed a cursory glance with its tangled sheets, dislodged pillows, and made the decision to sleep elsewhere.

'Don't even think about it.'

Danielle turned at the sound of that silky drawl, and watched him move into the room.

'I don't want to sleep with you.' Bald, brave words, spoken with quiet determination.

'Correction…you don't want to have sex with me.' He waited a beat. 'In this instance, *sleep* is the operative word. And we share the same bed.'

'No.'

'I wasn't aware I gave you an option.'

Anger flared anew. 'Go to hell!'

His gaze speared hers. 'Believe you don't want me to take you there.'

'Oh?' She was like a runaway train on a track leading to disaster. 'And what—' she flung an arm in the direction of the *en suite* '—was that happening in there? A *guy* thing? Or a lesson in subjugation?'

'You have a foolish mouth,' Rafe warned with chilling softness.

'If you wanted a meek, subservient wife you should have married someone else.'

'Instead, I chose you.' He paused, spearing her an-

gry gaze with hateful ease. 'The purpose is specific...or have you forgotten so soon?'

Danielle tore her gaze away from his. 'If you touch
me again tonight I'll—'

'Fight me to the death? Scratch my eyes out?' He
leant over the bed, straightened the pillows and
hauled up the bedcovers. 'Be warned, I'm a light
sleeper.'

'What does that have to do with anything?'

'A warning, should you decide to go sleep some-
where else in the middle of the night.'

'You can't—'

'Watch me.'

'You're nothing but a tyrannical bully!'

He unfastened the towel knotted at his waist and
tossed it aside. 'I'll wear only so many insults.' He
slid in beneath the covers. 'Get into bed, Danielle.'

'What if I don't?'

Dark eyes pierced hers. 'I'll put you there.'

A lock of hair fell forward onto her cheek, and she
tucked it back behind her ear in an involuntary gesture.

Capitulation was born out of wisdom...for now.
Although she didn't feel particularly wise as she reluctantly slid into bed. In a final gesture of defiance
she turned her back towards him and hugged the edge
of the mattress.

Something that gave her little satisfaction, for he
merely snapped off the light, plunging the room into
darkness, and she lay there tense, listening to his
breathing slow into a steady rhythm.

How could he slip so easily to sleep? Too much

practice in the face of danger? Or a finely tuned mechanism that permitted him to wake at the slightest sound, the faintest move?

What had he witnessed in his youth to have created such a hard exterior? Had fate dealt him such a difficult hand that he had no heart?

Could the right woman change his perspective? Could *she*?

Dear lord, what was she *thinking*? Her sole purpose in his life was to produce a child, then, following the requisite time span, move on.

Besides, what woman would willingly welcome a man of Rafe Valdez's calibre into her life?

Many, she admitted with obvious reluctance. The size of his cheque-book guaranteed obsequious adoration from the trophy wife prepared to be both gracious hostess and a seductive mistress. In all probability, willing to gift him a child.

So why *her*, when he could have chosen any one of several young women?

Because she refused to conform, and frequently opted for confrontation? Even to her detriment?

Or was it simply *circumstance*, as he'd claimed? Let's not forget the d'Alboa lineage, she added silently.

Did it really matter?

With a faint sigh she attempted to ease her tense body. Curled into a tight ball on the edge of a mattress was not her normal sleeping position.

She was already beginning to feel the tightness in several muscles. And she hurt, inside and out. Her breast ached from his retaliatory bite, and she ran her tongue over the tissues inside her mouth where he'd heartlessly ground them against her teeth.

It would be so easy to indulge in a crying jag. Wasn't there some analogy that credited weeping as a release to soothe the soul?

One solitary tear spilled and ran warmly down her cheek, and she brushed it away in angry rejection.

It was a while before she slipped into an uneasy sleep, from which she stirred to Rafe's touch as early dawn fingered the day's first light through the shuttered windows.

His sexual appetite ran to night *and* morning? Maybe if she simply lay there…

Fool, she accorded minutes later as warmth flooded her veins. He played her like a finely tuned instrument, seeking an unbidden response that had her clinging to him like a craven wanton.

Afterwards she slept, and when she woke it was morning, the space in the bed beside her empty.

CHAPTER FOUR

DANIELLE rolled over, checked the time on the digital bedside clock, then she slid swiftly to her feet, collected her cellphone and punched in the requisite digits to connect with her mother.

'Good heavens, darling. I don't expect you to come in this morning,' Ariane protested. 'I can manage quite well on my own.'

'With two of us, we'll be able to sort the stock in half the time,' Danielle said lightly as she crossed to the walk-in wardrobe, selected jeans and a singlet top, then she tossed them onto the bed before collecting fresh underwear.

'Are you sure Rafe won't object?'

She tucked the small phone beneath one ear and began pulling on briefs. 'I don't see why he should,' she managed evenly. 'As far as I know there are only plans for the afternoon, and I'll be back in time.'

The jeans came next, and she stepped into them, then manoeuvred them up over her hips.

'Shall I collect you? I have the car, remember?'

Oh, hell. She'd forgotten. 'OK. I can be ready in twenty minutes. I'll meet you at the gate.' In one fluid movement she tugged off the T-shirt, then gave a yelp in surprise as the cellphone was taken out of her hand.

She made a quick lunge to retrieve it. 'Give me that!'

Rafe merely put the phone to his ear. 'Ariane? We'll meet you at the boutique.' And disconnected the call.

Danielle spared him an angry glance. 'What do you think you're doing?'

'I believe it's called helping out.'

She became aware of her semi-nudity, and hurriedly turned away from him as she reached for her bra, fastening it in record time before pulling on the singlet top, and slipping her feet into trainers.

'It isn't necessary,' she flung over one shoulder and she entered the *en suite* and closed the door.

He was still there when she emerged. She'd swept her hair into a knot atop her head, and her only concession to make-up was a touch of gloss to her lips.

'You've had nothing to eat.'

He too was attired in jeans, trainers, and a polo shirt that hugged his muscular shoulders and emphasised powerful biceps.

She caught up her cellphone, collected her purse and sidestepped him. 'I'll grab something later.'

'I shall see that you do.'

'I dislike tyrannical men.'

'I've been called much worse.'

'Without doubt,' she responded with an edge of mockery.

She reached the head of the stairs and ran lightly down to the ground floor, aware he followed close behind her.

The garage was accessed via a hallway leading off from the lobby, and minutes later he eased the gleaming top-of-the-range Jaguar through the gates, then headed towards Toorak Road.

The positioning of La Femme was ideal, situated in a small U-shaped modern complex comprising seven upmarket shops and a boutique café specialising in fine coffee and gourmet food.

Danielle had to give Rafe his due, for he'd consulted with Ariane over shop-fittings, ordered what she'd requested and ensured the re-fit was completed in time to orchestrate the shift of stock.

Not only that, in Ariane's eyes he'd changed from ogre to champion by sanctioning an order of new French imports commensurate with patrons' expectations.

With their line of credit reopened and Rafe Valdez's financial backing, the attitude of wholesalers' representatives had undergone a dramatic change.

New stock had arrived by courier yesterday, and a further delivery was promised for tomorrow.

'Just drop me outside,' Danielle instructed as Rafe slowed the car and pulled into the kerb. 'I'll get a taxi back.'

He cut the engine and followed her onto the pavement, arching an eyebrow as she cast him a studied glare.

'There's no need for your personal inspection.'

'On the contrary,' Rafe drawled. 'I make it a habit to check all my investments.'

The gold sign-writing on the shop window looked good, and she could see Ariane behind the plate glass checking boxes of stock.

Was it Danielle's imagination, or did her mother's

gaze linger a little too long? What was Ariane looking for? A sign Rafe Valdez had mistreated her daughter?

Danielle could have reassured there weren't any. At least, none that was visible.

'Shall we get to work?'

She cast Rafe a cursory glance. 'You intend to stay?'

'You object?'

'Of course not,' Ariane responded with a ready smile. 'The stock will need to be sorted according to style, colour and size. I'd like to organise the display cabinets and attend to the window dressing.' She referred to the floor plan and the list they'd compiled on Friday. 'I've already made a start. Danielle, you search and sort, and I'll stack.'

'What would you like me to do?'

'Fetch and carry,' Danielle declared, crossing to one of the large boxes and slitting open the heavy masking tape.

It took a while to unpack all the boxes, then stack individual packets in coded order in the numerous large pull-out drawers contained in waist-high cabinets lining each opposing wall.

'I'll go fetch drinks and something to eat,' Rafe indicated, breaking from the task of collapsing yet another large box. 'Any preferences?'

'I packed sandwiches and brought bottled water,' Ariane informed. 'They're in the fridge out back.'

Danielle rose to her feet from a kneeling position, and stretched her arms. 'I'll get them.'

'We'll join you, darling. It'll be nice to sit down for ten minutes.'

There wasn't a great deal of spare space in the storeroom. Shelves lined the walls from floor to ceiling, and there was a small table and two chairs, and a servery cabinet which held a sink, crockery, cutlery, an electric kettle and a small microwave.

Danielle retrieved sandwiches and drinks and set them on the table.

'All the grunt work is done,' she declared as she fetched glasses and began filling them with water.

'Thanks to you both,' Ariane agreed with satisfaction. 'There's just the display cabinets and the window.'

For the past two and a half hours she'd been supremely conscious of Rafe's presence. The fluid ease with which he moved, the occasional brush of his fingers against her own as she took each stack of packets from his hand. The way his gaze lingered a fraction too long.

It unsettled her. Worse, it evoked a vivid memory of what they'd shared through the night. And would again. The purpose was evident in his eyes, a deep slumberous passion that held its base in sexual desire…nothing more, nothing less.

The sandwiches were delectable, and Danielle elected to tidy up while Ariane began on the window. Rafe remained where he was, and she turned towards him.

'There's no need for you to stay. I'll make sure I return to the house in time to shower, change and be ready by two.'

He reached out a hand and tucked a stray lock of hair behind her ear. 'No.'

Her pulse quickened, and there was nothing she could do to quell the heat coursing through her veins. Each separate nerve end seemed to flare into vibrant life at his touch, and she silently cursed him anew.

With quick, economical movements she rinsed glasses, dried and replaced them in the cupboard, then she crossed the storeroom, aware he followed close behind her.

With care, Danielle created an artful window display with tulle and satin ribbons, then dressed three mannequins in La Perla. A large illustrated catalogue was propped against an antique satin-padded chair, over which she draped a suspender belt in French lace.

A concentrated scrutiny, a few adjustments, and Ariane conceded it perfection.

All that remained was the need to dress the interior glassed showcases, which Ariane assured she could easily handle on her own.

'Are you sure?'

'Of course, darling. Besides, you probably have plans of your own for the afternoon.'

The tennis party, Danielle remembered with dismay. Her first entrée back into the social scene. A quiet afternoon spent lazing on a lounger by the pool with a good book was infinitely preferable to a few energetic games of tennis. Not to mention bearing the circumspect scrutiny of the social set.

'Yes, we do,' Rafe concurred, not missing the fleeting cloud that momentarily dulled her eyes, nor divining its cause.

'In that case, you must leave.' Ariane checked her

watch. 'It's almost one.' She leant forward and brushed her lips to Danielle's cheek. 'Have a good time. Thanks for your help.'

'I'll see you tomorrow.'

The boutique had come alive, and it looked good…really good, Danielle conceded as she slipped into the passenger seat of Rafe's car.

'I'll drop you off in the morning, then arrange for a car to be delivered to you through the day,' he indicated as he pulled out into the stream of traffic.

She didn't particularly want to accept anything from him, but a car was a necessity. 'Thanks.'

'I've suggested Ariane interview prospective staff to fill in part-time when you aren't available,' he continued, and she rounded on him at once.

'What do you mean—*not available*?'

'You'll accompany me whenever I travel on business. There will also be occasions when you'll need to take time off to attend an early-evening function, or a specific charity luncheon,' Rafe informed smoothly, aware of her mounting anger.

'La Femme is a priority.'

'Your first loyalty is to me.'

'My apologies,' Danielle offered facetiously. 'For a moment I forgot that I'd been bought and paid for.'

'Don't push it.' His voice was silk-smooth and dangerous, and succeeded in feathering apprehension down her spine.

Lunch was a delicious paella, followed by salad greens, and it was almost two when Rafe pulled into a familiar driveway and parked at the rear of a line of cars.

Lillian and Ivan Stanich.

Danielle's heart sank. By attending this particular soirée, he was throwing her in at the deep end. She could imagine the guest list, and had it confirmed as they entered the house.

'Rafe, darling.' Lillian went with the air-kiss routine, then she took a step towards his partner, only to pause momentarily as recognition hit. 'Danielle?'

'My wife.'

The recovery was swift. 'How delightful. Congratulations.'

Really? How long would it take for the gossip scoop to circulate? Five minutes? And who will be the first to try ascertaining the story behind the news? Or had the rumour mill already begun with the relocation of La Femme?

'Come through to the terrace and join everyone for drinks. Ivan has already organised the games roster.'

Danielle summoned a smile and suppressed the silent wish to be anywhere else but *here*, and followed in Lillian's wake.

Not one to miss an opportunity, the society doyenne clapped her hands to gain her guests' attention and announced Rafe's marriage, adding with a delighted chuckle, 'We're the first to know.' Turning towards Rafe, she offered a wicked smile. 'You've kept this very quiet, darling.'

'As I do most things in my personal life,' he drawled in response.

'So you're not going to enlighten us with any details?' Lillian queried coyly.

He caught hold of Danielle's hand and brought it

to his lips. His eyes were dark, their expression unreadable, then after a few electrifying seconds he lowered their linked hands to his side and met Lillian's avid gaze.

'No.'

There was a suspended silence during which it would have been possible to hear a pin drop, then Lillian spread her hands and gave a tinkling laugh.

'This calls for a celebration. Ivan must fetch some champagne.'

Danielle made a surreptitious attempt to free her hand without success. In a deliberate gesture she leaned towards him and uttered in a quiet voice, 'Just what are you playing at?'

'Solidarity.'

'A *united we stand, divided we fall* stance?'

'Yes.'

'You surprise me.'

'Why?'

'I imagined you'd have no hesitation in throwing me to the wolves.'

His gaze was direct, his voice as smooth as silk. 'I take care of my own.'

But she wasn't *one of his own*. At least, not really.

There were, of course, voiced congratulations, and she kept a smile pinned firmly in place as she was greeted by former friends whose enthusiasm didn't fool her in the least. These were people who'd turned their backs when the chips began to fall, whose invitations had become remarkably absent, and who had quickly refused to acknowledge Ariane or herself in any way.

Now that she was Rafe's wife, they were eager to renew their friendship. An act which she viewed with extreme caution and a degree of cynicism

'*Querido,*' a feminine voice purred.

Danielle turned slightly to face a statuesque blonde who was perfection from head to toe. Sex appeal, more than her share of pheromones, and the self-assurance of a modern-day Circe.

'Cristina,' Rafe acknowledged.

The blonde switched her attention to Danielle, and proffered a superficial smile. 'How dare you steal him away from me?'

It was spoken in jest, but there was no humour in those cool grey eyes.

'Perhaps you should ask Rafe?'

A suggestion which didn't go down at all well, and unless Danielle was mistaken a war had just begun.

'One of your many conquests,' Danielle acknowledged as she sipped champagne.

'We dated on occasion.'

It was as well Lillian and Ivan began marshalling players onto the two tennis courts adjoining their property, and Danielle found herself paired with Rafe against Cristina and her partner.

Tennis whites were obligatory, and her short pleated skirt and singlet top didn't come close to the designer gear Cristina wore.

What was meant to be a friendly game became highly competitive as the beautiful blonde deliberately set out to trounce Danielle off the court.

Something she refused to allow to happen, and it

said much for her own skill at the game that she managed to return almost every shot.

As expected, Rafe was a superb player, and, aided by height, strength and a killer serve, they completed the first set with a two-game lead.

It was a knock-out tournament, and it came as no surprise when Rafe took them into the final to win by a narrow margin.

He looked as if the afternoon's exercise had been no more strenuous than a walk in the park, whereas another set would have killed her!

Barbecued prawns and kebabs were served at eight with a variety of salad greens, followed by coffee.

'Danielle, you really must join the girls at next week's luncheon. I'll forward an invitation.'

The *girls*, huh? There was a certain irony in the fact that where Lillian led, others would follow. 'How kind.' She would decline when the invitation arrived, citing her commitment to La Femme.

There were a few charities she'd willingly support...by gifting a cheque, rather than by putting in an appearance among women who displayed such superficial artificiality.

Rafe saw the polite mask and was aware of the effort it cost her to project a pretence. She looked fragile, and there were faint shadows beneath her eyes.

Hardly surprising, given he'd kept her awake for much of the night.

With care he drained the last of his coffee, and crossed to her side.

'Ready to leave?'

'Yes,' she responded simply, wanting only to get out of here. She'd had enough, she was tired, and bed had never looked so good.

Except *bed* meant sharing intimacy with a man who'd wreaked havoc with her ambivalent emotions. There hadn't been a moment through the day when just one glance at him brought forth a vivid image of the previous night. That mouth, those hands... Something stirred deep within at the thought.

Dangerous thoughts. It would be easier if he was an inept lover, more focused on his own pleasure than hers.

Minutes later they thanked their hosts and began bidding fellow guests goodnight.

Danielle slid thankfully into the car, and laid her head back against the cushioned rest.

'You played the game well.'

She turned her head to look at him. 'Are we talking tennis, or the social deal?'

He fired the engine and eased the car around the semicircular driveway, then gained the street. 'Both.'

'Ah, a compliment.' It was impossible to avoid a trace of mockery.

The drive was a short one, and it seemed only a matter of minutes when Rafe drew the Jaguar to a halt inside the garage.

All she wanted to do was shed her clothes, take a shower, then slip into bed...to sleep.

Except there was as much chance of that happening as flying over the moon, she perceived as Rafe followed her into the shower.

'Isn't this carrying *togetherness* a bit too far?'

He trailed fingers across her shoulders. 'You've caught the sun.'

This close, she was supremely conscious of his powerful frame, the musculature of his chest and shoulders. And his unmistakable virility. It was an overwhelming force that swamped her senses.

Eyes front, an inner voice taunted. Better yet, turn away from him. Caution warned that might invite more than she was prepared to deal with.

She noticed a thin white diagonal scar on his left ribcage. Non-surgical. The careless slash of a knife blade?

Her head lifted, and she paused to examine a scarred indentation close to his collarbone that looked suspiciously like a bullet wound.

There was also an unusual oriental symbol tattooed on his upper right arm, and she wondered why he'd kept it, rather than have it cosmetically erased.

'Battle scars?' she posed, meeting his steady dark gaze.

'From my less than salubrious past?'

'How *less than salubrious*?'

'Do you really want to know?'

Her expression didn't waver. 'It's part of who you are.'

There were parts of those youthful years he refused to share with anyone. The edge of his mouth took an upward twist. 'How…profound.'

She caught up the soap and attempted to ignore him. An impossibility, given the size of the shower cubicle and his proximity.

Seconds later the soap-bar was taken from her

hand, and she tossed him an angry glare. 'Must you? A seduction scene isn't high on my list of priorities.'

'Why not close your eyes and enjoy?'

Something that would prove a sure path to disaster. Already her body was beginning to respond to his touch, with warmth spreading through her veins, disrupting her pulse-beat.

'I don't want to go there. At least, not tonight.'

He caught the slight catch in her voice, sensed the fragility evident, and slid his hands to her shoulders. 'That bad, hmm?'

She ached, everywhere. It was ages since she'd worked out, months since she'd last played tennis. Gym membership had been one of the first things to go, along with sports' club fees.

Dear heaven. His fingers were working magic, easing out the kinks, soothing tight muscles. The temptation was very strong to do as he suggested and just close her eyes.

It would be wonderful to turn into his arms and rest against him, to feel his palms skim over the surface of her skin and soothe away the tension of the day.

Where had that come from? Rafe Valdez had only one objective, and that was to satisfy his libido, and to father a child.

With a silent derisory groan she moved out of his grasp, exited the shower cubicle, snagged a towel and fixed the ends together above her breasts, then emerged into the bedroom.

Rafe joined her just as she was pulling a T-shirt

over her head, and his gaze narrowed at the faint dis-colouring blemishes marring her skin.

It wasn't his practice to harm, and he had to ask why it bothered him this woman should bear the marks from his touch.

She possessed a slender lissom body, slim legs displaying good muscle definition, and there was a fluid grace in the way she moved.

'Why a cotton-knit T-shirt as sleep-wear, when you have access to various luxury creations in silk, satin and lace at La Femme?'

Danielle turned her head and sent him a challenging glance. 'Perhaps I chose this—' she paused and indicated the fabric with an index finger '—as a turn-off.'

'Since whatever you wear won't stay on long,' Rafe drawled, 'it hardly matters.'

She chose not to answer, and merely pulled back the covers and slid into bed, aware as she did so that he crossed the room, snapped a switch and plunged the room into darkness.

Seconds later she felt the faint depression of the mattress as he slipped in beside her, and she tensed, waiting for the moment he'd reach for her.

Except the minutes dragged by, and she closed her eyes as tiredness overcame any desire to conduct a post-mortem on the day's events.

It was in the early pre-dawn hours that she struggled against wakefulness as male hands caressed her thighs, then gently tugged the T-shirt over her head.

Her murmured protest had little effect as Rafe gathered her close and nuzzled the sensitive hollow beneath her earlobe.

Danielle pushed against him, then groaned out loud as his mouth trailed to her breast, lingered, then traced a downward path.

She tasted of woman, warm and musky, and he stayed there a while, savouring her, cradling her hips as she lost control.

It was with ease he nudged her thighs further apart, then he plunged deep inside, aware of the way she expanded to take him, and heard the breath hiss from her throat as he began to move, rocking gently back and forth until she dug her fingers into his shoulders and matched his rhythm.

Afterwards they slept, then rose to shower and dress.

CHAPTER FIVE

BREAKFAST was a leisurely meal eaten al fresco on the terrace, and Danielle filched the fashion segment of the newspaper while Rafe studied the financial pages as they enjoyed a second coffee.

He looked relaxed and at ease, bearing a pantherish grace as he leant back in his chair. His dark hair was well-groomed, his face freshly shaven. His shirt was unbuttoned at the neck, and his jacket and tie were spread over a nearby chair. A briefcase and laptop sat on the floor close by.

The successful corporate executive, she mused idly, who wielded power and authority with incontestable right.

There was an inflexible quality evident, a hardness that came from the will to survive against the odds.

At that moment he looked up, and she met his steady gaze.

'If you've finished, we'll leave.' He drained the last of his coffee, then rose to his feet, attended to the two top buttons of his shirt, reached for his tie and fastened it, then he shrugged into his jacket.

It was almost eight-thirty when he brought the car to a halt adjacent to the boutique.

'I have a business dinner this evening.'

Danielle unclipped the seatbelt and reached for the door-clasp. 'So don't wait up?'

He ignored the faint cynicism. 'A car will be delivered to you this afternoon.'

'Thank you.' She slid to her feet and closed the door, watching as he eased the Jaguar back into the flow of traffic.

Danielle unlocked the boutique and discovered Ariane had already arrived, and together they effected a few minor changes, checked the stock list, before moving on to discuss a layout for their proposed catalogue.

The morning's trade was brisk as women stopped by to check out the new premises and the range of stock. Some were merely curious, others were there to purchase.

A few former clients wandered in, bought, and attempted to repair a severed friendship.

It was, Danielle determined, superficial behaviour at best and motivated by a need to establish favour with her powerful husband.

Integrity ensured she project a polite façade. Business was *business*, and it was a matter of pride the boutique should succeed.

Lunch was a fifteen-minute break each, taken in succession, and there was a stock delivery mid-afternoon.

Soon afterwards a sales manager presented her with the keys to a BMW parked out front. An hour before closing time Danielle signed for a certified document delivery from a prominent city bank. Inside was a portfolio containing cheque-book, ATM and credit cards in the name of Danielle *Valdez*.

Rafe, she perceived. Keeping his end of the bargain.

It shouldn't irk her so much, but it did. She attempted to analyse why, and attributed the blame to Rafe having taken control of her life. Except honesty compelled her to admit she was responsible for giving him that option.

As if she'd had a choice!

Who, in their right mind, would settle for bankruptcy and poverty when offered the opportunity to grasp an advantageous financial alternative?

Yet it came with a high price. Would *she* be able to keep *her* end of the bargain?

Dammit, introspection was of no benefit at all, she determined, and busied herself replenishing drawers with stock from the back room.

At five-thirty they closed up, checked the day's takings, and uttered a quiet whoop of delight at the figures.

It was after six when Danielle entered Rafe's Toorak home, and on a whim she shed the tailored business suit she wore to work, donned a swimsuit and headed down to the indoor pool.

The land out back had been carved away to incorporate a lower level devoted to a private gym, indoor pool, a spacious shower and bathroom.

The water was cool, and she stroked several laps before emerging to snag a towel, then head for the shower.

Dinner was a chicken salad Elena had left prepared in the refrigerator, and accompanied by chilled juice it made for a satisfactory meal.

The house seemed much too large for one person...correction, two. The downstairs rooms were spacious, and ideal for entertaining. The formal dining-room held no fewer than twenty-two chairs positioned around a long rectangular table. The formal lounge held comfortable sofas enough to seat a similar number.

Danielle collected a glass of chilled water and settled herself in front of the television, viewed a few of many programmes available via satellite, then retreated upstairs to bed at ten-thirty.

At what time would Rafe return? She plumped her pillow and told herself she didn't care. The later the better, for then hopefully he'd be tired and not bother her.

Fat chance, she protested silently as she emerged from the depths of sleep to the brush of his lips against the curve of her shoulder.

His mouth became an erotic instrument as he brought her to wakefulness, and in the darkness she clung to him, qualifying her own satisfaction as a pleasant fringe benefit in an otherwise diabolical scheme.

It was when they shared breakfast next morning that Danielle remembered the BMW.

'Thanks for the car.' She waited a beat. 'And organising details with the bank.'

Rafe drained his coffee and poured himself another. 'I intend that you shall.' He speared her a musing glance. 'Thank me.'

His meaning was unmistakable, and she hated the warmth heating her cheeks.

'Delightful.' His voice was a teasing drawl. 'A woman in today's age who can still blush.'

'It's a knack you have.'

'An integral part of my charm,' he conceded with a faint edge of mockery.

She opted to forgo another coffee and rose to her feet. 'I told Ariane I'd be early.'

'*Hasta luego.*'

The days were busy as the boutique flourished, much to Danielle and Ariane's delight. Quiet times were rare, and they interviewed several women before selecting one as necessary part-time staff with the capability of temporary full-time work as and when Danielle or Ariane might be absent.

At night there was Rafe.

The pattern during that first week followed an increasingly familiar routine. They ate in, Rafe secluded himself in the study with his laptop and rarely emerged much before ten.

Danielle utilised a desk in one of the spare rooms and checked figures and stock numbers, searched numerous internet sites, solely for the purpose of streamlining La Femme and providing clients with the ultimate in luxury lingerie.

Proofs for the catalogue were in place, but she wanted to be sure the assemblage couldn't be bettered before handing it all to the printer.

Rafe appeared to be one of the fortunate few who could apply optimum effort to a hectic work schedule with a minimum of five hours' sleep. Less, given the regularity with which he reached for her through the night.

Each time made it more difficult for her to remain emotionally distant from him. He had the touch, the skill, and he applied the time to ensure her pleasure matched his own.

Saturday dawned bright and clear, the sun's heat soaring with high humidity levels guaranteed to try anyone not blessed with the comfort of air-conditioning.

Traditionally, a Saturday was one of the busiest trading days of the week, with those who worked office and professional hours utilising part of the day to shop without having to cram everything into a lunch-hour.

It was an excellent day to have Leanne, the assistant Ariane had hired part-time, come in to work. Especially as Danielle needed to leave an hour before closing time.

A dinner party, Rafe had informed the previous morning, to be held at the home of a prominent social hostess.

It didn't help that Danielle was delayed due to a severe traffic accident, or that it took time for a uniform to appear and redirect banked-up traffic.

As it was, she brought the car to a halt outside the main entrance with a refined squeal of the brakes, raced up the stairs two at a time and skated to a halt in the bedroom at the sight of Rafe in the process of tucking a snow-white shirt into his waistband.

He slanted her a dark penetrating glance as he slid

the zip fastening home on impeccably-cut black trousers. 'You're late.'

'So—shoot me.' The flippant response covered an agitation caused by screaming sirens...police, ambulance, fire truck, an all too vivid imagination, and a painful reminder of her own father's accidental death in a similar situation.

His eyes narrowed. She looked faintly spooked, her eyes were a little too bright, not, he was sure, caused by flying up the staircase like a whirlwind.

He discarded the tie he was about to fasten, and closed the space between them. 'What's wrong?'

A week, and he could read her mind, divine her emotions? Surely she wasn't that transparent? 'I don't have time for an explanation.'

Rafe caught her chin between thumb and forefinger, tilting it so she had to look at him. 'A few minutes is neither here nor there.'

It was private, personal, and she didn't want to talk about it. 'Please, I need to shower, dress and be ready—' she paused briefly '—in twenty minutes.'

'Thirty will do.'

He didn't release her, and she threw him a fulminating glare. 'What is this? An inquisition?'

'I can easily find out,' he said quietly. 'So why not tell me?'

'Relentless bastard, aren't you?'

'The first is true, the second inaccurate.'

The glare intensified. 'You're driving me mad.'

He traced the pad of his thumb along her lower lip and felt it quiver beneath his touch. 'So what else is new?'

She held out for a few long seconds, then chose capitulation and relayed the reason for her delay.

'Something that revived the memory of how your father died.' The knowledge explained her agitation.

Fact, not a query, she noticed, and couldn't help wondering how closely he'd tracked the life of Joaquin d'Alboa's son and the lives of his widow and child.

'Go have your shower.'

Danielle escaped, managing to emerge twenty-five minutes later, dressed, her make-up complete, with her hair swept high into a knot atop her head.

The classic slim-fitting black gown with its spaghetti-thin straps showed her slender shoulders to advantage, accented the elegant slope of her neck, and showcased the gentle upper swell of her breasts.

She suffered Rafe's swift appraisal as she fixed on ear-studs, then she caught up her evening purse and preceded him from the room.

As dinner parties went, this had to be one of the more lavish, Danielle determined an hour later as she stood at Rafe's side sipping vintage champagne.

At least fifty guests assembled on a spacious terrace adjacent to colourfully lit gardens with manicured flower beds, topiary, decorative paths and seats placed at strategic intervals.

Uniformed waiters proffered trays containing a mix of canapés and savouries, and drinks.

'I neglected to ask,' Danielle ventured quietly. 'Is this merely social, or a function to aid a needy charity?'

'Ostensibly charity.'

'To which you've contributed a generous donation.'

Rafe inclined his head. 'I lend my support to a few worthy causes.'

He looked impressive attired in a dark evening suit that owed much to its Italian tailoring, for it fitted him like a superbly moulded glove, accenting an enviable breadth of shoulder, a lithe, muscular frame.

It made her think of what lay beneath the fine clothing, and it was no hardship at all to recall that toned body unadorned, the texture of his skin, the strength of muscle and sinew.

The image of his mouth angling in to capture her own, the feel of his hands on her body, skimming lightly over her skin, the intense sensual pleasure…

Stop it. The words were a silent scream. She suffered his lovemaking because it was part of the deal. Dammit, it was a major part of the deal, given conception was the ultimate aim.

A fellow male guest crossed to their side and, after an initial greeting, engaged Rafe in a business discussion.

Danielle welcomed the distraction, excused herself and moved towards a waiter with the intention of replenishing her drink…something definitely non-alcoholic this time out.

She caught snatches of meaningless conversation, and she had just selected a glass of chilled mineral water when she heard someone speak her name.

Turning, she summoned a polite smile and kept it in place. Cristina. Tall, elegant, exuding the patina of *class* bred from extreme wealth and exclusive private-school education.

'You must enjoy being active on the social scene again after such an—' there was an effective pause '—unfortunate absence.'

Careful, Danielle bade silently. Keep it polite and simple. 'Yes.'

Something shifted in Cristina's icy grey eyes. 'Interesting how you and your mother managed to effect such a reversal of fortunes.'

'Isn't it?'

'What did you do, darling? Sell yourself?'

This had the potential to become nasty. 'If that were true,' she managed evenly, 'why would marriage come into the equation?'

'Something that is on the tip of everyone's tongue.'

Danielle managed a slight smile, and refrained from comment.

'So, tell me,' Cristina pursued. 'Why *you*?'

'Perhaps you should ask Rafe?'

'You can't be *that* good in bed.'

She'd had enough. Polite conversation was one thing. Snide comments were something else. 'No?'

The blonde's gaze assumed a speculative gleam. 'Hope you can keep up with him, darling. He's a lusty son-of-a-bitch.'

'Mmm.' She aimed for a smile that was both dreamy and sultry. 'Isn't he, though?'

She'd gained an enemy. If she'd had any doubt, the sudden flash of jealous rage merely confirmed it.

'Just for the record,' Cristina stated with deliberate

calm, 'a wedding ring on a man's finger doesn't faze me at all.'

'And you'll be waiting to catch him if I fall from grace?'

'*When*, sweetheart. Rafe doesn't stay satisfied with one woman for long.'

'Well, now, maybe I'll be the exception.'

The raking appraisal bordered on the insolent. 'I very much doubt it.'

'What do you doubt, Cristina?' Rafe queried with a practised drawl.

He possessed the silent grace of a jungle cat, appearing at their side without warning.

The blonde recovered quickly. 'We were discussing La Femme, darling. Its relocation will prove to be an enormous success.'

She was good, Danielle conceded, and wondered if Rafe bought it.

'You'll excuse us?' He caught hold of Danielle's hand and threaded her fingers through his own, then he lifted her hand and brushed his mouth across her knuckles, eliciting a sharp glance.

'Damage control, Rafe?' She attempted to pull her hand free, and felt his fingers tighten. 'I can take care of myself.'

'Cristina has all the instincts of a piranha.'

'She has her sights on you.'

'My bank balance,' Rafe corrected drily.

Danielle cast him an analytical look, intrigued by his features in profile, the angles and planes reflected by lighting and shadows.

It was a strong face, the sweep of his jaw, the wide

forehead, symmetrically positioned nose, and a mouth to die for.

'Nice to know you have no illusions,' Danielle said sweetly.

He smiled, and her stomach executed a backward flip. It gave him an almost boyish look. Although she doubted he'd ever enjoyed boyhood. He'd gone straight from child to man, fashioned by the harsh law of human survival.

'You have a sassy mouth.'

'It's one of my talents,' she relayed solemnly.

'Our hostess is about to announce the buffet.'

A sumptuous array of food was set out on an extended table, and Danielle transferred a few morsels onto her plate. Bite-size portions and cutlery forks made for ease of eating, enabling the guests to move at will, converge with whoever they chose, lending a pleasant informality to the evening's proceedings.

Fund-raisers took various forms, Danielle mused, and success depended largely on the generosity and ingenuity of the charity organisers.

Tonight's effort followed a familiar pattern...ply the guests with drink, allow time to mingle, feed them, then while they're relaxed and mellow, provide the main event.

In this instance, the main event was an auction of memorabilia.

A set of Baccarat crystal goblets purported to have held Cristal champagne served at the table of visiting European royalty. A jade pendant worn by a past premier's wife at a function attended by an Arabian prince.

Danielle's attention was riveted by one item on display. The jeweller's box was distinctive, together with the exquisite diamond bracelet it held. Hand-crafted, the linking design was unique, and she recognised it as a bequest gifted to her four years ago on the advent of her twenty-first birthday. Retaining the matching earrings had been a sentimental act, but the bracelet had been sold off last year in one of many desperate bids to maintain a cash flow.

What was it doing here, and *who*…? No, he couldn't have. She shot Rafe a penetrating glance, and could determine nothing from his expression.

The auction began, and the bracelet was tabled as once belonging to a member of the Spanish aristocracy.

Rafe began the bidding, and Cristina's participation drew interest, causing the bidding to escalate as others joined in. Soon it reached an amount that saw the bid for ownership reduced to two. For every bid Cristina made, Rafe topped it, until an obscene figure was reached and Cristina declined to increase Rafe's bid.

Had it been Rafe's intention to make a public issue of Cristina's defeat? Most everyone present couldn't fail to miss the connection between his bid for the bracelet and its original ownership.

The list went on, and bidding was intense, culminating in a considerable sum raised for a charity specialising in providing terminally ill children with their dearest 'make-a-wish' fantasy. This evening's event would fund a return trip to Disneyland for a young leukaemia patient, her mother and a registered nurse.

Afterwards there was coffee, and the successful bidders paid for and claimed their purchases.

Rafe returned to her side, extracted the bracelet from its case and fastened it onto her wrist. 'Yours,' he declared quietly.

She ran the tip of her fingers over the precious stones. 'Thank you. It belonged to my paternal grand-mother.'

He cast her a studied look. 'It was among jewellery acquired by my agent.'

Jewellery she and her mother had been forced to sell. 'You chose to donate something already owned, then buy it back? Why?'

'A whim, perhaps?'

Danielle doubted any action he took was motivated by something as frivolous as a *whim*. He was a superb strategist who calculated to win.

Guests began to disperse, and she joined Rafe in thanking their hosts, then walked at his side to the car.

It was a mild summer evening, the sky a dark in-digo studded with stars, and there was a freshness in the air that boded well for a fine day tomorrow.

The drive home didn't take long, and as soon as Rafe garaged the car Danielle slid from the passenger seat and walked through to the lobby.

Thank heavens tomorrow was Sunday and she didn't need to race the clock or the traffic. She fancied a lazy day, preferably spent catching up with some accounting work on her laptop, maybe taking time to meet Ariane for a coffee.

She made her way upstairs to the bedroom, slid off

the stiletto heels, then reached for the zip fastening on her gown, only to discover Rafe's fingers about to complete the task.

With the zip freed, he slid the shoestring straps over each shoulder, then let the garment slip to the carpet.

As the gown was fully lined with an inbuilt support bra, all she wore beneath it was a pair of black thong briefs.

Danielle felt him slide the pins free from the elegant twist, and her hair fell to her shoulders.

Rafe turned her to face him, and she stood still, her eyes watchful as he shrugged off his jacket, then he discarded his tie and loosened the top few buttons on his shirt.

He cupped her face and angled his mouth over hers in a kiss that coaxed and seduced, then became intent on possession.

His hands shifted, one fisting her hair while the other slid down her back and cupped her buttocks, drawing her body in against him as he deepened the kiss to something that was almost primitive.

He was wearing too many clothes, and he dealt with them, then lifted her against him and parted her thighs so the most sensitive part of her was pressed to the hard bulge of his arousal.

The gentle sliding movement he initiated nearly drove her mad, and she groaned in encouragement as he tore off her briefs and tumbled them both down onto the bed.

He entered her in one long thrust, stilled, then took it slow and deep as she expanded to fit him. The rhythmic tightening of her inner muscles almost caused him to lose control, and he fought against it as he drove them both high onto a sensual plane where there was only the intense joy of fulfilment, the exquisite sensation of two people completely in tune.

Rafe supported his weight as he rested against her, nuzzling the sensitive hollow at the edge of her neck, then he trailed his lips to her breast to tease and provoke the burgeoning peak.

He felt her body quiver in response, and he absorbed her faint groan as his mouth settled over hers in a kiss that started sweet and slow, then built into something so incredibly erotic it was impossible not to be completely caught up with renewed desire.

In one fluid movement he rolled onto his back, and she arched against him, exulting in the sense of power as she took him on a ride that teased, tantalised and tested his control. The brush of her hair against his chest, the trail of her fingers as she explored the shape and texture of his body...enjoying the faint hiss of his breath, the husky growl low in his throat.

'Are you done?'

'Hmm, not yet.' She teased one male nipple with the edge of her teeth, nipped, then suckled, and took pleasure in his indrawn breath.

'When you're through playing, *querida*...'

Playing? She bit him, the fine edge of her teeth drawing blood, then she arched against him in a movement that was distinctly feline and rode him deep, increasing the pace until they met at the sensual pinnacle, held, then joined each other in a spiralling free-fall that left them both slick with sensual heat and gasping for breath.

Dear lord…there was almost a reverence apparent as she rested against him. Her body still pulsed in tune with her ragged breathing, and she felt the light touch of his hands as he skimmed the surface of her skin, soothing her until she gradually stilled.

Would it always be like this?

A woman could become addicted to the intense passion they'd just shared. Add *love*, and it would be a dynamic explosive mix.

As much as she'd vowed to hate him, her body was at variance with her brain, becoming a finely tuned instrument beneath his skilled touch. For that alone she wanted to hate him afresh. And herself, for her lack of control.

On the edge of sleep, she felt the brush of his lips against her forehead, and she sighed, too enervated to protest or to move.

CHAPTER SIX

DANIELLE woke alone, and she stretched, considered burrowing her head into the pillow for another hour, then opted against it.

The sun was shining, the whole day lay ahead, and she intended to devote part of it to updating La Femme's records, followed by some retail therapy.

It was ages since she'd been able to do any serious shopping, and, given her husband's social schedule, she needed to replace a pair of stilettos and acquire a new gown.

She slid from the bed, showered, pulled on jeans and a cotton top, tidied the bedroom, then ran lightly downstairs to the kitchen.

Danielle settled for cereal and fruit, followed it with toast, and made fresh coffee.

There was no sign of Rafe, and no note to provide an indication of where he might be. The study? The downstairs gym?

Danielle poured a second coffee, leafed through the Sunday papers, then she collected her laptop and briefcase, set both on the informal dining-room table and began to work.

It was there Rafe found her more than an hour later when he entered the kitchen after a punishing session in the gym.

'Good morning.'

She lifted her head, and felt her heart leap to a quickened beat at the sight of him in shorts, sweat-patched T-shirt and trainers. 'Hi.'

He crossed to the refrigerator and extracted a bottle of chilled water, broke the cap, and downed half the contents in one long swallow before turning towards her.

'I'll organise for one of the upstairs rooms to be furnished as a study for you.'

'That isn't necessary. I like the flexibility of being able to work anywhere. Keeping the records up to date rarely takes me more than a few hours each week.' At least it had up until now.

Rafe shot her a penetrating glance. 'It'll be easier if you have your own office space.'

Case closed. She knew she should be grateful. So why was there a niggling resentment apparent?

He drained the water bottle, dispensed with it, then walked from the kitchen.

An hour later Danielle closed down the laptop, gathered papers into her briefcase, then deposited both upstairs, checked her watch, then caught up her bag and car keys, and went in search of Rafe to let him know she'd be out for the rest of the day.

Except he was nowhere in plain sight, and she wrote him a note, propped it on the kitchen servery, then headed towards the garage.

Her first destination was Brighton, and she parked, then wandered at will, pausing at a trendy café for a cappuccino before browsing in the shops.

Her cellphone rang as she was about to enter a

boutique, and she retreated onto the pavement and took the call.

'Where are you?' Rafe's voice was unmistakable, and she mentally counted to three before answering.

'Precisely? Brighton, outside a dress shop.'

'Does the *not sure when I'll be back* in your note indicate late afternoon or evening?'

'Does it matter?'

'Answer the question, Danielle.'

'I didn't realise I required your permission to go out of the house.'

'*Querida.*' His voice was a dangerous purr. 'Don't test my patience, hmm?'

'Am I doing that?' she queried sweetly.

'Would you be so brave, I wonder, if you were facing me in person?'

'Count on it.'

His husky chuckle sent shivers scudding the length of her spine. 'Shall we begin again?'

She didn't pretend to misunderstand him. 'Evening. I want to call by the penthouse.'

'Six, Danielle. We'll take your mother to dinner.'

He ended the call, and she keyed in the digits to reach Ariane and relayed the invitation.

'Nonsense, darling. It'll be cosier if we eat here.'

Danielle wasn't sure *cosy* was a good idea. Her dear *mama* would doubtless indulge her romantic heart with a surreptitious analysis of the state of her daughter's marriage, despite or because of its circumstance.

'I'll make one of my specialities.'

It was so long since Ariane had been able to entertain. Resigned, Danielle queried, 'Is there anything you'd like me to pick up?'

'A fresh baguette from the bakery, darling. Oh, and some lettuce.'

'I'll come early and help with the preparations.'

'No, it'll give me pleasure to have you as my guest.'

Danielle ended the call, replaced the phone in her bag, then dedicated the next few hours to choosing a new gown and shoes.

It was after four when she let herself into the penthouse, armed with flowers, a bottle of wine, together with the baguette and lettuce.

A tantalising aroma permeated the kitchen, and she greeted her mother fondly, glimpsed the sparkling gleam evident in Ariane's eyes as she stirred the contents of various pots on the cook-top.

'For you,' she said with affection, gifting the wine and flowers, then she snagged a tea towel and fixed it at her waist. 'Now, what can I do?'

They worked happily together for the next hour, confident all was well, the serving dishes ready and the table set.

'Time to freshen up, I think,' Ariane declared.

The intercom buzzed, and Ariane released the external security door to allow Rafe into the building. Minutes later the chime bell sounded and Danielle added water glasses to the table setting while her mother let him into the apartment.

She heard their voices, his deep with its slight American accent, and sensed the pleasure in Ariane's greeting.

Danielle moved into the lounge, proffered a smile, and schooled her features as he crossed to her side, cupped her face and slanted his mouth over hers.

'What are you doing?'

'Kissing my wife.'

She wanted to slap him, and he knew, damn him! There was a humorous gleam evident in that dark gaze as he captured her mouth in a slow, sweet possession. A gesture that unnerved her, and brought pink colour to her cheeks.

It was a deliberate gesture, and one that would merely feed her mother's imagination. Which was precisely his intention.

'I thought we'd eat in,' Ariane declared. 'You'll be my first guests.' She sent her daughter a sparkling glance, then deferred to Rafe. 'What can I get you to drink? I have a nice chardonnay.'

The meal was a success, for her mother's culinary skills were notable, her delight in exercising them evident.

Cosy encapsulated the few hours they shared, and the developing rapport between Rafe and her mother was something Danielle viewed with caution.

There was a part of her that wanted to warn Ariane against a man who could manipulate circumstance at will. To advise Rafe's expressed affection was nothing more than an act, for it was laughable to contemplate otherwise.

His voiced interest in various framed photographs positioned on various items of furniture in the lounge sent Ariane delving into a drawer for more than one

family album, and Danielle deliberately absented herself on the pretext of making coffee.

She took her time, setting china onto a tray, adding
cheese and crackers to a plate, until the coffee had
filtered and there was no further reason for her to
delay a return to the lounge.

The fond hope the albums would be put to one side
weren't fulfilled, and she suffered through Ariane's
affectionate recount of foreign resort holidays and
various special-occasion photographs taken at different stages during her life.

It was too much information, acutely personal, and
left her feeling vulnerable.

'We must do this again,' Ariane enthused as Rafe
indicated they should leave.

'Indeed,' he agreed. 'As our guest. Danielle will let
you have the details.'

Danielle was silent as they rode the elevator down
to the basement car park, and Rafe walked to her car,
waited while she fired the engine, then followed in
his own vehicle.

They entered the driveway within seconds of each
other, and cut the ignition almost simultaneously.

Danielle gathered up the brightly emblazoned
carry-bags containing her purchases, then she entered
the foyer and made for the staircase.

'Your mother is a charming woman.'

'Yes, she is.'

Rafe followed her into the bedroom and began
loosening his tie. 'I'll ensure some of our invitations
include Ariane as a fellow guest.'

She deposited the carry-bags and stepped out of her

shoes. 'I know she'll appreciate that.' She slipped off her watch, removed the slender gold chain at her neck, and crossed to the *en suite*.

A leisurely shower, then bed. Tomorrow was another day, and there were a few items of stock due to arrive.

Danielle shed her clothes, turned on the water, then stepped into the shower stall. She picked up the soap and visualised the boutique window... She'd change the central mannequin's attire; maybe the black lace teddy—

The glass door slid open and Rafe stepped in. There was more than adequate room for two, but she resented him invading her personal space. Which was totally illogical, given the intimacy they shared.

'Must you?'

'You object?'

'Yes!'

He took the soap from her hand. 'Get used to it.'

'Look—'

'I'm looking, *querida*,' he drawled with amusement as he caught hold of her shoulders and turned her away from him. 'There was one photo in the album displaying a cute little birthmark.' His fingers trailed down her slender back to the curve of her buttock. 'Just about here. Ah, yes, there it is. How could I have missed it?'

Danielle wrenched out of his grasp, only to have him catch hold of her and turn her to face him.

Water cascaded against his back, and without thought she batted a hand against his shoulder, then clenched a fist and aimed it at his chest. 'Don't!'

His eyes stilled, the humour vanishing as if it was never there. 'You're treading dangerous ground.'

She raised stormy eyes to his. 'How would you feel if I began to examine *you* for any imperfections?'

'Aroused.'

'Of course,' she acceded with wicked cynicism. 'What else?'

'You want to make an issue of this?'

'Yes, dammit.'

'Why, when you have no hope of winning?'

'That doesn't stop me from trying!' What was the matter with her? To argue with him was madness. To do so when she was naked…insanity.

'What do you hope to achieve?'

She wrenched out of his grasp. 'If you don't mind, I'd prefer not to be used for sex tonight.'

Rafe pulled her back towards him and captured her head, tilting it so she had little option but to meet his gaze. 'And if I do mind?'

'You can go to hell.'

He was tempted to take her there. To show her the difference between taking and pleasuring. For a millisecond he almost did. Then he lowered his head and possessed her mouth, ravaging it in a manner that owed more to punishment than the desire to please.

He wanted her unbidden response, and he worked towards it, tormenting until he sensed her capitulation. Then he eased back, nipping the fullness of her lower lip with the edge of his teeth, teasing and provoking as she began to reciprocate, until the ardour was all hers and her hands lifted to link at the back of his neck.

In one swift movement he cupped her buttocks and raised her up against him, parting her thighs and plunging into her in one long thrust.

He watched her eyes dilate as she absorbed him, felt rather than heard her faint whimper at the suddenness of his invasion, sensed her body tense momentarily, then relax as he kissed her. Gently, with a sensitivity that made the breath catch in her throat.

Then he began to move, and she moved with him, caught up in the mesmeric passion of his possession. Helpless against a primitive hunger that changed her into a shameless wanton.

Danielle had no perception of time, and it seemed an age before she rested her head into the curve of his shoulder, totally spent.

Afterwards he moved beneath the water and cleansed her with a gentleness that almost made her want to weep, and she stood as he blotted the moisture from her skin before towelling himself dry.

On the edge of sleep she became vaguely aware that he caught hold of her hand and brought it to his lips.

The following few days were busy. Danielle effected a stunning window display that drew several compliments.

Business was brisk, although Wednesday proved to be a day where everything that could go wrong, did.

The courier failed to arrive as promised on the morning run, and the client sailed into the boutique prior to lunch expecting to collect her special order, only to become irate on discovering it wasn't there.

Apologies did little to appease, despite an assurance the order would certainly be included in the afternoon run.

It wasn't, and incurred a diatribe accusing La Femme of ineptitude, carelessness, together with promoting client dissatisfaction and a threat to take business elsewhere.

Danielle made a call to the supplier, and was informed they'd received a cancellation on that specific order, hence the reason why it hadn't been included.

A quick check with Ariane confirmed what Danielle already knew. Neither of them had initiated the cancellation. Leanne was excluded on the grounds she only worked on a Thursday, Friday and Saturday. The order had been faxed through on Monday, and today was Wednesday.

'Any ideas?'

Danielle gave her mother a thoughtful look. 'I could be wrong.'

'Sabotage?'

'I hate to think it might be a possibility.' Her teeth worried her lower lip, and her eyes hardened. 'From now on we confirm each order by electronic mail with a specially devised code known only to you, me, and the supplier.'

She picked up the phone and organised the arrangement.

Nevertheless, it perturbed her. The relocated La Femme was proving to be highly successful. The boutique provided a wide range of imported stock and the level of patronage was good.

If it was sabotage, then *who*?

Cristina? Did her vindictiveness extend this far? Danielle didn't like the way the mental maths added up. If Cristina was responsible she'd have to get irrefutable proof before she could take any action. Supposition and suspicion weren't sufficient evidence.

It preoccupied her during the drive home, adding an edginess to her demeanour. What she needed was some rigorous physical activity in order to expend excess nervous energy.

A workout in the downstairs gym, followed by several laps of the pool appealed, and she wasted little time exchanging her working clothes for a bikini, then she pulled on shorts and a T-shirt and sped lightly downstairs.

It was a spacious room, containing a bench-press, electronic treadmill, exercycle, punching bag and weights. There was a locked wall cabinet containing a variety of martial arts weaponry…at least one of which could be considered illegal. Unless he held a license.

'Admiring my collection?'

He had the tread of a cat, and she turned slowly to face him. He was dressed in sweat pants and T-shirt, and had a towel draped round his neck.

'You're a martial arts exponent?'

Rafe crossed towards her with a fluid grace not found in most men. 'Does that surprise you?'

Very little about him surprised her. 'No.' There was a quality to him she hadn't quite been able to pinpoint…the spiritual attunement of mind and body, the supreme discipline of each, and the acquired skill of using both as an art form.

He rested his gaze on her attire. 'You want to work out?'

'Punch something,' she amended succinctly.

He detected the edge to her voice and wondered at it. 'Care to tell me why?'

'Not particularly.'

He battened down his amusement. 'Want a pair of boxing gloves?'

Danielle cast him a dark glance. 'I'm serious.'

'That bad, hmm?' He was tempted to take the fine edge of her anger, turn it into passion, and enjoy the process.

Instead, he crossed to a set of built-in cupboards along one wall, extracted the gloves and returned to her side. 'Give me your hands.'

He taped them, then moved to the punching bag and held it still. 'Ever used one of these before?'

'No,' she denied, following him. 'But it'll do.'

'In place of *who*?'

She was silent for a few seconds. 'I'm not sure yet.'

Rafe offered a few basic instructions. 'Go for it.'

She did. Until he stopped her after a series of blows, and when he tore off the tape she crossed to the treadmill, set the controls at a medium speed and kept up the pace until she felt she'd had enough.

Rafe was within her peripheral vision, and she could only admire his fluid grace of movement as he completed a series of martial arts exercises. Control and discipline in practice form; lethal in combat.

Her energy spent, she left the gym and moved to the indoor pool.

It took only seconds to strip down to her bikini, and she took a running dive into the crystal-clear water.

Danielle lost count of the number of laps she stroked before a dark head surfaced close to her own, and Rafe matched his pace to her own.

It was a while before she called a halt and trod water at the far end of the pool.

'Had enough?'

'Yes.'

'Feel better?'

'Some.'

'Then let's get out of here, shower, and go eat.'

She levered herself onto the tiled edge, then got to her feet and reached for a towel. 'I'll cook.'

'We could dine out.'

'I do a great steak salad.' She caught hold of her hair and squeezed out the excess moisture. 'Elena has the makings in the refrigerator. Served with Turkish bread and hummus, it'll be divine. Trust me.'

It was. Eaten at the table positioned on the terrace, and accompanied by a superb cabernet sauvignon wine.

It was a peaceful scene, overlooking the landscaped lawns with their neat garden borders, the various flowering bushes and shrubbery.

Danielle had a sudden glimpse of what it would be like with children...there would a swing seat, a slide, and a variety of outdoor toys. A dog to love and provide fun and laughter, and indoors a cat to curl up on a few favoured chairs. And the nursery, with its cot, bed, bookshelves and toys. A rocking-horse, and a rocking-chair so she could sit with a child snuggled in her arms.

A child. The reason for this marriage.

Could she already be pregnant? It was a possibility, but, given her own calculations—most likely not.

How long would it take? A silent bubble of wry laughter rose and died in her throat. Given Rafe's dedication to propagating progeny…not very long at all.

'Ariane reports business continues to show a markedly increased turnover.'

Danielle took a sip of wine, then held the stemmed goblet in her hands. 'Yes.'

'You have reservations?'

He was quick. Too quick, she perceived as she caught his discerning look. Had Ariane relayed the mystery of the cancelled order and the resultant ire from their dissatisfied client? Should *she*?

There was a part of her that wanted to deal with it on her own. Surely it couldn't prove too difficult, even if Cristina had covered her tracks?

'No,' she ventured. The success of the boutique was vitally important. To Ariane, to herself. It was a matter of pride, and integrity.

'*But?*'

'Why do you imagine there is one?' She hadn't meant to sound so cynical, but Cristina and her trouble-making potential rankled.

Rafe leaned back in his chair and examined her

features. Something was bothering her, and he meant to find out what it was.

'We're attending a photographic exhibition on Friday evening at the Simpson Gallery.'

'Updating the coming week's social calendar?'

'Yes.'

'Oh, *joy*.'

'Don't be facetious.'

'Perhaps it's simply an aversion to being on display.'

'Given time, our union will become old news.'

He was right, but it didn't help much. Especially with the spectre of Cristina constantly looming in the background.

'Sunday we've been invited to join friends for a few hours in the afternoon. Volleyball on the beach, followed by a barbecue.'

'What if I have plans of my own?'

'We compromise.'

She'd ensure they did, just for the hell of it. 'How about taking in a movie at the cinema?'

'We'll be on the Gold Coast next week.'

'Excuse me...*we*?'

'I have business there,' Rafe relayed with marked patience.

'I can't leave the boutique.'

'Yes, you can. Leanne will work Thursday and Friday.'

She wanted to hit him, badly. 'I would have preferred you discuss it with me first.'

The sun was going down, fading the sky and dimming the landscape beneath it. Soon everything would be shrouded in varying shades of grey and pewter.

Remote sensors activated electric garden lights, illuminating the grounds in a soft glow.

Without a further word she rose to her feet and began gathering up china and cutlery, then carried them through to the kitchen. Within minutes she'd restored order, and she ran lightly upstairs to retrieve her keys and purse.

The need to escape, if only for an hour, was paramount.

'Going out?'

Danielle turned and saw Rafe framed in the bedroom doorway. 'Yes.'

'I'll get my jacket.'

Resentment flared, and lent her eyes a fiery sparkle. 'I'm going alone.'

His stance didn't alter. 'I go with you.' His voice was pure silk. 'Or you don't go at all.'

Anger intensified as she threw him a furious look. 'I don't want to be around you right now.'

'Tough.'

'Dammit! You can't—'

'Yes, I can.'

'Why are you making this such a major deal?' she demanded, sorely tried, watching warily as he moved into the room.

'Because no woman of mine goes out into the night alone.'

'I am not your *woman*.'

A faint smile curved the edge of his mouth. 'Yes,' he acceded in an indolent drawl. 'You are.'

'Not in *any* sense.' She was so angry she could spit, and irked no end that he found it amusing.

He caught up a jacket, hooked it over one shoulder, then he slanted her a quizzical glance. 'Let's go.'

'I've changed my mind.'

'We could always have an early night.'

His implication was clear, and she clenched her hands in anger. 'Sex.' She threw him a fulminating look. 'Is that all you think about?'

'With you, it isn't a hardship.'

She acted on impulse and aimed a stinging slap...except it was intercepted before the palm of her hand could reach his cheek.

In seeming slow motion he tossed his jacket onto a chair, then he pulled her close and fastened his mouth on hers in a punishing kiss that reached right down to her soul as it invaded, plundered and conquered.

Danielle fought him at first, beating her fists against his ribs, his back, anywhere she could reach. Except it did no good at all, as he simply hauled her up against him.

His arousal was a potent force, and she struggled against him until her brain registered what her body had already accepted.

The need to respond was uppermost, and the knowledge caused a silent groan of despair as she attempted to wrench herself from his grasp.

She managed it, only because he released her, and she stepped back a pace as she fought to control her rapid breathing.

'Do we go, or stay?'

He sounded so cool, it merely heightened her anger, and she raised stormy eyes to his. '*I'm* going out. Alone.'

'We've already done that. You don't want to do it again.'

'You're not my jailor!' She moved past him, and quickly descended the stairs. Her car stood in the garage, and she used the remote modem to lift the automatic doors, then slid into the driver's seat and ignited the engine.

At that moment the passenger door opened and Rafe slipped into the front seat.

Rafe doubted she had any particular destination in mind, and he didn't offer a word as she cleared the gates, then headed towards the city.

Southbank suited her mood, for there were several cafés and coffee bars from which to choose, plus the pleasure of sitting outdoors and watching the world go by.

Maybe if she ignored Rafe she could pretend he wasn't there?

Fat chance, she concluded minutes later as she chose one café, selected an outdoor table, took a seat, and ordered a latte.

'A short black,' Rafe indicated, then sank back in the chair and subjected the woman opposite to an encompassing appraisal.

'Are we going to sit in silence, or attempt to communicate?'

Danielle met his gaze with equanimity. 'Pick a subject.'

'Whatever it is that's bothering you.'

'*You* bother me,' she retaliated. 'You make plans without consulting me, and expect me to conform.'

'For you to conform is part of the deal.'

'Of course.' Her eyes darkened. 'Let's not forget *the deal*.'

His expression didn't change, although his voice was a silky drawl. 'Careful, *querida*.'

The waiter delivered their coffee, and Danielle stirred in sugar, then took an appreciative sip.

'I don't want to leave Ariane with the total responsibility of La Femme.'

Her mother was more than capable, and in normal circumstances she'd have no hesitation in absenting herself for a few days. Except she had an instinctive feeling that Cristina was intent on causing mischief. The more she thought about it, the more she was convinced the leggy blonde was behind today's contretemps.

The concern was what else Cristina had planned.

'Two days isn't a lifetime.'

The fact he was right didn't help at all. 'You're not going to give in, are you?'

He added sugar and stirred the dark brew. 'No.'

Danielle looked at him, and saw the unrelenting resolve evident. A man no sensible person would choose as an enemy.

Without a further word she finished her coffee, then rose to her feet, extracted a note from her purse and had Rafe close his hand over hers.

'You take independence too far.' He summoned a waitress, handed her a note from his wallet, then followed Danielle out onto the boardwalk.

Attired in black trousers, a casual cotton shirt un-buttoned at the neck, he looked the antithesis of the high-powered corporate executive. Yet there was something about him that attracted a second glance.

The evening air was fresh, and there was a breeze teasing the length of her hair. A few stray tendrils brushed her cheek, and she tucked them behind an ear.

A wolf-whistle pierced the air, but she didn't even glance towards the admirer, unaware she was the target of his appreciation. Nor did she see the chilling look Rafe threw in the man's direction.

Soon they turned and retraced their steps, and Danielle heard the laughter as they passed various tables, the chatter as couples enjoyed a late meal.

They reached the car and she handed Rafe the keys before slipping into the passenger seat.

The drive home didn't take long, and inside she made for the stairs, uncaring whether he followed or not.

Minutes later she shed her clothes, slid into bed and snapped off the lamp. Sleep didn't come easily, and she lay awake in the darkness for what seemed an age before Rafe quietly entered the room.

She heard the faint rustle of clothes being removed, and had a vivid image of him discarding each garment, that broad-shouldered frame, taut midriff, the flex of muscle and sinew, the satin-smooth olive skin.

Heat flooded her body, and the familiar ache deep within longed for his touch. Dear heaven, why did her body act independently from the dictates of her brain?

She didn't want him. *Liar.* There was a need to lose herself in the physical act, to experience again and again the primitive, magical sensuality he was able to arouse.

And just for a little while she wanted to be transported to that special place where it was possible to pretend what they shared was more than...just sex. Albeit very good sex.

For a moment the knowledge shocked her.

How could she even *think* her emotions could be involved? What was she...*crazy*?

She hated Rafe Valdez for the scheme he'd devised.

Except *hate* didn't form any part of what she felt as he reached for her. Dislike and apathy weren't even contenders as her body sang at his touch.

He had the skill, the knowledge to drive a woman wild, and as she went up in flames she didn't spare a thought for anything except the man, the moment, and the glorious, exhilarating ride.

CHAPTER SEVEN

DANIELLE couldn't help but wonder if Cristina had garnered an invitation to every function listed on the city's calendar for the social élite.

Coincidence or design? Given the glamorous blonde's intent to cause mayhem, it had to be the latter.

It was interesting to watch the society matrons work the gallery. A gracious word here, an overt hint there, and guests were rallied for the next event, be it social or a fund-raiser.

'Pensive thoughts?'

She turned towards Rafe and offered him a stunning smile. 'Observing.'

One eyebrow rose. 'Cristina?'

'However did you guess?'

'Any particular reason?'

She made a play at removing an imaginary speck from his immaculate jacket. 'She wants you. Can't you tell?'

'And that bothers you?'

'Why should it?'

Amusement lurked in that dark gaze, and a lazy smile curved the edges of his mouth. 'Let's examine the exhibits. The ones on the wall,' he added, placing a hand at her waist.

'You're killing me,' Danielle murmured. He had

no pretensions to grandeur, and merely played the role society expected of him. Whereas she'd been born into a class structure that lauded its peers, only to discard them when the chips began to fall.

The exhibits were many and varied. Harsh black and white, subtle shades of grey. An abstract collage that caused interest due to its demand for individual interpretation.

Breathtaking beauty vied with stark reality, and Danielle stood transfixed by the print of a child with cherubic features and eyes so incredibly sad their expression tugged her heartstrings.

She moved close, read the descriptive explanation printed beneath, and wanted to weep. A Bosnian child captured in a war-torn land, and deprived of family. Such innocence, so much grief.

Danielle felt a pulse thud at the edge of her throat. The thought of a child of her own suffering in any way almost killed her.

The fierce maternal instinct caught her unawares. It also endorsed the real reason for her marriage to Rafe Valdez.

She'd counted on her dislike of him. Putting up with sex as a means to an end. Playing a part in public, whilst leading separate lives in private.

Except it wasn't quite working out the way she'd envisaged.

No matter how hard she tried, it was becoming impossible with each passing day to distance her emotions, for he had only to touch her, and her pulse raced to a quickened beat.

It was all very well to abide by the adage *take each*

day as it comes...the days were fine. It was the nights—

'Rafe, darling.'

Danielle turned slightly at the sound of that husky feminine voice.

Cristina. Who else?

'I'd value your advice on a business proposition I'm considering.' The blonde offered Danielle a faint smile. 'You don't mind if I steal him for a few minutes?'

'Go ahead.' The proposition was undoubtedly a foil, but why should she care? Except she did, and that rankled more than she wanted to admit.

Fool, she derided silently. What possessed you to imagine you could become intimately involved with a man like Rafael Valdez, and keep your emotions intact?

Could he control *his* emotions?

Without doubt. The weak and undisciplined didn't survive the city streets. He'd acquired a sophisticated veneer during his rise and rise within the financial sector, and he fitted well into the social scene. However, the ruthlessness was evident beneath the surface, a heartless savagery that boded ill for any adversary.

For Rafe, she was the chosen vessel to conceive and carry his child, to provide essential maternal succour during its vulnerable early years. Once that had been achieved, it would be a case of mission accomplished, and she'd be released, financially taken care of as a salve to his conscience. Except men of Rafe's ilk didn't possess a conscience.

So, *get over it*, she chastised silently. Abide by the deal, and move on.

'Danielle. How nice to see you again.'

A familiar voice, and she turned with a ready smile. 'Lillian.'

'I'm endeavouring to organise something a little different as a fund-raiser. I thought possibly you and your dear mother might be interested in hosting a private showing of intimate apparel at La Femme. Invitation only, of course. We'd hire seating, provide the models, serve champagne and orange juice, bite-size appetizers. Included in the ticket price would be a voucher offering a ten per cent discount on items purchased at La Femme. What do you think?'

'I'd need to discuss it with Ariane,' Danielle said evenly. 'We'll also require detailed costing.'

'My dear, the costing isn't an issue. All I require from you is La Femme as the venue. The ten per cent discount will be your contribution.'

It was an attractive proposition, given the invited guests would undoubtedly spend, and spend well. 'What numbers are you considering?'

Lillian offered a triumphant smile. 'I thought fifty guests, seated in double rows of ten on each side, with two rows of five just inside the entrance.'

Naturally the boutique would need to be closed to the public during the showing. 'What time-frame are you looking at?'

'Two hours. Say, from two until four in the afternoon, tentatively mid-week, two weeks from now?'

'Put it in writing, Lillian, then I'll get back to you.'

'My dear, I already have.' She reached into her

bag, extracted an envelope and handed it to Danielle. 'Ring me tomorrow with your answer.'

Ariane would go for it, she was sure. It meant good business for La Femme, and profit was the name of the game.

Danielle moved between the exhibits, murmured an acknowledgement to a few people she knew, then paused in front of an enlarged print of a Harley Davidson motorbike. She couldn't decide who commanded more attention…the bike or the long-haired, black singlet-clad, heavily tattooed man who sat astride the seat.

'Some women's fantasy,' a familiar voice drawled, and she felt Rafe's touch at her waist.

'Hmm,' she agreed. 'All that pulsing power.'

'Are we talking about the bike here, or the man?'

She didn't miss a beat. 'Oh, the *man*. Bikes don't do it for me.'

'Image is everything?'

She cast him a studied look. 'You changed yours.'

'To fit the mould I shaped for myself?'

'Yet beneath the fine clothes, the practised sophistication, is the core of the person you were. That doesn't change.'

'So, in your opinion, I'm still a veteran of the Chicago streets.'

'You're Rafael Valdez,' she submitted solemnly. 'A man who fits easily into any background, and someone only the foolish would challenge.'

His eyes were impossibly dark, but humour lurked at the edge of his mouth. 'Is that a compliment?'

'A statement.'

He could shed his acquired image as easily as he'd assumed it. Become again what he had once been. It was there, something indefinable in his stance, the look of him. A waiting, watching quality, the hint of acutely attuned senses. In the name of survival, and protection of his own.

Did she come into that category? It was a thought she chose not to pursue.

'You spoke with Lillian?'

'Yes. She offered an interesting proposition.' She relayed it to him. 'What do you think?'

Progress, he acknowledged, aware that a week ago she wouldn't have mentioned it, let alone asked his opinion. 'Lillian has connections, and it will be a good advertisement for the boutique.'

It matched her own conclusions, and she was about to say so when she had the uncanny sensation she was being watched. With unhurried ease she turned slightly and became trapped in Cristina's gaze.

Venom glittered in unmasked brilliance for all of a few seconds, then it was gone, and Danielle suppressed a faint shiver. Such hatred!

'Can we leave?' She needed to get out of here, feel the fresh evening air on her face, and put as much distance as possible between her and the glamorous blonde.

If Rafe sensed the reason behind her request he gave no indication, and five minutes later she breathed a sigh of relief as the car eased out onto the main street and headed towards Toorak.

Numerous cafés were open, with patrons lingering over coffee at outdoor tables along the sidewalk. Rafe

drew into the kerb and parked, and together they selected a table, ordered, then relaxed as they waited
for their coffee to be served.

Rafe's cellphone pealed, and he took the call, spoke
for a few minutes, then cut the connection.

'Business?'

'I need to access the computer, and email data
through to New York.'

'Do you want to leave?'

'It can wait.'

He worked long hours and took minimum leisure
time. Even then leisure connected with business. He
could more than afford to cut some slack, delegate.
Except he knew from experience that when you took
an eye from the ball, the game suffered. Besides, he
enjoyed the adrenalin rush of planning a deal and having it reach a satisfactory conclusion.

He'd come a long way in the past ten years. He'd
acquired a reputation, wealth, social standing, and he
possessed the trappings that went with them. Fine
homes in different countries, a wife. Soon he would
have a child. An heir of his own blood to inherit everything he'd worked for.

Danielle d'Alboa *Valdez*. A woman who didn't
hide her dislike of him, and was honest enough to
enjoy what he offered without artifice. It made a refreshing change.

How would she react, he wondered, if he relayed
he'd deliberately tracked Ariane's financial decline
and fall from social grace with marriage to her daughter in mind? That it hadn't been a simple deal, but a
well thought-out and carefully orchestrated plan?

That, instead of a few months in the making, the deal had formed in his mind as long as a year ago?

She'd been right in accusing him of using her to his advantage. But not solely for her aristocratic connections. It was her pride and her courage that attracted him. And her honesty. For that alone he'd been prepared to pay the price. It was precisely those qualities he wanted in his child.

Rafe drank the strong dark brew and watched her with an indolence he knew she found unsettling.

She had the sweetest mouth, generously curved, and the delicate features of an angel. He felt himself harden at the mere thought of her unbidden response to his touch, and he shifted slightly in his chair.

It had been a while since he had felt the need for a woman the way he wanted her. How her flesh quivered when he kissed the curve at the base of her neck. The leap of her pulse when he held her, and the soft moan that escaped her throat when he suckled at her breast.

As for the moment he possessed her...it was like grasping hold of something incredible.

He drained his coffee, waited until she finished hers, then he pulled out a note and rose to his feet.

It took only a matter of minutes to reach home, and he resisted the urge to follow her upstairs. Work, he reminded as he crossed to the study and booted up his computer. An hour, two at the most, then he could join her in bed.

It was closer to three when he slid beneath the covers and gathered her close. He was fully aroused and needy, yet he took it slow until her response matched his own, and her unbridled passion became the sweetest gift as he led her towards ecstasy, then held her as they both went over the edge.

CHAPTER EIGHT

VOLLEYBALL, swimming, followed by a barbecue meant layered dressing, and Danielle donned a bikini, added a wrap-around skirt and matching top, then she tossed Lycra gym shorts and top into a gym bag, together with a towel, bra and briefs, minimum make-up and sunblock.

'Ready?'

'As ready as I'll ever be for a fun afternoon in the sun.' If Cristina happened to be among the guests, she'd scream.

Rafe added a towel to his gym bag, closed the zip, then led the way down to the garage.

He looked incredibly fit attired in fatigue-style shorts and a chambray shirt, his tall frame and breadth of shoulder emphasised by the casual attire.

He displayed an electric energy, a raw sensuality that made fools of women and reminded some men of their own inadequacies.

Dynamite. In the bedroom and out of it, Danielle accorded as Rafe brought the car to a smooth halt in the driveway leading to their hosts' stylish home.

Open-plan living, with an abundance of marble floors, modern furniture, and magnificent outdoor accoutrements, for there was a pool, a tennis court, and direct access to the beach.

Guests were already assembled on the spacious terrace, and she summoned a smile as she moved into their midst, greeting acquaintances. Women who had previously ignored her now gave the impression of being her very best friend.

It rankled, perhaps more than it should.

There were cool drinks, bite-size appetizers, and the ambience was casual. Designer gear was *de rigeur*.

'You're very quiet.'

She turned to the man at her side, and offered him a stunning smile. 'Forgive me, I didn't realise scintillating conversation was required.'

Rafe's eyes gleamed with musing cynicism. 'Our host will announce the volleyball event any time soon.'

'Thus providing the women an opportunity to cavort with the men, all in the name of sport.'

'*Cavort, querida*? I can think of a more pleasing way to expend physical energy than sport.'

Danielle directed him a level glance. 'I seem to recollect you did that last night.'

His soft, husky laughter almost undid her. 'Obviously I failed to make much impact.'

They both knew there was no truth to the statement. She'd reacted to his touch like a finely tuned instrument in the hands of a maestro. And barely restrained begging for more.

'I'm not into ego-stroking.' A flash of colour, the sound of tinkling laughter caused her to glance towards the French doors. 'I'll leave the lovely Cristina to make up for my loss.'

'Where do you think you're going?'

'Why, to mix and mingle,' she murmured. 'I don't intend to stay and watch her seduction technique.'

'You'd leave me to cope alone?'

Her mouth curved with wicked humour. 'Something you'll achieve with one hand tied behind your back,' she accorded, and turned towards the glamorous blonde. 'Cristina,' she acknowledged with pseudo-politeness. 'If you'll excuse me?'

'Of course, darling.'

Danielle wandered towards the bar and had her glass refilled with soda, then she glanced out across the bay, admiring the tranquil scene. Azure sky, blue ocean bearing colourful craft tacking across its surface. Cruisers, motorboats, families enjoying a weekend outing.

Inevitably her gaze skimmed back to Rafe, and she examined his features in profile. The strong jaw, the broad cheekbones, and well-groomed dark hair.

Cristina was intent on commanding his attention, and from here it looked as if the blonde was pulling out all the stops. The beautiful practised smile, the tilt of her head, the light touch of brilliantly lacquered nails against his forearm.

Charm personified, Danielle alluded, and dismissed the faint twinge of jealousy. To experience jealousy you had to care, and she didn't. So why did it irritate the hell out of her to see Cristina paw the man who'd paid for a child and several years of her life?

Almost as if he sensed her appraisal, he turned his head and slanted her a long, studied glance.

With a deliberate gesture, she took a long sip from

her glass then began an earnest discussion with the person standing close by.

It was perhaps as well their host chose that moment to announce the volleyball would commence.

What wicked wit had thought to place Cristina on the same side as Rafe and Danielle on the opposing side? Worse, the glamorous blonde had stripped down to a bikini. Grr!

This is the beach, Danielle silently chastised. Except fun was one thing; outright flaunting was something else.

Later, the players switched sides and Danielle found herself lined up next to Cristina. Not a good move, proven when she somehow managed to trip and land in the sand, orchestrated by a deliberately placed leg.

Well, two could play at that game. Except during the ensuing ten minutes she didn't get a chance to return an elbow jab or a stinging kick to a calf muscle.

It was a relief when the first round concluded and they retired to the pool while the remaining guests began their game.

Cristina executed a dive that showcased the perfection of her slender form. Danielle merely slid in from the pool's ledge.

She trod water as Rafe moved to her side. His eyes were dark, his gaze level, and she almost died as his mouth closed over hers in a kiss that tore the breath from her throat.

'What do you think you're doing?' she demanded the instant he lifted his head.

'Do I need a reason?'

'Yes.' With that she swam away from him, levered her body onto the side, then gathered up her towel, located her gym bag, and made for the guest pool-house.

It didn't take long to shower and change, and she emerged from the stall into the tiled lobby to discover Cristina waiting her turn.

'Pretty little scene you managed to engineer in the pool.'

This was getting tedious. 'I don't believe I owe you an explanation,' Danielle responded as she swept her hair into a careless knot atop her head.

'Watch your step,' Cristina warned, and Danielle met the blonde's gaze via mirrored reflection.

'All the time.'

'You don't stand a chance against me.'

She turned round to face a woman she knew to be her enemy. 'Be specific.'

'Figure it out, darling.'

'Are you threatening me?'

'You mean you need to ask?'

'Good luck, Cristina.' Her voice was a silky drawl, and she glimpsed a flash of rage before it was reined in.

'I never leave anything to chance.'

Danielle had had enough, and without a further word she effected a dignified exit.

The barbecue got under way around seven, with seafood kebabs, prawns, fish, and a variety of salads. Washed down with champagne it was a veritable feast.

The sun began to slip down beyond the horizon,

and dusk turned into dark. Electric lamps sprang to life, illuminating the terraced gardens and pool, and the sea became grey, almost black, as a silvery moon appeared in a star-studded velvet sky.

Coffee was served, and Danielle was conscious of Rafe's presence as they mingled among fellow guests.

It was after ten when the evening drew to a close, and she sat in silence as Rafe traversed the short distance home.

Indoors he re-set the alarm and followed her upstairs to their room.

'Nothing to say?' Rafe drawled as he began discarding his clothes.

'It was a pleasant afternoon, the food was great,' Danielle accorded matter of factly. 'Tomorrow's another day, I'm tired.' She shot him a piercing glance. 'Will that do?'

He crossed to her side, then hunkered down and examined her leg, pressing his fingers into her calf muscle.

'Must you?' she demanded, then winced at the sudden pain. 'That hurt.'

He massaged the muscle lightly, then unbent his length. 'You'll have a bruise.' His hand moved to her ribcage, and she slapped his forearm.

'Don't.' A useless directive, for he didn't take the slightest notice. 'Ouch.'

'I'll get some cream to reduce the bruising.'

'I don't need it.' She turned away from him, and stepped into the *en suite*. Within minutes she'd removed her clothes, donned a T-shirt, removed her make-up and brushed her teeth.

When she emerged into the bedroom he was standing beside the bed, tube in hand.

'Oh, for heaven's sake. Give it to me.' She went to take it from him, only to have him ignore her and apply the cream. 'Must you play nursemaid?' she vented angrily. 'Your ex-mistress is a vicious bitch.'

He finished with the cream, tossed the tube onto a nearby pedestal, then captured her face and lowered his mouth down to hers.

'That isn't going to work,' Danielle said the moment she could speak.

'I can see it won't.' He angled his mouth and took her deep.

When he lifted his head her eyes were glazed with passion, her lips pink and slightly swollen. He returned for more, grazing the curve of her mouth with the edge of his teeth before trailing to the edge of her neck and nuzzling there.

He sensed the silent groan in her throat, and caressed the vulnerable hollow where her pulse leapt to a quickened beat, then he pulled her gently down onto the bed.

Thursday morning they took a flight to Coolangatta Airport, then rode a taxi to the Palazzo Versace situated at Main Beach overlooking the broadwater.

The hotel itself was a drawcard for the tourists, and each of the privately owned condominiums provided a luxury only the wealthy could afford.

Italian in design, the mosaic tiles in the foyer were an art form, and Danielle gasped in sheer delight as she preceded Rafe into a luxurious condominium with views over the water.

Furnished completely by Versace-designed accoutrements, right down to cushions, china, cutlery, crystal.

It was, in a word, beautiful, and she told him so.

'Enjoy, *querida*,' Rafe bade indulgently. 'If you need to contact me, do so on my cellphone. I'll book dinner.'

It was a few years since she'd last visited the Coast, and she intended to explore. First priority was the apartment itself, the amenities, then she wandered into the adjacent Marina Mirage shopping complex, lingered in one of the cafés over a latte, and walked to Tedder Avenue at Main Beach, which had remained just as trendy as she remembered.

There was also the knowledge she wasn't pregnant, and she didn't know whether to be pleased or peeved at the discovery.

It was almost five when she entered the apartment, and she collected fresh underwear and headed straight for the shower.

Minutes later she gave a startled gasp as the door slid open and Rafe stepped into the tiled stall.

'Must you?' Danielle demanded fiercely.

'Why not relax and enjoy?'

'Forget seduction, it won't do you any good.'

They'd been intimate every night for almost three weeks. He didn't need for her to spell out the *why* of it.

His hands skimmed down over her shoulders and

rested on her breasts. 'There are many ways to indulge one another.'

'None of which I'm buying.'

A husky laugh left his throat an instant before his
mouth captured hers, and the kiss left her wanting,
needing more, much more.

It was a while before he lifted his head, and he
traced the sensitive curve of her lip, his eyes as dark
as her own.

'So be it.' He patted the firm cheek of her bottom.
'Now go.'

She did, and was almost dressed when he entered
the bedroom. All she'd packed was a change of
clothes and an elegant evening trouser suit in red silk.
Black stilettos and matching evening bag completed
the outfit, and she swept her hair into a smooth twist.

The restaurant overlooked the broadwater, and the
food was to die for, so artistically arranged on the
plate it was almost a sin to disturb it.

It was, Danielle decided, nice to be alone with him.
No other guests at the table with whom she felt compelled to exchange polite conversation. And no possibility of Cristina intruding.

'Did you buy the condominium off the floor plan?'

'Two,' Rafe corrected imperturbably. 'One for my
own use, and one to lease as an investment.'

Given the location and design, the value could only
escalate.

'I gather your business meeting this afternoon was
successful?' As if it would be otherwise.

'Yes.'

She lifted her glass and took a sip of wine. 'What time is our flight out tomorrow?'

'Late morning.'

Such a brief stay. Would they return in the not too distant future?

'Yes. In a few months,' Rafe drawled, and saw her surprise. 'You have expressive features.'

'Not so *you*.' It was impossible to read him, and she wondered if she ever would.

'Coffee?'

They took their time with it, then Rafe settled the bill, and they strolled along the boulevard, enjoying the night sounds. Luxury cruisers lay moored at the marina, and the numerous cafés lining the broadwater were busy with the boutique coffee crowd.

Rafe reached for her hand, and she linked her fingers through his.

Less than a month ago she'd sworn to hate this man, yet with each passing day there appeared a subtle shift in her emotions.

He was her husband, her lover. In time he would become the father of her child. Was it possible he could also be her friend?

And when their relationship was reduced to *friends*, how would she deal with it?

Not well, a tiny voice taunted. The knowledge slammed into her brain and settled there, sending her into contemplative silence.

Fool, she accorded silently. The wine has gone to your head. Rafe Valdez had presented her with a business proposition, which she'd accepted on his terms.

A business proposition their relationship would remain. Even if it killed her.

The days settled into a familiar pattern, and there was a sense of achievement as well as pleasure in seeing La Femme go from strength to strength with increased clientele and soaring profits.

At night Danielle dealt with the shimmering passion Rafe was able to evoke. Electrifying and incredibly sensual, it fed a primitive hunger and left her wanting more than just an enjoyment of the physical act.

Planning for Lillian's proposed fund-raiser took precedence as she conferred with Ariane and calculated the extra stock required, ensured the orders were placed in time for delivery.

The day duly arrived, and organisation was the key; that and lunch on the run, Danielle reflected as she closed the boutique, ensured the notice announcing a private showing was clearly visible, then she checked out the seating, adjusting a chair here and there to ensure they were staggered to enable guests seated in the rear row would be able to view the parade with ease.

A magnificent floral arrangement held centre place against the mirrored wall behind the counter…a *good luck* gift from Rafe.

'What do you think?'

'Darling, it looks wonderful,' Ariane enthused.

The caterers had not long delivered a variety of appetizers, and a large cooler out back held the champagne and orange juice.

The afternoon's programme had been rechecked twice, the lingerie and underwear set out in order.

Three models were due any minute, together with Lillian and a few volunteers to help out.

CDs were ready in the disc player, and it was just a matter of waiting for the guests to arrive.

At that moment Lillian breezed through the door with her volunteers, and two of the models followed close behind.

'There's a slight change of plan,' Lillian informed. 'The third girl we contacted to model has called in sick, and I've managed to find a replacement. It's so kind of Cristina to fill in at such short notice.'

At that moment the tall blonde entered the boutique and swept towards them.

Cristina? Saving the day, or employing subterfuge?

Danielle summoned a smile and subdued the desire to snarl. 'Kind,' she agreed, hating the role that forced her to be polite. 'The other models are in the fitting rooms. Leanne, our assistant, will go through the programme with you.'

Ariane checked her watch and moved with Lillian towards the entrance to greet the first group of guests.

By the appointed time all the chairs were filled, the champagne flowed, and the show was ready to begin.

So much thought and care had gone into its preparation, there was little chance of there being a hitch. Danielle had the programme memorised to the smallest detail, and the tension began to build as the first segment was shown.

After considerable deliberation, it had been decided to begin with sleepwear, then finish with the more daring thong briefs and minuscule bras. Three models, three colours in each category of styles.

La Femme now carried a full and varied stock of top French, German and Belgian labels guaranteed to please the most fastidious buyer.

Silk pyjamas in ivory, pale peach and cream drew murmurs of approval; exquisite full-length nightgowns and negligées were also a hit; the length changed with each round, until the most frivolous almost-there line was shown. Silk wraps in glorious colours followed.

So far, so good, Danielle breathed as there was a brief break while Lillian's volunteers refilled the guests' flutes with champagne and proffered appetizers.

'The feedback so far is excellent,' Ariane reported as they prepared for the next segment featuring slips in every length, colour and design, silk, satin, lace.

'Most everyone is marking items off on the programme,' Leanne informed. 'If they decide to buy you'll need to place a huge order for replacement stock.'

Dared she cross her fingers for luck? The temptation was almost irresistible.

The phone rang, and Ariane took the call, spoke a few words quietly, then she replaced the receiver and crossed to her daughter's side.

'Rafe, darling. He's in the area and will call in for a few minutes.'

A solitary man in a woman's domain? 'When?'

'He has just pulled up in the rear parking area.'

Danielle felt the tension headache accelerate. 'I'll

go let him in,' she managed calmly. Quite a feat when she felt anything but *calm* as she moved through the back room to unlock the door.

Rafe stood framed in the aperture, one hand casually thrust into a trouser pocket of his impeccably tailored business suit.

A dark angel, she accorded silently, and tamped down the slow-burning flame coursing through her body.

He shouldn't have this effect on her, and she assured herself she didn't covet it.

'What are you doing here?'

One eyebrow arched and his eyes assumed a humorous gleam. 'Is there a reason why I shouldn't be?'

Oh, hell, she had to marshal some control! 'It's unexpected.' She stood aside, then locked up behind him. 'The parade is in full swing.'

'It's going well?'

'I think so.'

Firm fingers caught hold of her chin and tilted it. *'But?'*

'Nothing.'

His gaze raked her features, caught the faint edge of pain evident, and brushed a thumb pad over her mouth. '*Nothing* gives you a headache?'

She managed to free herself from his grasp. 'Are you staying?'

He hadn't planned to. His original intention had been to move through the boutique, greet Ariane, Lillian, linger a few minutes to provide a little weight to the success of the parade, then leave.

Now he changed his mind. 'Will it disturb you if I do?'

Oh, my, what a question! 'I'm sure your appearance out front will *disturb* a few of the guests.' And delight one particular model.

His husky laughter sent warmth flooding through her veins. 'I'll try to be unobtrusive.'

'Sure, and pigs might fly,' she retaliated, and wasn't anywhere near quick enough to escape the brief hard kiss he bestowed on her mouth.

She shot him a dark glance as she reached into her bag, extracted a slim tube and took a few seconds to renew her lipstick.

Rafe's presence had just the effect Danielle anticipated, for the guests sat up a little straighter, smiled a little more brightly, and the models when they took the floor for the next segment seemed to possess a lighter step, their movements noticeably more provocative.

His eyes narrowed as he saw Cristina emerge, and his features remained expressionless as he observed the model's performance.

The blonde was trouble, and he had to wonder what lengths she'd gone to in order to replace the model contracted to appear at this afternoon's assignment. Somehow he doubted Lillian Stanich would have conspired to the change. It was more likely Cristina had enquired which models had been contracted, then offered one of them a higher fee to call in sick.

Exotic lacy teddies had little effect on his libido, although there was appreciation for the cut and style and the slender toned bodies of the girls who wore them.

He let his attention rest on his wife's features, and glimpsed the strain beneath her smile.

The parade was scheduled to conclude at four, and if he left immediately he'd still make his four-thirty appointment.

Danielle did her best to ignore him. Not an easy task when her mouth still tingled from his kiss, and she was battling with a mixture of resignation and anger at his presence.

Why didn't he go? Or was he deriving vicarious pleasure from watching near-naked young women parade in titillating underwear?

Satin bra and pants sets, briefs that ranged from hipster, bikini, to thong. The latter so minuscule the garment was a mere whisper of lace.

Cristina was in her element playing the role of seductive temptress as she circled the boutique, pausing every few steps to pose. Her gaze deliberately sought Rafe, and the tantalising sweep of her eyelashes, the soft pouting mouth, the witching smile all conspired to give the impression she was bent on reminding him what was on offer.

Danielle failed to see how anyone in the room could miss the blonde's blatant invitation.

The final segment concluded, Ariane relayed a gracious few words in thanks to Lillian for arranging the afternoon's gathering, and encouraged the guests to utilise their discount vouchers in aid of a worthwhile fund-raiser.

Coffee was served, together with petit fours, and

Rafe lingered only long enough to speak with Lillian, then he took his leave. But not before Cristina way-laid him on some nefarious pretext.

Danielle deliberately focused her attention on the guests lining up at the counter with their programmes and their discount vouchers.

Business was brisk. In fact, it was so good, a number of guests were still lingering in the boutique when it came to closing time.

Lillian, an exemplary organiser, had arranged for the hire firm to collect the chairs at five, together with the cooler, and after the final guest had departed Ariane, Leanne and Danielle began cleaning up and restoring order.

Consequently it was almost seven when Danielle entered the house, and she made for the stairs.

Rafe's car was in the garage, so obviously he was home. Hopefully he'd already eaten and was en-sconced in the study.

She reached the bedroom and entered the *en suite*, intent on filling the spa-bath, then she discarded her clothes, pinned up her hair, and sank into the warm water.

Bliss, she accorded silently as she switched on the jets, then she leant her head back and closed her eyes.

Danielle lost count of time as she reflected on the successful afternoon in terms of stock exposure and sales. The only fly in the ointment had been Cristina.

'That bad, hmm?'

Her lashes swept upwards at the sound of Rafe's voice, and her eyes widened as he hunkered down and handed her a flute of champagne.

He touched the rim of his flute to hers. 'To a successful afternoon.'

He looked vaguely piratical in dark jeans, his shirt unbuttoned and the sleeves turned back. This close he was a threat to her equilibrium.

'I forgot to thank you for the floral display,' Danielle offered politely.

'My pleasure.'

'It was thoughtful of you to stop by.'

He smiled, at least one step ahead of her. 'But a severe case of overkill to have stayed for more than an hour, hmm?'

She swept him a killer glance. 'The guests positively *glowed* in your presence.'

'My sole interest was one of support.'

'Really?' She wanted to throw something at him. 'That's why you stayed? Forgive me for imagining it was just to leer at the semi-nude models.'

His husky laughter was the living end.

'*Querida*, I was far more tempted just looking at you, knowing what lay beneath that chic business suit, aware that it's mine for the taking,' Rafe drawled, 'than viewing exotic underwear on women who have no appeal for me whatsoever.'

'Cristina didn't seem to think so,' she shot back.

'Naturally, as an exhibitionist with an impossible ego.'

'As far as she was concerned, she was giving a private showing just for *you*.'

'Jealous?'

She picked up the sponge and threw it at him.

He fielded it easily, tossed it back into the spa, then

he uncurled his lengthy frame. 'You want I should join you?'

'If you get in, I'll get out,' she offered succinctly, and felt her eyes widen as he pulled off his shirt and reached for the snap fastening on his jeans.

'I wouldn't bank on it.'

Danielle scrambled to her feet as he discarded his jeans, briefs, toed off his trainers, and he grasped hold of her arm as she attempted to step out of the tub.

'Let me go!'

There was something almost pagan about him as he joined her, a raw sexual energy that was infinitely primitive.

'Don't.' She tried to evade him, and found herself pulled down into the cradle of his arms.

'Relax.'

How could she *relax*, for heaven's sake?

Even as she struggled, his hands slid up her arms and he began kneading the tight muscles at the base of her nape.

Oh, God, that felt good. So good, she breathed silently, giving in to the magic of his touch.

After a few minutes she couldn't help herself. 'You do that very well.'

She felt the brush of his lips against the curve of her shoulder.

'One hopes it's not the only thing I do well.'

She could hear the amusement evident in his voice, and her body began to throb as sensation swirled, reaching every nerve-end until she felt as if she was on fire.

'What do you want? A score on a rating from one to ten?'

Laughter rumbled from his throat. 'Heaven forbid.'

'I'd like to get out now.'

'We're not nearly done.'

His hands left her shoulders and slipped to cup each breast, stroking the firm contours, then exploring each burgeoning peak.

The tactile touch ignited a flame deep within, and she groaned as his hand slid down over her stomach to the apex between her thighs.

All it took was a circling sweep and sensation spiralled, taking her high. His lips caressed her nape, and she arched against the sensual probe of his fingers. She cried out as he stroked the sensitive clitoris, convulsing at the intense oral stimulation, and she made no protest as he scooped her into his arms and stepped out of the spa.

Rafe snagged a towel and blotted the excess moisture from her skin, then dragged the towel over his body before leading her to the bed.

One tug and the bedcovers slithered onto the floor, then he pulled her down with him, entering her in one deep thrust.

It was she who began to move, she who dictated the pace, and she exulted in the power a woman could have over a man. Aware of the animalistic passion, and raw intensity that consumed them both as they climaxed, then tumbled in a glorious drift of sensual emotion.

Afterwards she slept, and it was almost midnight when they ventured downstairs to replenish their energy levels with something as prosaic as food.

CHAPTER NINE

SHARING breakfast on the terrace was a relaxing way to kick-start the day, and Danielle took a generous sip of strong coffee as she let her gaze wander over the gardens. Antonio's efforts with the lawns, the plants, showed tremendous care and dedication, and the visual effect was stunning. The couple's work hours coincided with her own, which meant they entered the house after she left and were gone by the time she returned.

Toorak was a well-established moneyed suburb, with a pleasing mix of modern and old homes, some of which stood in spacious grounds.

Rafe's home was no exception, and high walls lent an air of privacy and seclusion, despite the suburb's close proximity to the inner city.

'I have a week of meetings in Paris and London,' Rafe informed as he drained the last of his coffee. 'We fly out tomorrow.'

The *we* rankled. 'I suppose you've already discussed this with Ariane, Leanne is prepared to work, and the whole thing is a *fait accompli*.'

Rafe inclined his head. 'Would you have preferred a time-wasting argument?'

'You won't give me the option to refuse?'

There was an edge of humour apparent. 'Do you want to?'

She opened her mouth, then closed it again. *Paris.* She'd have the opportunity to visit the lingerie houses, revisit a few of her favourite places... A winsome smile curved her lips. 'Who would protest about a trip to Paris?'

Even in the cold, drizzling weather of a northern hemispheric winter, Paris still retained its magic.

Danielle dismissed the misty fog hanging heavily on the air, buttoned her coat and swung the woollen scarf round her neck.

It had been five years since she last visited, and there were places she wanted to explore, an art gallery, the Left Bank, a favoured café she'd haunted during her sojourn in this beautiful city.

The skies might be grey, but her mood was as bright as a rainbow.

She adored the ambience, the sense of history apparent. A place where battles had been fought long before, the generations of Parisians who'd walked these streets, the architecture...

It didn't matter that Rafe would be tied up in business meetings all day. There was the Louvre, Notre-Dame, and no visit to Paris was complete without viewing the city from the Eiffel Tower. St-Germain-des-Prés...

Danielle sighed, and quickened her footsteps, intent to make the most of the few days she had here.

There was the thrill of being able to shop, and, although she could have gone crazy with Rafe's credit card, she resisted the temptation by being selective. Very selective. A gift for Ariane, something small for Leanne, and a token for Elena.

It was after six when she entered their luxury hotel on the Avenue des Champs-Elysées and took the lift up to their suite.

Rafe was already there, his jacket discarded and his tie pulled free as he poured himself a drink.

He took one look at her pink cheeks and sparkling eyes, then he crossed the room and took her mouth in a lingering kiss.

'Good day?'

'Wonderful.' She offered him a smile that curled round his heart and tugged a little. 'You?'

'The French like to haggle.'

'A stand-off, huh?'

'You could say that.'

'And you won't give in.' It was a statement, not a query.

'No.' The deal, if it was cut, would be on his terms.

Danielle deposited the signature carry-bags onto a chair, and began unbuttoning her coat.

Rafe slid his hands inside its warmth and pulled her close to nuzzle the sweet hollow beneath her ear-lobe. 'Come share my shower.' His palms slipped low to cup her bottom, drawing her in against his arousal.

He wanted her, needing the sweetness, and more than anything he wanted to lose himself inside her, to hold her close and temporarily forget the frustrations of the day.

Then, he determined, they'd dress and go some-where for dinner, eat fine food, drink a little wine, then stroll back to the hotel.

'I'm not sure that's a good idea.'

His lips brushed the edge of her jaw and settled on the edge of her mouth. 'No?'

'We might not get out of this suite.'

'And that's a problem?' He nipped the soft fullness of her lip, then soothed it with his tongue.

'This is *Paris*,' Danielle said simply, as if that said it all, and he chuckled an instant before he conducted a slow sweep of her mouth.

She kissed him back, and couldn't help the way her body responded as he deepened the kiss with a hunger that matched her own.

Their clothes were an impossible barrier, and they dispensed with them, letting them drop where they stood.

Rafe took a few seconds to throw back the bed-covers, then he tumbled her down onto the bed. He buried his mouth in the valley between her breasts, then tantalised each peak, rolling the tender nipple with his teeth in an action that held her on the brink between pleasure and pain.

Danielle arched up against him, circled one male aureole with her tongue, savoured it, then she nipped the hard pebbled nub...and felt his sharp indrawn breath.

Emboldened, she reached for him, tracing the satin-smooth skin sheathing his male shaft with a feather-light touch before sliding low to cup him.

His husky growl urged her to tease and tantalise, before conducting an erotic circling movement that had every muscle tensing in his body.

'Careful, *querida*,' he warned softly, and lowered his mouth to hers in an oral imitation of the sexual act itself. Then he entered her with one powerful thrust that took him to the hilt.

The feeling of enclosure was acute, given his sheer size, and he rocked a little, easing the pressure as her muscles caught his rhythm.

She hadn't thought it possible to feel like this every time, and she held on in a mutual slaking of desire that swept them high.

Was that her voice crying out? Begging? The thought fled as she became caught up in such a tide of emotion that she shattered into a thousand pieces at the moment of climax.

Dear heaven.

There wasn't a single word she could utter as he disengaged, then scooped her into his arms and carried her through to the *en suite*.

Cataclysmic whispered through her brain long minutes later as they soaped each other. Earth-shattering sex, she added silently.

Half an hour later they emerged from the hotel and walked briskly in the cold night air. They could, probably should, have frequented one of the hotel's restaurants, and not ventured outdoors.

However, fine restaurants lined the streets and avenues radiating off the Champs-Elysées, and they didn't need to walk far before they ventured into an élite establishment, where Rafe requested, in faultless French, the *maître d'* find them a table.

The wine, the food, both were superb; a true gourmet delight, Danielle complimented as she declined dessert and requested coffee.

Rafe had the look of a satisfied cat...a sleek panther, she decided, all too aware of the power beneath the Italian tailoring, the crisp white shirt.

Even thinking what he could do to her set all her nerve-ends on edge, and renewed warmth invaded her body.

He knew. She could tell from the indolent gleam in those dark eyes, the warm curve of his mouth.

'Danielle? *Danielle* d'Alboa?'

The voice was familiar, the man's features even more so.

'Jean-Claude?' There was disbelief in her voice, then soft laughter emerged from her throat as she lifted her face to receive his salutary kiss to each cheek. Her eyes sparkled. 'I don't believe it.'

'It is I who does not believe you are back in Paris, *chérie*.' He glanced from her to Rafe, and back again. 'Are you not going to introduce us?'

'Of course. Jean-Claude Sebert, Rafael Valdez.'

'Her husband,' Rafe drawled, intent on claiming ownership.

Danielle sensed the faint warning edge in his tone, and briefly wondered at it.

'Jean-Claude is an old friend,' she explained. It had been *years*, at least five, and he'd been very good to her. 'Please, you must join us. We were just about to order coffee.'

'*Chérie*, you are sure I am not intruding?' He glanced towards the man who had put a ring on her finger, and wondered at the wisdom of annoying him.

Rafe gestured towards the vacant chair. 'Please.'

'So, tell me, Rafael, how you managed to capture this delightful creature.'

'By presenting her with an offer she couldn't refuse.'

'I see.'

'I hope you do, my friend,' Rafe drawled, and, lifting a hand, he signalled the waiter to bring coffee.

'It seems so long since I last saw you,' Jean-Claude declared. His shoulders lifted in a Gallic shrug. 'Yet not so long.' His mouth curved into a warm smile. 'You are even more beautiful now than you were then.'

A mischievous smile widened her lips. 'And you are even more the flatterer, *oui*?'

'Ah, you know me well.'

'Jean-Claude was an art student at the Sorbonne,' she relayed, aware of Rafe's watchful gaze. 'We met whilst taking a tour of the Louvre. He was determined to set the world on fire with his art.'

'And have you?' Rafe queried with deceptive indolence.

'Not the world. Just a small part of it.'

'How small, Jean-Claude?' Danielle teased. 'You always were incredibly modest.'

'My work hangs in some of the galleries.'

Coffee was delivered by a waiter, and served. Danielle added cream and sugar to hers, while both men took theirs black.

'How long are you staying?'

'Only a few days,' Rafe informed, and saw the other man's disappointment.

'Tell me how things are with you. Have you married?'

'Briefly. It didn't work out,' he relayed with an eloquent shrug. 'Now I bury myself in my work.'

'I'm sorry.'

'Yes, I do believe you are.' He sipped his coffee, finished it, then rose to his feet and withdrew a note which he placed on the table.

Rafe waved it aside, but the Frenchman didn't pick it up.

'If you'll excuse me?' He brushed his fingers to her cheek. *'Au revoir, chérie.'* He turned to her husband. 'Rafael.'

She watched as he disappeared out onto the pavement, then she picked up her cup and sipped its contents.

'No, he wasn't,' she offered quietly, challenging Rafe's level gaze.

He didn't pretend to misunderstand. 'Did you love him?'

'He was there for me when I needed him to be,' Danielle said quietly. 'After someone I thought I loved proved to be more interested in the d'Alboa heritage than he was in me.' Her eyes were clear, with just the merest shadow of remembered pain. 'Jean-Claude picked up the emotional pieces and helped me put them back together again.'

And fell in love with her, Rafe added silently, wondering if she'd known.

'It appears I may have misjudged him.'

'For which you won't have the opportunity to make amends.'

'You didn't maintain contact?'

'It wouldn't have been fair,' she qualified simply.

Rafe summoned the waiter, and paid the bill. 'Shall we leave?'

They walked a while, pausing every now and then to peruse the shop window-dressing. The night was alive, with people seated in numerous cafés, the aroma of food and strong coffee redolent on the evening air.

There was a sense of timelessness, a vibrancy she hadn't experienced in any other major city in the world. Perhaps she was just viewing it with new eyes, but it seemed different.

Or maybe it was *she* who had changed. Fashioned by circumstance and the loss of a lifestyle she'd taken for granted. The realisation that dignity and integrity were more important than possessions and false friends.

It was late when they returned to their hotel suite, and Rafe crossed to the desk, opened his laptop, then set to work. 'I'll be a while.'

'Fine.' She'd slip into bed, and hopefully be asleep when he joined her.

She was, and an hour later he stood looking down at her features in repose, aware of the inner beauty of her soul. It tugged at him, awakening something deep within.

The following few days passed much too quickly, for there wasn't sufficient time to fit everything in.

Rediscovering the city was a wonderfully exhilarating experience as Danielle became reacquainted with the familiar and enchanted by the new.

It would have been fantastic to be able to take a

month instead of three days to explore. However, she managed to seek out two élite lingerie boutiques and elicit a preview of the new season's styles.

There was too much to see and do to linger long in any one of the many trendy cafés lining the boulevards and avenues, and she returned to the hotel each evening in time to shower, change, dine, then explore the city by night with Rafe in attendance.

All too soon they boarded a flight to London, and spent two days and a night there before returning home.

The telephone pealed, and Danielle crossed from the mannequin she was dressing to the counter to take the call. Ariane was engaged in the fitting room with a client.

'Good afternoon. La Femme. Danielle,' she intoned pleasantly.

'Have you received my replacement brief?' a feminine voice demanded with autocratic arrogance on identifying herself.

The client from hell. 'I was able to purchase the same colour, style and size whilst in Paris. It's here for you to collect at your convenience.'

There was a faint pause as the woman digested the information. 'I'll be in tomorrow.'

Great, Danielle perceived with a slight grimace. The woman seemed bent on causing trouble, returning a pair of briefs she'd purchased at the lingerie showing, insisting a small slit in the lace had been there at the time of purchase. Something both Ariane and Danielle knew not to be true, for each garment underwent a rigid check on delivery, and wasn't added to the stock shelves without inspection.

Which meant the slit had occurred after purchase. Whether it had been deliberate action or the result of an accident was debatable.

A lengthy and very vocal diatribe about careless workmanship, an accusation La Femme was selling falsely labelled goods at highly inflated prices indicated a deliberate attempt to denigrate.

Hence, Danielle had kept the receipt and packaging as proof.

It disturbed her, and made for extra caution. If the client had been Cristina the motive would be clear. But both complaints in the past ten days had come from different women.

It was something of a relief when several days went by with no mix-up with any special order, no one returned a supposedly flawed garment or lodged a complaint.

The boutique thrived, the catalogue went out, and on a social level it proved to be a very quiet week.

'Would you mind if I invite Ariane to dinner?' Danielle queried over breakfast Friday morning, and incurred Rafe's measured glance.

He had the power to render her helpless with just a look, and she wondered how he could sit there so calmly when only hours before they'd shared earth-shattering sex. Dammit, she could still *feel* the power of his possession, the acutely sensitised erogenous zones he was able to play with such innate mastery.

'Tonight?'

Get a grip. A silent admonishment that was of no help at all!

'I thought Sunday, unless you have plans.' She bit into the last morsel of toast, then followed it down with coffee.

'Sunday's fine.'

'I'll cook.' She wrinkled her nose at his faintly raised eyebrow. 'You doubt I can?'

'Did I imply otherwise?'

Just for that, she'd plan something incredibly exotic!

Rafe drained his coffee and rose to his feet. 'Don't wait dinner.'

'I won't be home. It's late-trading night,' she reminded, and followed him from the room, snagged her jacket, briefcase, then trailed him to the garage.

'Mmm,' Rafe murmured appreciatively as he entered the kitchen late Sunday afternoon. 'Something smells good.'

She looked cute in cut-off denim shorts and a singlet top. Her hair was caught into a pony-tail, she wasn't wearing a skerrick of make-up, and she had a smear of flour on one cheek.

He moved in and caught her close, only to have her slap his forearm. An action which had no effect at all as he leant down and fastened his mouth on hers.

When he lifted his head he took satisfaction in her slightly glazed look, although she recovered much too quickly for his liking.

'If you're going to stay in the kitchen you can be

useful.' She indicated a stack of pots and pans. 'You want to wash or dry?'

He'd served his time in a few restaurant kitchens in exchange for food. 'Go freshen up.'

She didn't need second bidding, and when she returned ten minutes later the kitchen had been restored to its sparkling best.

Ariane arrived at five, presented Rafe with a bottle of chilled wine, and laughingly spread her hands when Danielle refused her help.

It was a fine meal, and well worth the effort. Afterwards they took their coffee out on the terrace.

The air was fresh, the sky a deep indigo with a sprinkling of stars, and Danielle was loath to admit it had been a long time since she'd felt so relaxed.

CHAPTER TEN

'ARE you sure you don't mind if I leave early?' Ariane queried with an air of concern.

'Mid-week, and five o'clock?' Danielle queried with a smile. 'The boutique isn't going to suddenly experience a rush of clients. Now *go*. I can handle closing up.'

Twenty-five minutes later Danielle checked her watch and switched off the deck with its selection of CDs chosen for subtle background music. In a few minutes she could lock the front door, retrieve the cash float, then close up and leave.

The heat of the day would hit as soon as she exited the boutique's air-conditioned interior, and she conjured up an image of Rafe's pool, its cool, silky water. The thought of indulging in a few leisurely laps appealed before she showered and changed to attend a sculpture exhibition. An invitation-only affair, it was a private showing for a select coterie of proven clients and collectors of the sculptor's works.

Her mind strayed to the contents of her wardrobe. Black always made a statement, but perhaps—

The sound of the electronic door-buzzer surprised her, for it was rare for anyone to enter the boutique at this hour.

The young man's motorcycle gear and helmet

shouldn't provide any reason for her sudden instinctive spurt of alarm.

'Is there anything in particular I can help you with?' Danielle queried as she moved towards him.

Maybe he was here on behalf of a girlfriend, and had size, colour, style memorised or written down.

He indicated a mannequin to his left. 'Do you have that in black in a size ten?'

It took only a minute to open the appropriate drawer and extract the briefs. She double-checked the size tab, then crossed to the counter for tissue and ribbon, the carry-bag that was their trademark packaging.

Hard hands caught hold of her arms, and she cried out in shock as they were wrenched behind her back.

'What the hell are you doing?'

'Shut up.'

The motive had to be robbery, but she was damned if she'd accept it without a fight.

Quick reflexive action with the heel of her shoe found purchase, and she heard a grunt as she was pushed down onto the floor.

She struggled in vain, hating the ease with which he held her down. He had her hands in a crushing grip, and she was half-sitting, half-kneeling on the floor.

She didn't even think, just aimed her head at his leg and sank her teeth into a trouser-clad thigh.

Then she screamed in agony as fingers caught hold of her hair, wrenching her head back, and a resounding slap cracked against the side of her face.

'Bitch.'

Danielle's eyes watered with the force of the blow.

'Take the money and go.'

She heard the sound of masking tape being torn from its roll, followed by a harsh snort of derision, and she fought like a tiger before her captor successfully bound her wrists together.

Her hair, once caught into a sleek twist, now tumbled loose, and her breathing came in ragged gasps from her exertions.

He pushed his face close to hers. 'Try that again, and you'll wish you were dead.'

The look she cast him held a mix of disdain and fury.

'Nothing to say?' he taunted. His eyes were cold, cruel. With deliberate movements he reached out a hand and cupped her jaw.

'Don't...*touch* me!' Her anger was very real.

His smile held an evil calm. 'Try to stop me.'

She kicked out at him in a last-ditch attempt to harm as he grabbed hold of her legs. Masking tape at her ankles, then her knees made any further movement impossible, and she swore at him.

She watched as he opened the cash register, stuffed notes and coins into his pocket, then leant down and caught her chin in a punishing grip.

'By the time you get help I'll be long gone.'

He swept the briefs off the counter onto the floor, then disappeared out the door.

Danielle wriggled out of her shoes, then inched her way towards the phone. Dammit, who would have thought masking tape could be so effective?

If she could open a drawer and somehow retrieve the scissors, she might be able to cut herself free.

It took time, but she managed it. First her ankles, then her legs, her thighs. Once the scissors slipped, leaving a nasty scratch.

At least she could get to her feet and reach the phone. Dialling wasn't easy, and she punched in a wrong number, then had to start over.

Rafe picked up on the third ring. 'Valdez.'

'Someone has just robbed the boutique,' she relayed calmly. 'I need to file a police report.'

She heard him swear. 'Are you OK?'

Shaken, angry, but not hurt. 'Yes.'

'I'm on my way.'

He was there in five minutes.

Minutes during which she managed to wrestle with the scissors and slice through the tape binding her wrists.

He took in the scene at a glance, his features a chilling mask as he crossed to her side.

His eyes were impossibly dark as he caught the reddened patch marking her cheek. 'He hurt you.'

'It could have been worse.'

Rafe cupped her face. He brushed his fingers gently over her cheeks, then leant down and kissed her. A soft open-mouthed gesture that almost fractured her into a hundred pieces.

'Tell me.'

She did, quietly, although her voice shook a little as he tucked the hair back from her face.

'OK, let's call it in.'

Rafe's influence ensured an officer was on the

scene in record time. Realistically, there was little that could be done other than file a report. The boutique hadn't been trashed, the money taken comprised a one-hundred-dollar float, and she wasn't injured. The fact the intruder had worn leather gloves meant there were no fingerprints. By not removing his helmet he'd made recognition and identification impossible.

They'd run a check, question if anyone had seen anything, but the chance of someone memorising a license plate was next to nil, and the entire episode would end as just another incomplete file.

Rafe saw the police officer from the premises while Danielle collected her bag and followed him to the door.

'I'll see you at home.'

She incurred his sharp glance. 'I'd rather you didn't drive.'

'Why?'

'Indulge me, *querida*.'

'I'm fine,' Danielle insisted, and she was. Despite a niggling suspicion the robbery hadn't been a random act, but a premeditated one with a purpose.

He saw the determination evident, glimpsed something beneath it, and made a decision to postpone pursuing it until later. For now, he wanted her out of here.

There were calls he needed to make to step up security. He made the first from his cellphone as he followed her home, and had the satisfaction of knowing his instructions would be implemented the next day.

Both cars eased to a halt into the spacious garage

within seconds of each other, and Rafe led her upstairs to their room, filled the spa-bath, then crossed to her side.

He tended to the buttons fastening her jacket, and she batted at his hands.

'I can undress myself.'

'So you can,' he drawled, and slid the jacket from her shoulders before reaching for the zip at her waist.

'We'll be late for dinner.' As a protest, it was feeble.

'So, we'll be late.'

The skirt fell to the carpet, closely followed by her half-slip and briefs. He unclasped the clip on her bra, then cupped each breast and brushed a thumb pad back and forth across the nipple.

Her flesh responded, heating to his touch, and sensation quivered deep inside, piercing in its intensity.

She could close her eyes and willingly go wherever he chose to lead.

Without a word he divested his clothes, and her eyes darkened, their dilation almost total.

The breath hissed between his teeth as he caught sight of the long scratch on her inner thigh, and she glimpsed white-hot rage as he sought to bank it down.

'The scissors slipped when I cut through the tape.'

His eyes narrowed. 'Did he touch you?'

'Not in the way you mean.' The fact he could have sent shivers scudding down her spine.

Rafe led her into the *en suite*, closed the taps, activated the jets, and stepped into the spa-bath to settle her in front of him.

There was something incredibly sensual in being

bathed by a lover. The smooth slide of soap-slicked hands over her skin, the light perfume that rose with the steam, teasing her nostrils, the touch of his lips at the sensitive curve between her neck and shoulder.

It was heaven to lean back against him, to let her lashes drift down, and just *be*.

She felt him move, then a brush stroked gently through the length of her hair, and she murmured her appreciation.

After he was done he massaged her shoulders, the kinks she hadn't realised were there, then he turned her round to face him and kissed her.

There was no demand, little hunger…just an open-mouthed gentleness that made her want to weep.

Danielle moved in close and wound her arms around his neck, needing the reassurance, the warmth and heat of him.

To be treasured, loved, adored by this man was not something he offered. But for now, what she had was enough. To long for more was a foolishness she couldn't afford.

Slowly she lifted her head and brushed her lips lightly against his own. Her smile held genuine humour as she rose to her feet and stepped out from the bath. 'Have you forgotten we're due to put in an appearance at Daktar's exhibition?'

'I'll phone and cancel.'

Danielle pressed a finger to his mouth. 'I'd like to attend.'

'Are you going to tell me why?'

He was too clever by half. 'I could be wrong.'

'And if you're not?'

She snagged a towel and wound it round her slender curves, aware Rafe closely followed her actions.

'I need to deal with it.'

She would, but with considerable help, he determined as he followed her into the bedroom and began to dress.

Tomorrow there would be security cameras installed in front and out back of the boutique. As well as an alert button with direct access to a top security firm. What was more, a guard would be present from the time the boutique opened until it closed.

And he'd plan his own investigation. If someone had it in mind to frighten her, or worse, for whatever devious means...they'd pay dearly for their efforts. But first he'd ensure every preventative precaution was in place.

Irrespective of her approval, or otherwise.

It was after eight when they entered the Gallery, and Danielle accepted a flute of champagne from a hovering waiter.

Invitation only ensured the cream of the social élite were in attendance, the women resplendent in fine gowns and displaying jewellery sufficient to warrant the presence of a security guard.

Clever use of concealer beneath her make-up meant the mark on her cheek didn't show, and she'd chosen her gown with care, aware the blush-rose colour highlighted the texture of her skin, the bias-cut design accenting slender curves. Seeking a sophisticated image, she'd swept her hair into a sleek twist, added a decorative clip, and opted not to wear jewellery.

Danielle wandered at will, pausing here and there

to examine the fluidity and style of more than one sculpture which took her eye.

Rafe didn't leave her side, and he made a mental note as she returned to a particular item, a remarkable bronze eighteen to twenty inches high, set against a background of concave mirrored panels, so that every angle was captured.

'It's stunning,' she accorded simply. She could picture it in the boutique. Standing on a marbled column to the left of the counter, set against softly draped silk. It would be a focal point, and capture interest.

She referred to the glossy catalogue and blanched at the price. Perhaps not. She'd need to increase the boutique's insurance just to cover the sculpture's replacement value.

'Rafe, Danielle. How nice to see you again.'

Danielle turned and offered Lillian Stanich a smile in greeting.

'Lillian,' Rafe acknowledged with considerable charm. 'Will you excuse me for a few minutes?'

'He's quite something, isn't he?' the society doyenne commented musingly.

'Something,' Danielle agreed solemnly, and heard Lillian's tinkling laugh.

'You make a delightful couple, my dear.'

'I'll tell Rafe you said so.'

'I'm arranging another fund-raiser next month. I'll ensure you receive tickets.'

'You'll include Ariane in the invitation, I hope?'

'My dear, of course.'

'Thank you.'

'Now, if you'll excuse me?'

Alone, she cast the sculpture a wistful glance, then moved to the next exhibit. Seconds later instinct caused her to glance across the gallery, and there, a striking figure in red, was Cristina.

If the blonde was surprised to see Danielle she hid it well, and after a few seconds of riveting eye contact Danielle raised her champagne flute a few inches in a silent salute, then watched as Cristina crossed the floor.

'I didn't expect to see you tonight.'

As a greeting, it lacked any pretence to gracious-ness, and Danielle deliberately widened her gaze. 'Any particular reason, Cristina?'

'How was Paris?'

'Romantic, despite grey skies, cool temperatures, and rain.'

'A city for lovers.'

'Yes.'

Cristina took a tentative sip of champagne, then ran a red-lacquered nail round the flute's rim. 'Don't fall in love with him, darling.' The smile became a bril-liant facsimile, although there was icy venom evident in those cold grey eyes. 'It's fatal.'

Danielle caught sight of Rafe an instant before the blonde turned slightly and offered him a killer smile.

'We were just talking about you.'

He curved an arm along the back of her waist, and sensed the tension in her stance. 'Home, I think.'

'Cristina would like another champagne.'

'Would you mind, *querido*?'

'I'll summon a waiter.' He lifted a hand, clicked

his fingers, and within seconds a waiter appeared, bearing a tray of drinks.

'Spoilsport,' Danielle murmured quietly, and felt the pressure of his fingers increase.

'Shall we leave?'

'Good heavens,' Cristina mocked. 'So early?'

'He has seduction in mind,' Danielle declared with a singularly sweet smile, then tilted her head towards him. 'Don't you, *querido*?'

The Spanish endearment held a certain cynicism that wasn't lost on the glamorous blonde, and her eyes glittered vengefully for a second before she successfully schooled her expression. 'In that case, have fun, darlings. No doubt we'll run into each other again soon.'

Danielle watched as Cristina disappeared across the room. She had the beginnings of a headache, and she felt incredibly fragile.

'We've remained long enough,' Rafe declared firmly, not fooled in the slightest, and she made no protest as he led her towards the exit.

In the car she leaned back against the head-rest and closed her eyes, glad of the dim interior as Rafe eased into the flow of traffic and headed home.

Fifteen minutes later she entered the bedroom and began to undress, aware of his close scrutiny as he discarded his jacket, his tie, and began unbuttoning his shirt.

'Would you care to tell me what that was all about?'

'No,' she said simply. She walked into the *en suite*,

removed her make-up, her briefs and bra, then pulled on a T-shirt.

When she emerged he offered her a glass filled with water and two tablets. 'Take these, and get into bed.'

Her head felt as if it didn't belong to her body, and she swallowed the medication, then slid in between the sheets.

The last thing she remembered was Rafe switching off the light, the room's darkness, and the relief of blissful oblivion.

Breakfast was a leisurely meal eaten out on the terrace, and, at Rafe's insistence, Danielle rang her mother and relayed what had happened the previous evening, listened to Ariane's shocked incredulity, and gave what reassurance she could.

'Yes, of course I'll be in this morning,' she declared before replacing the receiver.

'I've organised for a security firm to install a state-of-the-art system in the boutique,' Rafe informed as she refilled her glass with juice.

Her hand paused, and she replaced the jug onto the table. 'Excuse me?'

'You heard.'

'There's no need—'

'My prerogative, Danielle,' he declared hardly. 'No negotiation.'

'The hell there isn't!'

'A team of men are due to arrive early this morning. There should be minimum interruption.'

She felt like stamping her foot in frustration at his high-handedness.

'Are you sure you're OK?' Ariane queried with concern the instant Danielle entered the boutique.

'I'm fine,' she reiterated firmly. She felt like a chick with two over-anxious parents, except Rafe's attention was the antithesis of paternal!

'A few faxes, darling. One from Paris confirming our enquiry, another from the supplier informing a delay with an order.'

'Give me a moment and I'll check the emails.'

'I've just made coffee.'

The electronic buzzer sounded, and Danielle moved forward to greet the man who had just entered the boutique.

His proffered business card confirmed his status with the security firm, and the men had hardly begun work when a smartly dressed young woman entered the boutique, presented her credentials, and insisted she'd been contracted by Rafael Valdez as in-house security officer.

'I don't believe this!' Danielle declared angrily as she crossed to the phone and dialled Rafe's cellphone.

He answered on the second ring, listened to her tirade, then directed with controlled calmness, 'Maris stays. End of story.'

'I don't need a damned bodyguard!'

'Live with it, Danielle.'

'We'll discuss this when I get home.'

'If you wish.'

She had the feeling she could *wish* all she liked, but the result would be the same, and she cursed him afresh as she cut the call.

'I'm conversant with your computerised register,

and familiar with sales techniques,' Maris informed
with practised efficiency. 'I can double as a sales assistant, and in this situation I'd advise going for that
angle.'

Cut and dried, Danielle concluded, and winced as
one of the workmen activated an electric drill.

It was going to be one hell of a day!

She silently seethed through most of it, and by midday she had the explanatory patter down to a fine art
when clients queried the workmen's presence.

Not only a security system, but cameras positioned
out back as well as in the main salon.

The boutique was, she told her mother, more
heavily secured than a bank.

'Darling, Rafe has your best interests at heart. Last
night was most unfortunate, but it could have been
much worse.'

Dammit, she knew that. And, beneath the anger,
she was grateful in a reluctant sort of way.

However, it didn't stop her from launching into a
verbal attack within minutes of entering the house.

Danielle found him in the study, intent on figures
up on the computer screen, and he pressed the *save*
key as she entered the room, then he leaned back in
his chair and gave her his full attention.

'Why didn't you consult me?' she demanded without preamble.

Did she realise how beautiful she looked when she
was angry? He banked down his amusement and settled in for the fight.

'It's a done deal, *querida*,' he drawled, watching
as she attempted to rein in her indignation.

'OK,' she qualified as she crossed to stand in front of his desk. 'I'll go along with the alarm system.' She placed both hands down onto the polished surface. 'I'll even concede to the cameras.' Her next move was to lean forward and glare at him. 'But Maris? *Really*, Rafe. Maris is definite overkill!'

'She's in my employ,' he said succinctly. 'I pay her salary.' His gaze locked with hers. 'End of story.'

Danielle picked up the first thing that came to hand and threw it in his direction, watching with detached fascination as he fielded and palmed it neatly, then placed it down onto the desk.

With easy lithe movements he rose to his feet and crossed round to where she stood glaring at him in open defiance.

'You have something you want to prove?'

'*Yes*. Just for once I'd like to see you diminished in some way.'

He lifted a hand and caught hold of her chin. When had want and lust become *love*? He couldn't pinpoint the exact moment. Only that it had.

'You succeeded,' he intoned indolently. 'Last night. Knowing someone had got to you. Imagining how badly you could have been hurt.'

What was he trying to say...that he cared? The thought almost destroyed her.

For several seemingly long seconds she couldn't tear her gaze away from his, and she stood locked into immobility.

There was something unreadable in those dark eyes, and she felt her anger deflate. 'I'm sorry.'

He smiled, and traced the outline of her mouth with

the pad of his thumb. 'Yes, I do believe you are.' He dropped his hand and swept it towards a box sitting on the credenza beneath the window. 'Go open it.'

She stood still for a few seconds, unable to wrench her gaze away from his, then she crossed to the credenza and carefully undid the tape.

There was considerable packing, and she took time to distribute the foam chips, gasping almost soundlessly as she glimpsed the mirrored panels.

The sculpture she'd admired at the gallery.

'You bought it?' she queried with incredulous reverence.

'I thought it would look good in the boutique.'

Danielle carefully replaced the foam packing, then turned to face him. She didn't know whether to smile or cry. 'Thank you.'

'I shall see that you do.'

He was teasing her, and she knew it. But it didn't stop the anticipation of the night ahead as she sat through dinner, logged figures into her laptop, then showered and prepared for bed.

It was she who reached for him, and although he revelled in the slide of her fingers, the tentative exploration of her mouth, it was *he* who took control of the pace, *he* who led them both towards a tumultuous climax that left them both bathed in sensual heat.

'Why do you always have to win?' she demanded huskily, and heard his equally husky reply.

'Because I can.'

CHAPTER ELEVEN

'DARLING, you're looking pale,' Ariane voiced with concern a few days later. 'Are you coming down with something?'

'I don't think so. I just feel a bit tired, that's all.'

'Perhaps you're overdoing things.'

Danielle shot her mother a quizzical look. 'No more than usual.' She could hardly confide Rafe kept her awake at night, and most often reached for her in the early dawn hours.

'Is it possible you might be pregnant?'

She went into instant recall on pertinent dates, then slowly shook her head. 'I doubt it.'

Yet she visited a pharmacy, bought a home pregnancy test, and sank down in a heap when it showed positive.

How could she be pregnant? *Stupid question.*

A doctor's appointment confirmed it.

'Eight weeks.'

'That can't be right,' she protested.

'My dear, I assure you it is.'

'But I had a period last month.'

'Did you notice any irregularities?'

Her brow furrowed. It had been unusually light, lasting less than half the usual time, and she said so.

She listened in stunned silence as the doctor offered a medical explanation. Registered the need for blood tests, and accepted the request form. Then she got to her feet and left the surgery with an appointment card held in her hand.

Dear heaven. A child. *Her* child.

The reality hit as she slid in behind the wheel of her car and drove back to the boutique.

She could hardly hide the news from her mother. Ariane had a right to know.

So, too, did Rafe.

Oh, God.

'It's a *yes*,' Ariane deduced within seconds of Danielle walking in the door. 'Oh, darling, what wonderful news,' she enthused, catching her daughter close in a fond embrace.

Is it? She should be ecstatic at achieving the first stage of the deal. *So why wasn't she?*

Because it meant there was now a firm time-limit fixed on the length of her marriage.

'Are you going to ring and tell Rafe?' Ariane queried gently, witnessing her daughter's conflicting emotions.

'I'll wait until tonight.'

It would give her some breathing space, although the day was pleasantly busy and allowed her little time to think.

Which was probably just as well, she determined as she entered the house shortly before six.

In normal circumstances, she would have booked a table at a favoured restaurant and relayed the news over fine food, wine and candlelight.

Instead, she mentally tussled with words all through dinner and gave up trying to find the right ones as she pushed away a half-eaten plate of seafood paella.

'Not hungry?' Rafe posed, watchful of her desultory efforts.

'Not really.' *Tell him.*

'Something is bothering you?'

There was never going to be the *right* time. 'I had an appointment with the doctor today. I'm pregnant.' There, it was done.

Something flared in his dark eyes, then he banked it down. 'I assume you have a due date?'

Conception had occurred within ten days of their marriage. 'Mid-July.' She managed a smile, although it didn't quite reach her eyes. 'Stage one is now complete.'

He was silent for a few seemingly long seconds, and his gaze seemed to sear her soul. 'How do you feel?'

Oh, my. How did she answer that? Flippancy came to mind, but she chickened out at the last second. 'Fine.'

'You will, of course, transfer to the care of an obstetrician, and cut down your hours at the boutique.'

'No.'

He didn't move, but he assumed a dangerous stillness that succeeded in sending an icy shiver down the length of her spine. 'No?'

How could a single word have the potential to initiate so much havoc?

'I'm young and healthy,' Danielle qualified reasonably. 'If the GP indicates I require specialist care, then so be it.' She drew a calming breath and released it.

'As to the boutique…I intend working right up to the last few weeks.' A spark of anger lit her eyes. 'It's my body, and my child. At least at this stage we're inseparable.' She had to get away from him, albeit temporarily, and she rose to her feet, intent on putting as much distance between them as possible.

His hand snaked out and snagged hers before she had a chance to move more than a single step.

'Let me go.' It was a plea wrenched from the depths of her heart, and one he chose to ignore as he pulled her close.

'Your body, my seed,' Rafe declared with chilling softness. He brought her hand over her stomach and covered it with his own. '*Our* child.'

How could he say that? Already the foetus was a living entity she'd carry in her womb for another seven months, nurture and love every day of its infant years…only to have to step back and share a small part of its life.

As crazy as it seemed, she was already contemplating her separation from a child who had yet to be born.

And Rafe…how could she bear to have him walk away from her, stand by and watch him remarry, provide step-siblings for *their* child, and lead a life totally separate from her own?

Worse, how could she possibly exist without him? *Dear God.*

Realisation hit with shattering impact. *Love?* She couldn't have fallen in love with him. It wasn't possible. Dammit, *love* didn't form any part of the deal!

It had to be hormones wreaking havoc, one part of

her brain rationalised, while another part silently wept.

'I'll cancel out of tonight.'

She heard the words and felt her stomach plummet. Opening night at the theatre where actors would portray their parts in a prominent Australian playwright's new play. How could she have forgotten?

The thought of dressing up and playing the social game left her less than enthused. However, it was a prestigious event and their absence would be noticed.

'Why? Pregnancy doesn't suddenly make me a fragile flower.'

The musing warmth of his smile could have melted her heart, and almost did. Her mouth trembled slightly as he pressed his lips to her forehead.

'I didn't imagine for a moment that it would.'

They entered the auditorium ten minutes before the first act was due to commence. Tickets had been sold out well in advance, and it appeared many notable patrons of the arts were in attendance.

Danielle was supremely conscious of Rafe's close proximity as they mixed and mingled.

'Rafe. Danielle. I was hoping you'd make it.'

Oh, Lord. Cristina. Looking, Danielle had to admit, absolutely stunning in an ivory silk gown. Her male companion wasn't someone she'd seen before, and she banked down the uncharitable thought the blonde might have rented him for the night.

'I believe we're seated together.'

No small feat in the manipulation stakes, Danielle accorded silently. Fortunately the electronic buzzer sounded, signalling patrons to take their seats, and she was saved from having to make polite conversation.

Naturally Cristina managed to seat herself next to Rafe, and Danielle stifled murderous thoughts as she took the seat to the left of him.

He caught hold of her hand and threaded his fingers through her own, and didn't even wince as she dug her nails into his palm.

The orchestra began, the lights dimmed, and the curtain lifted in a majestic sweep.

Danielle attempted to pull her hand free without success, and she fixed her attention on the stage, focusing on the actors who entered it.

Three acts, two intermissions. During the first intermission she excused herself and utilised the powder room. Something for which she seemed to have developed a more frequent need of late.

When she emerged it was to discover Cristina deep in conversation with Rafe. Although, to be fair, the blonde was doing all of the talking.

Danielle joined them, and her eyes widened slightly as Rafe caught her hand and lifted it to his lips.

'What are you playing at?' she demanded in a quiet voice as they traversed the carpeted aisle to resume their seats.

'Reassurance.'

'Yours, or mine?'

The second act captured her attention. Well, most of it. She was too aware of Cristina's possible machinations, and pride forbade she check if the blonde's lacquered nails were resting on any part of Rafe's anatomy.

A further need to utilise the powder room during the second intermission caused Danielle to wonder if a weak bladder was a pregnant woman's curse. She would, she decided, have to buy a book and become acquainted with all the facts!

Fortunately there wasn't much of a queue, and she emerged to discover Cristina making a play at refreshing her make-up in front of the long mirrored wall.

There had to be a purpose for the blonde's presence, and a single guess at the cause was one too many.

Why waste time? 'Presumably it isn't coincidence you followed me in here?'

'It would be a pity if La Femme suffered a few setbacks.'

'Is that a threat, Cristina?' Danielle took a moment to apply colour to her lips, then she capped the tube and tossed it into her bag. 'If so, I'll ensure you're first on the list when the police investigate any further problems.' She paused fractionally. 'It might pay you to remember it's Rafe who owns La Femme, and his connections.'

'Darling, I haven't a clue what you're talking about.'

'No?'

Cristina's eyes narrowed. 'You're a little pale, darling. Not feeling well?'

'I've never felt better.' An extension of the truth, but she was entitled to bend the rules a little.

'One might think—' She came to a halt, her eyes widened, then narrowed down. 'You're not pregnant?'

'Actually, *yes*.'

Cristina's features displayed a gamut of emotions, none of which was attractive. 'Why, you *bitch*.'

'Not the most pleasant manner in which to offer congratulations.' The outer door opened, and Danielle took the opportunity to escape.

Rafe was immersed in conversation with Lillian, and it was something of a relief to hear the buzzer signalling a return to their seats.

'You were gone a while.'

'The powder room is a popular place.'

The lights dimmed, the orchestra began, and the final act got underway.

It was late when they returned home, and Danielle smothered a yawn as she ascended the stairs. It had been all she could do to remain awake during the third act, and as soon as she reached their room she shed the elegant amethyst silk evening suit, removed her make-up, and crept into bed.

'Tired?' Rafe queried as he drew her close, and at her murmured affirmative he brushed his lips to her temple, then prepared to sleep.

It was a beautiful day, with only the merest drift of cloud to mar the azure sky.

Danielle made a mental note to ring the supplier as she eased the car out of the driveway and headed towards Toorak Road. A newly released style of matching bra and briefs was proving popular, and she needed to increase La Femme's existing order.

All of a sudden a streak of blue appeared in her

peripheral vision, she heard the sickening jolt of metal against metal and she was flung forward.

It happened so unexpectedly, so quickly, she didn't have a chance to *think*, let alone brace herself. Although she must have instinctively stamped on the brake, for seconds later the car jumped the kerb and came to a halt a mere whisper away from one of several large trees lining the avenue.

Hell.

She sat there shaken for all of a few seconds, then reality hit, and she reached for the seat belt, released it, and slid out from behind the wheel.

There was concern for the other driver, a need to check damage to her car, and details…she'd need to record details for insurance, log in a call to the police…

'Are you all right?'

Danielle heard a male voice, had the same query echoed by another, and looked round for the other car. Which was nowhere in sight.

'Hit and run,' someone said, adding a vehement, 'Bastard.'

Disbelief clouded her features. 'You're kidding me, right?'

'I think you should sit down, miss.'

Before I fall down? Heavens, I'm made of stronger stuff than that, she wanted to assure, except shock temporarily robbed her of her voice.

'I'll call the police.'

'And the ambulance.'

'I don't need an ambulance,' Danielle protested,

and extracted her cellphone. She should call Ariane and explain she'd be late.

'Stay exactly where you are,' her mother instructed after demanding to know of any injuries. 'I don't give a damn if the car is driveable. Don't you dare move.'

'I'm—' *Fine*, she'd been about to add, except Ariane had already cut the connection.

The rear end of the BMW looked incredibly normal, and there didn't even appear to be so much as a scratch on the bumper.

A police car cruised to a halt, its lights flashing, bare seconds ahead of Rafe's Jaguar, and Danielle momentarily closed her eyes against the sight of him.

A tall, dark angel, she accorded seconds later as he leapt from the car ready to tear someone apart.

As long as it wasn't *her*.

Rafe reached her first, uncaring that he'd broken the speed limit getting here, or that he'd pulled to a screeching halt and caused the cop to pause mid-stride, turn, and check him out.

He completely ignored the steely-eyed appraisal, and if there was going to be any verbalised caution he'd deal with it later.

For now his total focus was Danielle. Dear God, if anything had happened to her… He closed his eyes against such an anguished visage.

It helped to put his hands on her. The instinctive reassurance of touch, and he didn't give a damn who saw him cradle her face and angle his mouth down over her own.

His own reassurance level moved up a notch at her initial response, and it rose a little higher as she pulled out of his grasp. Not that it did her much good, for he merely reined her in again.

'Must you?' Danielle hissed in protest.

His eyes were incredibly dark, his features etched as if from stone as he searched her face. A muscle bunched at the edge of his jaw, then relaxed as his mouth partly slightly, and the tension that had wound through his body like a steel coil from the instant he'd taken Ariane's call began to dissipate.

'Yes.'

She glimpsed something evident she was afraid to define, and for a heart-stopping second everything around her faded as her gaze locked with his.

Did the world stand still? She was willing to swear that it did.

'I need some details, miss.'

And the spell was broken. She turned and saw the uniformed cop standing within touching distance, heard the buzz of voices, and in the distance the wail of a siren.

'I don't need an ambulance,' Danielle reiterated, but no one appeared to be listening. Grr!

With a drawn-out sigh she began recounting the lead-up to the moment of impact…which didn't provide much, for there had been no warning.

The cacophonous siren subsided with a growl as the vehicle drew to a halt, and she suffered a string of questions, contradicted Rafe's assurance he'd ensure she was taken to hospital, then protested volubly as he collected her briefcase, locked her car, and put her in his.

'Just take me to work.'

Rafe pulled out from the kerb, aware he had five minutes before she realised he wasn't going anywhere near the boutique.

She reacted pretty much as he expected, and he reached out, caught hold of her hand and lifted her fingers to his lips. 'Shut up.'

If he thought that gentle salutation was going to win her over, he had another think coming. 'There is nothing wrong with me!'

He spared her a quick, controlled smile. 'Humour me.'

Danielle drew in a deep breath, then released it. 'Where are we going?'

'We're nearly there.'

There was an exclusive private hospital, geared in advance to admit Danielle d'Alboa Valdez into a private suite.

'This is ridiculous,' she flung in a low undertone as she was instructed to undress and get into bed. She cast Rafe a dark look as he prowled the room, and she checked out the cotton gown. Ties to the front, or back? Dammit, she shouldn't even be here at all!

'Here, let me help you.'

He was there, unbuttoning her jacket, easing it off and then tossing it over a chair.

'I can manage.'

He didn't take any notice, and she pushed at his hands as he reached for the zip fastening on her skirt.

'You're in my face, Rafe. Go away.'

'Not a chance.'

She was down to her bra and briefs when a nurse

bustled in, and she indicated her underwear. 'Do I get to keep these on?'

'All of it off,' the nurse responded far too cheerfully, and pointed to the hospital gown. 'Ties to the back.'

'Charming,' Danielle muttered as she complied.

Brisk efficiency resulted in what seemed to be a barrage of tests, questions and an ultrasound, followed by a visit from the obstetrician.

'The baby is fine.'

'Now do I get to go home?'

'Tomorrow. We'll keep you in overnight. Rest, observation.'

'Is that necessary?'

'It's a precaution,' the obstetrician assured, and with a warm smile he turned and left the suite with the nurse following close on his heels.

'I think I'd like to be alone,' Danielle voiced quietly. Rafe loomed large in the room, a tall, brooding entity whose presence seemed to swamp her. 'Would you please leave now?'

Rafe turned away from the window and the scene he'd been studying below. There were questions that needed to be asked; answers he would demand. And calls he had to make.

He crossed to the bed, resisted the urge to cage her in, and satisfied himself with a light, sweeping kiss that left him hard and wanting.

'I'll be back later.'

She could only nod in acquiescence, and when he was gone she laid her head back against the nest of pillows and closed her eyes.

Hit and run. An action which meant a deliberate attempt to harm. Cristina? Had the knowledge of Danielle's pregnancy tipped her from obsession into paranoia?

And if so, could it be proven?

The staff delivered lunch, Ariane rang, the florist delivered a floral bouquet with an accompanying card signed with Rafe's slashing signature, and she spent time leafing through a selection of magazines before slipping into a fitful doze.

Ariane visited on her way home from the boutique, presenting a La Femme carry-bag with an exquisite nightgown and negligée set, plus a pair of satin mules.

'For you,' her mother revealed, hiding maternal concern behind a warm smile. 'A hospital gown is not a good look.'

She kept the conversation light, deliberately refrained from mentioning she'd relayed each and every suspicious incident to Rafe together with her own suspicions, and left when staff delivered dinner.

Danielle had just freshened up when Rafe entered the suite, and she didn't resist when he fastened his mouth over hers in a brief, hard kiss. Then he pulled her close and teased her lips with his own, gently with a lingering softness that brought her hands up to link together at his neck.

'Have you had dinner?' A prosaic query which didn't come close to what she wanted to say.

'Later.' He gathered her into his arms, crossed to a nearby chair, then settled her onto his lap.

'Busy day?'

'Yes.' He'd gone into immediate action, called in

a few favours, gathered facts, then arranged a meeting
with Cristina, who had tried guile, tears, and followed
them with an avowal of undying love. His response
had been a chilling warning, and the advice to leave
town within twenty-four hours or face legal charges.

It was *nice*, Danielle decided, to rest in his arms.
She could feel the reassuring thud of his heartbeat,
smell the exclusive cologne he preferred to use, and
sense the clean male scent of him mingling with body
warmth to create an essence that was uniquely his.

Perhaps it was delayed shock, but she was beginning to feel quite tired, and a night alone in a hospital
bed didn't seem nearly as unattractive as it had a few
hours ago.

CHAPTER TWELVE

'WE NEED to talk.'

Danielle had been home an hour, and in that time she'd been plied with tea and bite-size sandwiches.

They were seated on the terrace, overlooking the gardens.

'I have only one question.' Rafe's voice was deadly quiet, his features expressionless. 'Why didn't you confide in me?'

She met and held his gaze. 'I thought I could handle it on my own. What would you have had me do? Run to you, bleating like a baby with every piece of Cristina's nastiness? How was I to know she could be dangerous?'

'If you'd told me of her efforts to cause trouble, her first attempt would have been her last.' He caught hold of her chin and tilted her face towards him. 'And you wouldn't have suffered grief at her hands.'

He finger-combed her hair, lingered at her nape, then he brushed a thumb down the sensitive cord to rest in the hollow at the base of her throat.

The anger left as quickly as it had risen. 'She wanted what I had,' Danielle reiterated quietly. *'You.'*

Cristina had been too clever to show her hand, with the exception that the card she'd expected to play as a *trump* became the *joker*.

Rafe angled his mouth over hers in a kiss that

melted her bones, and it was a while before he lifted his head.

'When I think—'

She pressed a finger against his lips. 'It didn't happen. I'm fine. The baby's fine. You'll have your son or daughter.' *And my heart will break when I walk away,* she added silently.

His eyes became dark with an emotion she couldn't define. 'You think the child you carry is all that matters to me?' He closed his eyes, then opened them again. *'Por Dios.'*

'We have an agreement—'

'To hell with the agreement.'

'What are you talking about?'

'You.'

She didn't get it. Didn't dare begin to even think he could mean—

'Do you have any idea what I went through when Ariane rang to say you'd been involved in a car accident?'

'I imagine you were concerned—'

'That doesn't come close.'

Danielle's heart seemed to leap to a faster beat.

'Dios. They were the worst minutes of my life.' He slid his hand to her wrist and captured her hand in his. 'If I'd lost you—' He couldn't bring himself to finish the sentence.

She wasn't capable of uttering a word as the seconds ticked by. 'What are you trying to say?' she managed at last.

He didn't try to wrap it up in fancy words. There were only three that really mattered. 'I love you.'

'Rafe—'

'You're more important to me than anything or anyone in my life.'

If only he meant it! 'I think you're in shock,' Danielle said carefully.

'I have something for you.' He reached for his briefcase, retrieved a long envelope, and extracted a legal-looking document. 'Read it.'

She took it from his hand, and skimmed the legal-ese. There was no need for an explanation. In simple form, it rendered the agreement between them null and void. It already contained his signature and that of his lawyer.

'Look at the date.'

It was dated a day before the accident.

'I planned giving it to you at an appropriate moment,' Rafe declared, and glimpsed the moisture shimmering in her eyes. 'Don't,' he groaned, and watched helplessly a single tear escape and roll slowly down her cheek.

Women's greatest weapon. He gathered her into his arms, nestling her head into the curve of his throat as he held her close.

'The obstetrician suggests a holiday.'

He brushed his lips against her temple, then trailed a path to her mouth, savouring it gently as she began to respond.

'The Gold Coast condominium?'

'If that's what you want.'

She lifted her hands and linked them behind his neck, keeping him there, and it was he who carefully broke the contact.

He'd laid his heart on the line, and she hadn't said a word. For a moment he experienced the agony of her possible rejection. Good sex wasn't *love*. Yet he was willing to swear she cared... All he had to do was persuade her it was enough.

'I think I need to hear you say it again.'

There was no artifice, just a tentative wonderment and a melting softness that touched him in a way nothing else had.

With great care he cupped her face and tilted it so his eyes met hers.

'I love you.'

He thought she was going to cry, and he witnessed her effort to control the tears. Her mouth shook a little, then curved to form a tremulous smile. 'Thank you.'

'For loving you?'

'For giving me the most precious gift of all.'

Something twisted in his gut.

She caught the briefest glimpse of his indecision, and pressed her fingers to his lips. *'You.'* She was sure the warmth in those dark eyes would melt her bones. 'Your heart, your soul,' she said gently. 'I shall treasure them all the days of my life.'

Danielle felt his lips move beneath her touch, and saw the emotion starkly etched on his features.

'At first, I wanted to hate you. For a while, I thought I did. Then I realised the prospect of a life without you would be no life at all.' She trailed her fingers along the edge of his jaw, felt a muscle bunch there, then she traced his lower lip and lingered at its edge. 'I love you.'

His heart, which had been thudding loud in his chest, increased its beat, and for a few seconds he was incapable of speech.

She watched his expression transform, saw the intense warmth, the passion, the unguarded *love*, and there was wonderment that it was all for *her*.

There was also the knowledge she witnessed something she doubted he'd allowed anyone to see in a very long time...raw emotion that came direct from the heart.

He brushed his mouth to hers, then used his teeth to nip the fullness of her lower lip, lingering there before tracing a path to the vulnerable hollow at the base of her neck. And felt the answering kick of her pulse-beat as it moved in tune with his own.

Dear heaven, he had a burning need to hold her, to reassure himself she was alive, and *his*.

Rafe rose to his feet with her in his arms and carried her upstairs to their bedroom. He undressed her with such care it was all she could do to keep the tears at bay, and she watched unashamedly as he discarded his own clothes before sliding beneath the covers to gather her close.

He contented himself with stroking the slender curve of her back, the swell of her buttocks, the toned length of her thigh. His hand lingered at her hip, then covered her stomach, felt the slight thickness at her waist, and he brushed his fingers gently back and forth as if in silent reassurance to the growing foetus nurtured in its mother's womb.

He moved to her breasts, aware from her faint gasp of their sensitivity. Then he kissed her, with a gentleness that caused the breath to hitch in her throat as he began a slow exploration of her body with his lips...

It took a while, and he allowed her to reciprocate in kind, until she reached the most vulnerable part of his anatomy, when he stayed her seeking mouth and turned it to his own in a kiss that shattered them both.

Rafe held her through the night. Whenever she shifted a little he drew her close, simply because he couldn't bear to let her go.

His wife, the mother of his child. His life. To think he might have lost her...

If he slept, he was unaware of the stolen minutes throughout the night hours, and it was Danielle who slid carefully from the bed as dawn broke.

She shrugged on a robe and stood looking at him, drinking in the strong features softened in repose. There was the shadow of a night's growth of beard, and she almost reached down to trace a path across his cheek. Thick dark lashes with their slightly curled edges, and that mouth...

His eyelids swept up in one swift movement, the dark orbs instantly alert, then he saw her and he smiled, a slow, sweet curve that melted her bones.

'Hi.' His voice was a deep, husky drawl, and he extended an arm. 'Come here.'

'You have that certain look in your eye,' she teased, and saw his teeth gleam white.

'And what look is that?' He reached for her, drawing her gently back onto the bed.

'Hmm...dangerous.'

He buried his mouth against the sweet curve of her

throat, and she wove her fingers through his hair, absently finger-combing it as he eased open her robe.

'I can't think of a better way to wake each morning,' Rafe murmured as he bestowed a trail of lingering kisses along her collar-bone.

A delicious warmth invaded her veins. 'This could become addictive.'

'Count on it.'

Later they rose, showered, and took breakfast out on the terrace. It was a glorious day, with sunshine, blue skies and moderate temperatures.

Everything, Danielle thought with satisfaction, was right in her world. She had a husband who adored her, and whom she loved with all her heart. Their baby was growing inside her, safe and doing just fine.

Within a few hours they were due to fly to the Coast for a holiday. Their first together that didn't relate to business.

It would be wonderful, she perceived dreamily as she nibbled toast and sipped from her second cup of herbal tea.

And it was. Lazily spent days spent stretched out on poolside loungers beneath the shade of a beach umbrella. Sometimes they swam in the pool, or walked along the beach, and at night they had each other.

It had all the elements of a honeymoon, Danielle decided dreamily. And there, beneath the warm summer sun, it was possible to believe the past few months hadn't existed, and their lives together began from this moment on.

A trial by fire? Maybe, she conceded. But they'd

forged something very special, and she'd fight to the death to protect it.

The last night of their Coast sojourn was spent lingering over dinner, followed by a stroll along the beachfront in the moonlight.

'Happy?'

Danielle tilted her face up to her husband. 'Yes,' she said simply, and felt his arm tighten along the back of her waist.

He wanted to kiss her, draw her into him, and never let her go.

She linked her fingers with his. 'Enjoying the anticipation?'

'Witch,' he accorded in teasing remonstrance.

'It's part of my charm.'

'I think we'd better head back to the hotel.'

She laughed, a delightful throaty sound. 'Are you going to be this protective right through my pregnancy?'

'Count on it.'

She became serious. 'You won't object if I go back to work for a while?'

He'd been waiting for her to pose the question. 'A few hours a day,' he conceded. 'Preferably mornings, then you can take a rest in the afternoon.'

'OK.'

'Just—OK?'

She cast him a winsome smile. 'Yes.' It was all she wanted, something to keep her hand in. Besides, there was a nursery to plan, baby clothes to buy.

'Such docility.'

'Ah,' she began with teasing mockery. 'The love of a good man can do wonders for a woman.'

His eyes gleamed with humour. 'I think I need to take you in hand.'

'I adore the way you do that.'

'Adore?'

The teasing fled, and in its place was a sincerity that touched his heart. 'I love you. So much,' she added quietly.

'I know,' Rafe said gently. *'Dios mediante, querida.'*

EPILOGUE

JUAN CARLOS RAFAEL VALDEZ entered the world two weeks early, following a long labour which necessitated delivery by Caesarean section. Much to the relief of his father, who appeared ready to tear obstetrician and nursing staff limb from limb, and the bemused acceptance of his mother.

He squalled loud and long, stopping only when he was placed in his mother's arms, whereupon he yawned and promptly went to sleep.

Displaying his mother's relaxed temperament, Danielle sweetly reminded Rafe, despite bearing a striking resemblance to his father.

A comment which earned her a dark, brooding look that couldn't quite reach amusement for the lurking anxiety still prevalent from the birth.

A more doting father would be difficult to find, Danielle mused as she watched Rafe settle Juan Carlos into the crook of his arm at the christening.

In the three months of his short life, their son had become the centre of their universe.

'I think,' Danielle said as she gazed fondly down at her son, 'he needs a sister. Or a brother.' Her lashes swept up as she glimpsed the shock momentarily evident in her husband's features. 'Otherwise he'll be impossibly spoiled.' She offered him a witching smile. 'As an only child, I always longed for a brother

182

or sister.' She paused fractionally, and aimed for guile. 'Didn't you?'

'Danielle—'

His voice was a soft growl which she chose to ignore. 'Can't you just picture a little girl? Lovely dark curls, bright eyes, and the cutest smile?'

'*Amada*, no.' He was drowning here. 'Not yet, I don't think I could bear to—'

'See me in pain?' she finished. 'What nonsense. Women have been bearing babes since the beginning of time. Besides, the obstetrician advised a Caesarean section would be necessary for all future deliveries.'

All? They were going to need to have a serious discussion.

'We'll talk about it later,' Danielle murmured as the photographer assembled them together with Ariane for a family shot.

Later was long after the guests departed, dinner with Ariane had concluded, Juan Carlos had been fed, changed and settled for the night, and they were alone.

'Our time, *querida*,' Rafe accorded, drawing her into his arms. His lips nuzzled the sensitive curve at the edge of her neck, and had the pleasure of feeling her pulse leap at his touch.

'It's been a long day.' A beautiful day, filled with joy and pride, laughter and love. But nothing compared with the love she had for this man.

He was everything she could want, all she'd ever need.

She captured his head and brought his mouth down to hers. 'I love you.'

Her voice was husky with emotion, and his heart thudded to a quickened beat as he slid his hands to her buttocks and curved her into him.

He wanted her to feel what she did to him, to know even on the most base level what there was between them.

His mouth sought hers in a kiss that was surprisingly gentle, until she moved sinuously against him, and then there was hunger, raw, primitive, emotive.

It wasn't enough. It was never enough, and they helped each other shed their clothes, discarding them where they fell.

What followed was a ravishment of the senses, and afterwards they lay curled into each other, spent and gloriously *alive*.

A cry sounded through the baby monitor, and they both stilled as it was followed by another, and soon became a wail.

'I'll go.' Rafe released her and slid to his feet, shrugged into a robe, and disappeared through to the nursery.

He was gone a while, and, curious, Danielle grabbed up her robe and followed him.

There, seated in the rocking-chair, was Rafe with his son cradled against his chest. Juan Carlos had his head tucked into his father's shoulder, and was fast asleep.

'It was wind,' Rafe informed softly. 'I changed him.'

'And found it hard to put him down.'

His smile almost undid her. 'You know me too well.'

'What would the business sector have to say about a hard-headed negotiator known for his unrelenting stance if they could see you now?' she teased.

His eyes gleamed with humour. 'They'd envy me for being one of the luckiest men in the world.' And knew it to be true.

He rose carefully to his feet and transferred his son into the cot, then covered him with such tenderness it made her heart ache.

Juan Carlos didn't stir, and together they dimmed the night-light and moved quietly from the nursery.

In their room Rafe sat on the bed, angling his legs so he could draw her close.

Danielle laid her cheek on the top of his head and wound her arms around his shoulders. 'Are you so against having another child?'

'I think only of you, *amada*,' he said quietly, and felt her arms tighten around him.

'This is a beautiful home, with lovely grounds. Can't you just see three or four dark-haired children enjoying the advantages we can provide for them?' she queried wistfully.

He could deny her nothing. His life had never been complete until she came into it. And love…dear heaven, what it was to love such a woman, and have that love returned.

'A year, *querida*,' he qualified. 'Let us have a year to enjoy our son, before we add to our family.'

She brushed her lips to his forehead. 'Hmm, I love the way you compromise.'

He lifted his head and directed her a teasing glance. 'Only *compromise, amante*?'

She tilted her head to one side. 'Oh, I can think of another thing or two you're quite good at.'

'*Quite*, huh? Obviously I need to work on my technique.'

Danielle slanted her mouth to his, and slid the edge of her tongue along his lower lip, dipped inside briefly, then withdrew an inch or two. 'As in, beginning *now*?'

'Take that as a given, *mi mujer*.' He captured her face in his hands. 'All the days of my life.'

'Only days?'

'Sassy,' he accorded. 'Definitely sassy.'

'But you love me.'

His expression sobered, and the humorous gleam evident was replaced by naked sincerity.

'With all my heart.'

'*Gracias,*' she responded huskily, and leant into him, gifting him everything in a kiss that reached right down to his soul.

There was a part of him that would always be hard and unyielding, but not with her, never with her. She held the very heart of him, and she intended to treat the gift with the greatest of care...for the rest of her life.

The Pregnancy Proposal

HELEN BIANCHIN

CHAPTER ONE

SURPRISE, shock, were only two of the emotions swirling inside Tasha's head as she walked from the doctor's office and slid in behind the wheel of her car.

For seemingly endless minutes she sat staring sightlessly through the windscreen as the words echoed and re-echoed inside her head.

Eight weeks pregnant.

How could she be *pregnant*, for heaven's sake?

A tiny bubble of hysterical laughter rose to the surface. She knew the *how* of it... She just didn't understand why, when she'd taken the Pill as regular as clockwork and never missed.

Nothing was infallible, the doctor had informed as he listed a few exclusions. One of which proved startlingly applicable, pinpointing a nasty gastric-flu virus that had laid her low for a few days when she hadn't been able to keep anything down.

Including the Pill, obviously. Sufficient to throw protection from conception out the window for that month.

Dear heaven. The groan was inaudible as it echoed in her mind. What was she going to do?

She was twenty-seven, a corporate lawyer. A

good one. She had a career, a partner. Her life was carefully planned...

Pregnancy wasn't on the agenda.

She closed her eyes, then opened them again.

Jared. Her heart lurched in tandem with her stomach. What would his reaction be?

One thing was sure...his surprise would match or outstrip her own.

How would he accept fatherhood?

A few differing scenarios swept through her mind, from enthusiasm and warmth, support...to the opposite end of the spectrum.

No, a silent voice screamed from deep inside. Termination was out of the question. Without thought she placed a hand to her waistline in a gesture of protective reassurance.

There could be no question this child was Jared's...but it was also *hers.* And no matter how Jared viewed its existence, she intended to have it. Life as a solo mother wouldn't be a piece of cake, but she'd manage.

What if Jared proposed marriage? Oh, sure. Pigs flew, and cows jumped over the moon!

There was little doubt he viewed their relationship as permanent...well, as permanent as any intimate liaison could be. Commitment, *sans* the sanctity of marriage.

Until now, she'd been fine with the arrangement.

Except there was a third life to consider in this equation. Decisions would need to be made. Only then would she know which direction her life would take.

Without thinking she instinctively reached into her bag and retrieved her cell-phone, only to pause as she keyed in the first digit, then disconnect the call.

Jared was due in court this afternoon, and his cell-phone would be switched through to his rooms. Any direct contact would have to wait until this evening.

Besides, this sort of news should be imparted in person, not via a telephone!

She could, she decided, plan a special candlelit dinner, dress in a provocative little number, be openly seductive during the main, then deliver the news over dessert.

But not tonight. An unladylike curse slid from her lips with the sudden realisation they were due to dine out. A Law Society soirée, one of many organised throughout the year for differing reasons.

Tasha stifled a slip into black humour at the thought of imparting her news *sotto voce* as they mixed and mingled with the city's legal scions in the foyer of the grand hotel. Perhaps she could convey the information in a seductive whisper between the soup starter and the entrée?

He might very well choke, whereupon someone would have to administer the Heimlich manoeuvre...and that would never do.

Better, perhaps, to be more circumspect. She could always call into a babywear boutique, purchase a pair of white knitted bootees and place them on his pillow. How was that for subtlety?

Tasha's mind unconsciously slid to the man who was causing her so much grief...and didn't know whether to smile or shed a few tears at the reflection.

Jared North was known as one of Brisbane's most sought-after barristers. In his late thirties, he was a brilliant man in his chosen field with the verbal skill to reduce the most hardened criminal to an insecure incoherent in the courtroom and tear the defence attorney's testimony to shreds.

She'd first met him three years ago at a dinner for the legal fraternity. His reputation preceded him, and, while she'd seen his photo in newspapers and magazines, nothing prepared her for seeing the man in the flesh.

One look across a crowded room was all it took, and her insides began to melt. Tall, broad shoulders, the way he wore his impeccably cut suit set him apart from his associates. Hewn facial features sculpted by nature's hand gifted him a strong jaw, wide cheekbones, a perfectly symmetrical nose. Muscle and skin assembled to provide almost a Latin look, a throwback it was said to his maternal Andulusian ancestry. But it was the eyes, well-set, dark and knowing as sin, that pulled a woman in. There was the promise of innate sensuality and unbridled passion beneath the sophisticated façade. And something else she recognised at a base level, but didn't care to define.

That night it was as if the room and its occupants

faded from the periphery of her vision. There was only the man, and an awareness that fizzed her blood and sent her heart racing to an accelerated beat.

He crossed the room, slowly weaving his way towards her, pausing momentarily as one associate or another sought his attention. But his gaze caught and held her own, his intention clear as she waited for him to join her.

Afterwards she had no clear recollection of their conversation. Instead, she heard only the deep timbre of his voice, an intonation that hinted at education abroad. She became fascinated by his mouth, the sensual curve of his lower lip, the warmth portrayed when he smiled.

An astute, clever and dangerous man, she perceived, instinctively aware even then he would have a profound effect on her life.

After three months of dating Jared suggested she move in with him. Tasha opted to wait six months, unwilling to leap too soon into a committed relationship where lust formed a large part of its foundation.

Now, two years down the track, they shared his luxurious apartment in one of Brisbane's prestigious inner suburbs overlooking the river.

Life was good. Better than good. They devoted a lot of time to their individual careers, and each other, socialising on occasion. There was an apartment on the Gold Coast, less than an hour's drive south, where they frequently escaped for the weekend. Sun, sand and relaxation, it provided a different lifestyle to the one they each led through the week.

At no time had *marriage* been mentioned.

Tasha didn't want it mentioned, unless it was for the right reason...*love*. The everlasting, ever-after kind.

The beep from her pager was an intrusive sound, and she reached for it, read the message to call her office, and retrieved her cell-phone.

Minutes later she fired the ignition, eased her BMW out from the medical centre car park and gained the arterial road leading into the city.

It was a glorious day, the sky a clear azure with the merest drift of cloud. Lush green lawns, late-spring flowers provided colour and there was the promise of summer in the sun's warmth.

Brisbane's city-scape loomed in the distance. Splendid architecture in varying office towers and apartment high-rises of concrete, glass and steel. The wide river was a focal scenic point, together with a university, arts centre and the bustling Southbank with its many attractions.

Within minutes Tasha turned into a private key-operated inner-city car park, then drove to her allotted space and took the lift to the fifteenth floor.

The receptionist manning the front desk resembled a model from *Vogue* magazine. An admirable reflection of the head partner's dictum professional image was everything. Amanda certainly aided that, and then some.

'Your two-thirty appointment is delayed; you have messages on your desk.'

'Thanks.' Tasha summoned a smile in acknowledgement as she passed through Reception *en route* to her office.

Work proved a necessary distraction, and she checked her appointment schedule, ensured her secretary had the requisite paperwork ready for perusal, and gave instructions for three follow-up calls.

Two client consultations and a late-afternoon meeting brought the working day to a close. Something she viewed with relief, for her powers of concentration seemed to have zoomed off to another planet.

There had been moments when she was totally focused, others when a coloured illustration of a tiny foetus from the pages of the doctor's medical book proved a haunting intrusion.

So tiny, so alive.

For a moment she stood perfectly still, consumed by a fierce protectiveness that drove out rational thought.

Then she extracted her briefcase and slid in printouts with various notations she needed to examine in preparation for a meeting tomorrow, collected her laptop, walked out to the foyer and took a lift down to the car park.

The best thing to be said about peak-hour traffic was that it moved... This evening, the speedometer didn't register a notch over ten kilometres an hour through the inner city.

Her cell-phone beeped, signalling an incoming text message, and she activated it while she sat waiting for the lights to change.

Jared... *Delayed an hour.*

Tasha wasn't sure whether to be peeved or relieved. While there was a part of her that wanted to get Jared's reaction out of the way, there was also a certain reluctance.

Neither of which made much sense, she determined as she garaged her car and rode the lift to their apartment.

Situated on a high floor, it was one of two sub-penthouses in a prestigious apartment block on the river with splendid views of the city.

Spacious with cream marble-tiled floors, large expanses of floor-to-ceiling tinted glass, there were oriental rugs, modern furniture in cream and beige, with splashes of colour provided by modern works of art adorning the walls.

The lounge and dining-room were large, the kitchen and utilities modern, and the master suite was a dream with its large bed and adjoining bathroom. Of the three remaining bedrooms, Jared had converted one into a legal reference library with a desk, computer and electronic equipment for his own use. Another room held a day bed, and a desk which Tasha could use for her own needs. The third bedroom was a guest suite.

Tasha crossed into the kitchen, extracted a bottle of juice from the refrigerator and poured some into a glass, drank some, then she sliced cheese onto a biscuit and ate it.

Over the past week or two she had seemed inclined to want to nibble food at frequent intervals. Another symptom of pregnancy?

She'd have to buy a book and study it, she perceived as she walked through to the master suite.

Choosing what to wear didn't pose too much of a problem, and she tossed an elegant black evening suit onto the bed, then made for the shower.

It was a while before she emerged and, dry, a towel wound round her slender form, she began style-drying her hair. Dark sable, it tumbled in wavy curls down onto her shoulders.

Next came make-up, and she chose subtle shadings to highlight her gold-flecked dark brown eyes, then she donned fresh underwear and entered the bedroom.

Dressed, she slid her feet into black stiletto pumps which added four inches to her petite frame.

Selecting jewellery, she was in the process of fastening a pendant at her nape when Jared walked into the room.

Her gaze met his, and her stomach fluttered at the warmth evident in those dark grey, almost black eyes.

His jacket was hooked over one shoulder, he'd loosened his tie and he'd undone the top button of his shirt and removed his cufflinks.

He bore the faint shadow of a man who needed

to shave twice a day, and it lent him a slightly dangerous air.

Lethal, she amended as she felt her body stir in recognition of her attraction to him.

Passion, even in its mildest form, had the ability to liquefy her bones. All he had to do was look at her, and she was lost.

His mouth curved into a musing smile as he crossed to her side.

'Let me fix that for you.'

He was close, much too close. She felt her body quiver as his fingers brushed her skin, and she was conscious of every breath she took, the heightened sensuality as she caught the faint aroma of his cologne, the male heat that was uniquely his.

Tasha felt his hands shift to her shoulders, the brush of his mouth against the sensitive curve at the edge of her neck.

'Beautiful.'

She caught the slight huskiness in his voice, and deliberately stepped away. 'If you don't shower and change we're going to be late.'

There was a moment's silence, then he shifted and turned her round to face him. 'Bad day?'

The query was softly voiced, and she met his narrowed gaze with equanimity.

'Something like that.'

'Want to talk about it?'

Tasha shook her head. 'We don't have time.'

Jared caught hold of her chin between thumb and forefinger, and tilted it. 'We can make time.'

No, they couldn't. This was going to take a while if she was going to do it right. And there shouldn't be any distractions or time restriction.

She knew if she said the word, he would delay their departure for as long as it took. And part of her wanted to, very much.

His presence at tonight's event was expected. Reneging without good reason was unthinkable.

She managed a faint smile. 'It can wait.'

He cast her a brooding look, unable to define much from her expression.

'Really,' she assured.

'Later.'

It was capitulation, and she released a silent sigh of relief as he tossed his jacket down onto the bed, pulled off his tie, then began to discard the rest of his clothes.

Half an hour later she slid into the passenger seat of Jared's late-model Jaguar and sat in silence as he traversed the ramp to street-level, then eased the powerful car towards the city.

She'd gained a reprieve. But only a temporary one. At evening's end, Jared would have the facts and be aware of her options.

CHAPTER TWO

THE evening's legal soirée followed the pattern of those preceding it...superb venue, tastefully decorative bite-size food offered on silver platters by an array of uniformed waitresses, while the drinks stewards hovered, presenting guests with champagne and orange juice.

It was all very elegant, Tasha observed. Dinner suits and black tie for the men were *de rigueur*, and the women excelled themselves in gowns of varying design, length and colour.

There were colleagues to greet and spend time engaging in pleasant conversation before moving on. Notable peers who were important to acknowledge.

She found it vaguely amusing to be partnered by one of the latter, aware of the difference between dignified patronage and obsequious awe as members of the legal fraternity sought Jared's attention.

Something he handled with friendly professionalism, never faltering in recalling a name or the firm for whom they worked.

'How do you do that?' Tasha asked quietly.

A slight smile curved his mouth, tilting the edges and deepening the vertical line slashing each cheek. His eyes were dark and held a musing gleam. 'Memory training.'

16

Something he'd honed to perfection during his law-school days. An asset that was equally lauded and feared by his contemporaries.

She selected a canapé from a proffered tray and bit into it, then took a sip from her glass...orange juice, when she would normally have chosen champagne.

Dinner was a splendid meal, the food superb, and their table companions provided interesting conversation.

There were the customary speeches, and Tasha listened attentively, aware throughout the evening she was merely acting an expected part.

If Jared noticed, he gave no sign, although there was more than one occasion when she became aware of his lingering gaze, and she caught the faintly brooding quality evident.

His presence at her side was a constant, and she was supremely conscious of him, the light touch of his hand at her waist, the warmth of his smile.

All she had to do was look at him to feel the blood pump faster through her veins, and sensation unfurl deep within. It became a fine kind of madness that was entirely sensual as heat consumed her body and liquefied her bones.

Those large hands could wreak magic to each and every pulse-beat, and his mouth... Dear heaven, even thinking about what his mouth could do wrought havoc with her senses.

Almost as if he knew, he reached for her hand and threaded his fingers through her own. His thumb-pad soothed the criss-cross of veins pulsing rapidly on the inside of her wrist, and she curled her fingers, letting the fingernails bite into his flesh a little.

Did he know what he did to her? Without doubt, she alluded wryly. She'd been *his* from the start, ensnared by the power, the sheer male magnetism that was his alone.

The question that needed to be asked...and answered, she ventured silently, was how she affected *him?* Sexually, what they shared together was good. Better than good. Earth-shattering. She'd have sworn on her life his loss of control wasn't faked.

But was it *love*...or merely lust? Sadly, she couldn't be sure.

'Let's get out of here,' Jared drawled as he pulled her close. 'The evening is just about done, and we've fulfilled our social obligation.'

His gaze narrowed fractionally as he caught the edge of weariness evident on her features, the faint shadows beneath her eyes. Dammit, she looked fragile. The onset of a virus? She'd admitted to a difficult day at the office, which was most unlike her. She excelled with challenge of any kind.

Tasha made no protest, although the thought of exchanging a social comfort zone for what would inevitably prove an explosive situation accelerated her nervous tension.

It took a while to escape, for there were certain courtesies to observe, and Tasha sat quietly in the car as Jared sent it purring through the city streets.

They entered the apartment close to mid-night...the witching hour, Tasha acknowledged, and wondered at the irony of it.

'Coffee?'

'No, thanks.'

Jared closed the distance between them, and glimpsed the faint wariness evident in her gaze. He caught her chin between thumb and forefinger and tilted it.

'You've been as nervous as a cat on hot bricks all evening.' His musing drawl had an underlying edge to it. 'Why?'

There was no easy way to impart her news. She hesitated, reflecting on a few rehearsed lines she'd silently practised...in the office, driving from work, during the evening...and discarded each and every one of them.

'Tasha?' A slight smile widened his mouth. 'What did you do? Earn a traffic violation? Over-extend your credit limit?' The last was an attempt at hu-mour, and he caught the faint roll of her eyes before she shook her head. 'No?' He brushed his thumb over her lower lip, felt its slight quiver, and ditched any further attempt to lighten the situation. 'I take it this is something serious?'

Oh, man, she reflected ruefully. You don't know the half of it.

'Do I continue to play twenty questions, or are you going to tell me?'

She threw out the soft approach and went for hard facts. 'I'm pregnant.'

Was it benefit of courtroom practice that allowed no expression to show on his features? There was no surprise or shock, and Tasha pre-empted the question she thought he'd be compelled to ask.

'I had a doctor's appointment late this morning. He confirmed it.' She spread her hands in a helpless gesture, then sought to explain how and why the Pill hadn't been effective. 'I thought I had a lingering virus.'

Of the many scenarios she'd imagined depicting his reaction, she hadn't counted on his silence.

She looked at him carefully. 'I won't consider a termination.' This child is mine, she cried silently. But so much a part of *you*. The thought of relinquishing its chance to life almost killed her.

Dear heaven, why didn't he say something... *anything*.

'Did I ask that of you?'

All afternoon and evening she'd been on tenterhooks worrying about his reaction, agonising if the existence of a child might spell the end of their relationship.

'We'll get married.'

Her whole body stilled. 'Why?' *Because you love me?*

'It's an expedient solution.'

She felt as if her heart tore, then shattered into a thousand pieces. 'I don't want a marriage based on *duty*. And I sure as hell don't want my child to be brought into a loveless arrangement.'

Jared's eyes darkened. 'Loveless?' A muscle bunched at the side of jaw. 'How can you say that?'

'Have either of us mentioned the word *love*?' He hadn't, not once. And because he hadn't, neither had she. 'We're sexually compatible.' On a scale of one to ten, she'd accord what they shared as a twenty. Mind-blowing. She hadn't experienced anything like it, and doubted she ever would with anyone else.

'We've been incredibly indulgent, with no thought to changing the relationship in any way.' She paused, aware she was dying inside. 'Pregnancy wasn't part of it. Nor was marriage.'

'You're carrying our child.'

'Marriage doesn't necessarily have to follow.'

'I'm proposing that it does.'

She held his gaze. 'Answer me honestly. If my pregnancy wasn't an issue, would you have broached the subject of marriage?'

Please give me the reassurance I want, *need*, she silently begged. Sweep away my doubts and uncertainties by saying just one word, *now*.

His expression didn't change. 'I imagine so, eventually.'

She felt as if a sword pierced her heart, and it took considerable effort to keep her voice steady. 'I don't want you as a husband out of a sense of obligation.'

'Two years together and you question my obligation?'

It wouldn't do if she crumbled at his feet. 'Two years during which either one of us has been free to walk away,' Tasha said quietly. 'My definition of marriage comprises love and a permanent "till death us do part" significance. If you had wanted that, you'd have suggested marriage before now.'

'Which you choose to interpret as me preferring an open relationship with no legal ties?'

His slight hesitation together with his choice of words had provided an answer.

'Yes.'

'And you couldn't possibly be wrong?'

Do you know how desperately I want to be wrong? She felt like railing at him. *I love you.* I want to be with you for the rest of my life…as your wife, the mother of your children. But not, dear God, as a second-best choice borne out of duty. I'd rather be alone than know I'd forced you into a role you didn't want.

'I don't think so.'

'But you're not sure?'

'Don't use counsellor tactics on me. Save them for the courtroom.'

Without a further word she turned and walked down the hall to the master bedroom where she caught up her wrap, a few essential toiletries, and made her way to the guest room. Only to come face-to-face with Jared.

She registered the suit jacket hooked over one shoulder, the loosened tie and the semi-unbuttoned shirt. It lent him a rakish look and succeeded in activating a spiral of sensation she fought to restrain.

'What do you think you're doing?' His appraisal

was swift, and his eyes darkened as she made to move past him.

'Sleeping in the spare room.'

She could sense the tension in his large body, the tightening of muscle and sinew as he exercised control. 'The hell you are.'

The deadly softness of his voice issued a warning she elected to ignore. 'I don't want to have sex with you.'

His gaze hardened, a fractional shift of his features that reminded her of a panther's stillness the moment before it leapt to attack. 'I accept that. But we share the same bed.'

And risk succumbing to his brand of subtle persuasion?

She was all too aware it would only take the glide of his hand on her hip, the familiar trail to her belly and the gentle but sure fingers seeking the soft folds at the juncture of her thighs to rouse her into semi-wakefulness and turn to him in the night.

By the time she remembered, it would be too late, and she'd be lost. 'I don't think so.'

'Tasha—'

'Don't.' She lifted a hand, then let it fall to her side. 'Please,' she added. 'I want to be alone right now.'

It was the *please* that got to him.

'We need to talk.'

'We've already done that.' Her voice was even, calm, when inside she was breaking apart. Hurting so badly, so deeply, she'd probably bear the scars from it for the rest of her life.

His gaze locked with hers, the force of his will vying with her own for long, timeless seconds, then he moved aside to let her pass.

The guest room held its own linen closet, and she undressed, donned her wrap, removed her make-up, then she made up the bed, slid between the cool percale sheets and switched off the bedlamp.

Sleep came easily, but she woke in the early hours of the morning, momentarily disoriented by her surroundings until she remembered where she was and why.

The bed was comfortable, but she wasn't curled in against Jared's muscled frame as he held her close, even in sleep. She missed the steady beat of his heart, his reassuring warmth. The way he seemed to sense when she stirred during the night, how he'd gather her in and press his lips to the curve of her shoulder.

Inevitably it would lead to lovemaking, and she delighted in the fact he could never get enough of her. Secure in the relationship and what they shared.

Not any more, a tiny voice taunted. You blew it.

It was then the tears began to well, spilling over to slip in slow rivulets to her temples and become lost in her hair.

Tasha lay awake, staring at the darkened ceiling until the grey light of an early dawn crept between the shutters, giving the room shape and form, followed by subtle shades of colour.

It was too soon to rise and meet the day, and any further hope of sleep was out of the question. She could slip into the master suite and retrieve what she needed to wear into the office. Except she'd encounter Jared...something that was unavoidable, but she'd prefer to face him when they were both dressed. Which meant she'd need to wait until six-thirty, when he left the apartment for his daily work-out in the downstairs gym.

At six-forty she took a leisurely shower in the hope it would ease the tiredness. It didn't, and she brushed her hair until her scalp tingled.

With care she tidied the bed, caught up the clothes she'd worn the previous evening, and entered the master suite.

The large bed bore witness of Jared's occupation, the covers a tangled mess, the pillows bunched at different angles. So he hadn't had an easy night of it, either.

Somehow the thought gave her pleasure as she crossed to the large walk-in wardrobe.

Clothes were everything, and she began with her sexiest underwear, pulled on the sheerest tights, added a new suit she'd bought only the week before but hadn't worn, and slid her feet into killer stiletto-heeled shoes. Then she collected her bag of cosmetics and returned down the hall to the guest suite.

Make-up was both an art form and a weapon, and she took extra care with its application, highlighting her eyes before sweeping her hair into a smooth chignon. A touch of perfume, and she was about as ready as she'd ever be to face whatever the day might bring.

Any hope of escaping the apartment before Jared's return died as she entered the kitchen and saw him seated at the breakfast table sipping black coffee as he scanned the morning's newspaper.

His usual routine on return from the gym was to shower, shave, dress, eat, then leave for the city.

This morning he'd chosen to reverse the process, and the sight of him in sweats, his hair ruffled from exertion, and looking incredibly *physical* sent the blood racing through her veins.

He lifted his head and his gaze seared hers. It gave him no pleasure to see the carefully masked signs showing she hadn't slept any better than he had.

'Coffee's hot.'

Tasha made tea, added milk, slid bread into the toaster, then peeled and ate a banana as she waited for the toast to pop. When it did, she spread honey, and carried both tea and toast to the table.

Begin as you mean to go on, she bade silently. Anything less is a compromise you don't want to make.

'I'll arrange an apartment of my own within the next few days,' she said quietly. She took a deep breath, then released it slowly. Her throat felt as if it were closing over, and she swallowed in an attempt to ease the restriction.

'You think I'll allow you to do that?' His voice was quiet, much too quiet.

She was willing to swear she stopped breathing, and for a few timeless seconds she wasn't capable of summoning a coherent word.

'It's not your decision to make,' she managed at last.

'No?' The silky tone held something she didn't care to define.

'My child, my body.' It was as if she was hell-bent on treading a path to self-destruction.

'Our child,' he corrected. 'Our decision.' He stood to his feet, aware he outmatched her in height, size and weight. He caught the faint flicker of alarm in her eyes and derived satisfaction from it. Dammit, he'd take any advantage he could get.

She stood her ground. 'I've already made my decision.'

'Change it.'

She checked her watch. 'I have to leave, or I'll be late.' She collected her briefcase and walked from the apartment, then she took the lift down to the basement car park, slid into the BMW and sent it up to street-level.

Focusing on work took all her concentration, and it didn't sit well when a para-legal pointed out something she'd missed, when she should have picked up on it. A minor error, but it gave her pause for thought.

Tasha's lunch was a sandwich she sent out for, which she ate at her desk in between contacting real-estate agents. The sooner she tied up a lease on an apartment the better, and she made appointments to view at the end of her working day.

The afternoon didn't fare much better, and it was a relief to join the building's general exodus shortly after five.

Her first appointment didn't work out. She could have ignored the female agent's over-the-top presentation if the apartment had lived up to expectations. It didn't, and what was more the rental was way overpriced.

The second was an improvement, but Tasha didn't like the location.

'I can get you anything you want if you're prepared to pay,' the agent snapped. 'Both apartments I've shown you are in the price-range you quoted.'

'I have a few others to see tomorrow,' she dismissed coolly. 'I'll get back to you.'

Going home held a new connotation. She was very aware the apartment and everything in it belonged to Jared. Clothes and select items of jewellery comprised her possessions. She'd given up a lease on her own apartment and her furniture had been put in storage when she'd moved in with Jared.

The muted ring of her cell-phone sounded from inside her bag, and she retrieved it, checked the caller ID and felt her stomach muscles tighten. Jared.

'Where in hell are you?'

'Three blocks away at a set of traffic lights,' she answered reasonably.

'It's almost seven. You didn't think to call and say you'd be late?'

'I lost track of time.' The lights changed and cars up front began to move. 'Got to go.' She cut the connection before he had a chance to respond.

Jared was standing in the lounge, hands thrust into his trouser pockets, when she entered the apartment. The adopted casual stance belied the tense set of his features.

'Perhaps you'd care to explain?'

There was nothing like the truth. 'I was viewing apartments with an agent.' She began loosening the buttons on her jacket, only to pause part-way when she remembered all she wore beneath it was a bra…a very skimpy number that was little more than a scrap of moulded red lace.

Tasha saw his eyes flare, then harden as she refastened the buttons.

'A useless exercise. You're not going anywhere.'

Calm. All she needed to do was to remain calm. 'I don't believe you have the right to tell me what I can or can't do.'

Jared lifted an arm and indicated the room. 'Why move out when we can share this apartment?'

See you every morning, every night? Separate bedrooms, separate meals, polite conversation? And die a little every time? 'I don't think so,' she responded with a politeness that belied her emotions.

'Tasha.' His voice held a silky warning she chose to ignore, and her expression held a mix of fearless pride.

'I have no intention of denying you access,' she managed quietly.

'To you?'

She didn't misunderstand his implication. 'To the child,' she elaborated.

'Unlimited time. Your place or mine, but I don't get to stay?'

'I don't want the child to sense its father might only be a temporary entity who might choose to walk out of its life at any time.'

His gaze hardened measurably. 'You must know I would never do that.'

'Perhaps not.' She waited a beat. 'However, your future wife may not be so keen to welcome a child from a previous relationship.'

'As you will be my wife, that doesn't apply.'

One fine eyebrow arched in silent query. 'Another proposal you expect me to accept, when I know that, had it not been for the child, marriage was never your intention? Thanks, but no, thanks.'

A muscle tensed at the edge of his jaw. 'I don't recall saying marriage wasn't my intention.'

He was good, very good. But wasn't it the skill of his chosen profession to utilise words to their best advantage? To confuse the defendant and cleverly persuade admissions which otherwise might be withheld?

'You didn't need to.'

'You're being ridiculously stubborn.'

'Am I?' She drew in a short breath and released it. 'I guess that's my prerogative.' It took considerable courage to hold his gaze. 'If you'll excuse me, I need to go freshen up.' She checked her watch, and grimaced ruefully. 'I'm already late.'

'Late for what?'

Jared's voice held an ominous thread she chose to ignore. 'Eloise rang to say Simon is out of town for a few days, and I suggested we meet for dinner.'

'A girls' night out?'

'Yes.' She moved past him and entered the bedroom she'd occupied the night before. It didn't take long to freshen up, repair her make-up and re-do her hair.

Jared watched her emerge into the lounge, and experienced the familiar surge of desire. She was everything he wanted, all he needed. Dammit, she was *his*.

The thought of any other man coming near her…worse, being given the right, almost undid him.

Did she have any conception of how he'd managed to get through the day without seriously impairing his reputation?

'Tasha.'

She turned as she reached the door, watchful as he closed the distance between them. 'Yes?'

'You forgot something.'

A puzzled frown creased her forehead. Purse, keys… 'I don't think so.'

'This,' he murmured as he cupped a hand to her face and brushed his lips to her own, lingered, then he deepened the kiss to something warmly evocative before lifting his head.

He smiled faintly at her slight confusion, aware of her response for an unguarded instant. 'Drive carefully.'

Oh, God, she agonised as she rode the lift down to the basement car park. Why did he have to do that? She could still feel the slow sweep of his tongue on her own, the pressure of his mouth. Not to mention the quickened beat of her heart.

She made a quick call to Eloise from her cell-phone to say she was running late, then she drove the car to street-level.

Traffic was heavy, with a number of vehicles heading for the city, and it was almost eight when she entered the restaurant.

'I'm so sorry,' Tasha offered as she slid into the seat opposite Eloise.

The attractive blonde smiled and indicated her half-empty glass of wine. 'A gentleman had the waiter bring me champagne with his compliments. And a note offering his—er—services for the evening.'

'Naturally you declined.'

'It was tempting,' Eloise relayed solemnly, and Tasha bit back a mischievous laugh. She'd known Eloise since their pre-teen years when they'd commiserated over pimples, teeth braces, and lusted after the male television and movie stars of the moment.

Relationships, they'd experienced a few, and supported each other when they fell apart. Now Eloise was happily married to Simon, and Tasha was with Jared...and pregnant.

Tasha picked up the menu. 'OK, what are we eating?'

The drinks waiter arrived, and she requested chilled mineral water.

'I'm driving.' It was a weak excuse, and she knew it.

'So am I,' Eloise stated. 'But one glass won't pitch either of us over the legal limit.'

They ordered, choosing an entrée, skipped the main, and settled on fresh fruit, cheese and crackers instead of dessert.

'It's no fun being virtuous.'

Tasha sipped from her glass, then replaced it onto the table. 'Speak for yourself.'

'I thought Jared might have been with you.'

'Disappointed?'

'Not in the least. We rarely get to go out on our own.'

'Without the men of the moment.'

'OK, what gives?'

Tasha picked up her glass and took a leisurely sip. 'What makes you think anything does?'

'Too many years of friendship. Are you going to talk, or do we continue to pretend nothing's wrong?'

Eloise would know soon enough, so it might as well be now. 'I'm pregnant.'

'You're kidding me.'

'I wish.'

'What do you mean, *you wish*? Maybe the timing isn't right, but Tasha…a baby. I think it's wonderful.' She leaned forward. 'So when's the wedding?'

'There isn't going to be one.'

'Excuse me?'

'I'm not going to marry Jared.'

'This is serious stuff.' Eloise pushed her plate to one side and leaned forward. 'Didn't he ask you?'

'Yes.'

'And you refused? Are you insane?'

Quite possibly. 'I don't want marriage just because it serves a purpose.'

'Stubborn,' Eloise declared with brutal honesty. 'You're being ridiculously, pathetically stubborn.'

'*Stubborn,* huh?'

'Forget the dream, and go with reality. Marry the man.'

'Sure,' Tasha agreed. 'And wonder if it'll last? If he'll be enticed by the excitement of an affair…singular or plural. Consign the wife and child to one side and indulge in extramarital sex.'

'Many marriages exist and survive in those circumstances.'

'More fool the wives who condone them.'

'You'd be surprised how many do.'

'In exchange for the mansion, social and professional status, overseas trips…not to mention their husband's wealth,' Tasha concluded cynically.

'Better the legal advantage of wife, than mistress.'

'So…why not me? Is that what you're saying?'

'What will change?' Eloise demanded. 'You

adore the guy, he clearly adores you. Dammit, you've lived together for two years. So, the pregnancy wasn't planned. So what? It happened, and it can't be undone. Well, it can, but, knowing you, you wouldn't consider abortion as an option.'

'No.'

'You'll deny your child a live-in father and the stable relationship of two full-time parents…because of stubborn pride?'

'You don't understand.'

'Take a reality check, Tasha.'

'You didn't settle for anything less than love.'

'If you remember, it was a rocky path to the altar.'

Rocky was an understatement, she reflected. An engagement that was more *off* than *on*. Yet Eloise and Simon had resolved their differences, and as far as she could tell the magic that had shimmered beneath the surface was still there.

'So you think I'm being a fool?'

'Yes.'

There was nothing like the honesty given from the benefit of a long friendship! 'Yet you know I'm going to do it my way, regardless?'

'I don't have the slightest doubt.'

Minutes later another waiter presented them with a tastefully decorated platter of fresh fruit, assorted nuts, cheese and crackers.

'Enough about me,' Tasha dismissed as the waiter took their order for tea and coffee. 'How's business?' Eloise was a high-flying executive in a public-relations firm who dealt with an interesting range of clients.

'Hectic.' The attractive blonde grimaced slightly. 'Simon's flight arrives from Tokyo an hour before mine departs for Sydney.' She rolled her eyes. 'We'll be lucky if we catch sight of each other. There's a lot to be said for the nine-to-five daily grind.'

'As opposed to fame and fortune?' Simon dealt in corporate real estate, worldwide, setting up multi-million-dollar deals involving buildings, hotels. Formerly based in New York, he'd made his home in Brisbane following his marriage to Eloise.

'I guess it would be selfish to want both?'

'Not possible,' Tasha opined solemnly.

'Because there's no such thing as a perfect world?'

'Something like that.'

It was almost eleven when they left the restaurant. The adjacent parking area was well-lit, and Eloise's car occupied the bay next to her own.

'I'll be in touch,' Eloise promised as she unlocked her door. 'Take care, Tasha, and think about what I said.'

'Shall do.'

The possibility Eloise was right didn't escape her as she followed her friend's car onto street-level.

It was a beautiful night, the sky a deep indigo sprinkled with stars and a sickle moon. Bright lights, colourful neon, traffic. Reflections of the sky-scape evident in the smooth waters of the city river.

Self-castigation was not an uplifting experience, Tasha determined as she took the exit lane from the bridge.

What was wrong with her? Why not accept Jared's proposal, enjoy being Mrs Jared North, gift her child legitimacy, and to hell with her high ideals?

She needed her head read. Anyone else would go eagerly into the marriage and be content with whatever Jared offered. She knew he cared for her. So what if lust was a poor substitute for *love*?

Any number of women would be willing to settle for less, given Jared's personal wealth, professional and social status. He was a generous man, in bed and out of it. Wasn't that *enough*?

Was she a fool for wanting it all?

The answer had to be an unequivocal *yes*.

CHAPTER THREE

THE apartment was quiet as she entered the foyer, and she crossed to the kitchen, withdrew bottled water from the refrigerator and filled a glass, drank some, then she made for the hallway.

Was Jared home?

The sudden thought he might have gone out resulted in a frown. He would have rung, surely? Or at least left a text message on her cell-phone.

'Enjoy your evening?'

He stood framed in the aperture leading to the room he used as a study. One wall was lined floor to ceiling with bookshelves, another wall contained a long credenza. There was an antique desk which held his laptop surrounded by legal files, and a thick yellow legal pad.

Attired in black jeans, a white chambray shirt unbuttoned at the neck with the sleeve cuffs carelessly turned back, his hair slightly ruffled as if he'd dragged his fingers through it, he looked vaguely piratical, even satanical.

Dark eyes, dark hair, olive skin, his expression unfathomable as he stood regarding her.

Tasha felt vaguely defensive, even wary. Normally she'd have moved in close, reached up and kissed him, sure of her welcome, the feel of his arms closing around her slender form as they pulled her in and he deepened the kiss.

Sometimes they'd talk, but most often he'd simply sweep an arm beneath her knees and carry her into their bedroom. Fast and furious, slow and gentle…one would inevitably follow the other in a long loving far into the night. Often the talking waited until morning as they showered together, ate breakfast, dressed for the day.

Now Tasha remained still, unfamiliar uncertainty meshing with an undeniable sexual attraction. 'Yes.'

Jared didn't move, and she contemplated walking straight past him to the spare bedroom.

Except there was a waiting, *watching* quality to his stance. A silent warning she instinctively knew she'd do well to heed.

'Working hard?' It was a light query, and unnecessary. He was one of a few people she knew who could survive on four or five hours' sleep and face whatever the day held with energy and purpose.

Razor-sharp was a superlative often used in reference to Jared North's mind power, his memory recall. Very little, if anything, escaped him.

'A few more hours should do it.'

The faint drawling quality sent prickles of unease up her spine. They were both being excruciatingly polite. Too polite, she perceived, aware there was a degree of anger beneath the surface of his control.

With her? Of course with her! The pregnancy was her fault. Well, not entirely, but she could have, *should* have been aware of the consequences and ensured extra precautions were taken. Except she hadn't given the possibility of pregnancy a thought.

Divine intervention? A *test* by the Deity to determine the strength of their relationship?

Oh, dammit, Tasha cursed silently. She was really losing it!

'Goodnight.' She made to step past him, only to pause as his hand closed over her shoulder. Firm fingers cupped her chin, tilting it so she had no choice but to meet his gaze. 'Don't.' Dear heaven, he was so close, too close. 'Please,' she added quietly.

Jared touched a finger to her lower lip, and he offered a faint smile. 'Afraid, Tasha?'

'Of you? No.'

'So brave.' His voice held a mocking tinge she chose to ignore.

It took courage to project *cool* when her pulse felt as if it was jumping out of her skin. 'Is there a purpose to this?'

'Does there need to be one?'

'Yes,' she managed evenly.

'By all means...' His mouth closed over hers in a gentle exploration, teasing, evocative, as he held her there.

For an instant she began to respond, the instinctive inclination automatic, then reaction set in and she strained against him, unsure whether to feel relieved or disappointed as he let her go.

'You don't play fair.' Her breath hitched a little as she sought control.

'Did you imagine I would?'

She looked at him, caught the stillness in that dark gaze, and recognised the need to act with her head and not her heart.

'No.' Beneath the sophisticated façade there was a primitive ruthlessness apparent, a hard strength coupled with indomitable power. Characteristics that made him a man feared in a court of law...and out of it.

A sensual man, she added silently, practised in the art of lovemaking and pleasing a woman. Intense passion and great *tendresse*...he employed both with considerable skill. Yet there was also the hint of sweet savagery, well-leashed, but exigent none the less.

A tiny shiver slithered the length of her spine. Jared North was someone no one in their right mind would choose to have as an enemy in any arena.

'I'm going to bed.' She turned away from him and took the few steps necessary to bring her level with the spare bedroom.

'Sleep well.'

Tasha ignored the faint irony in his voice, and chose not to respond as she entered the room. She turned on the light switch, then closed the door quietly behind her and stood leaning against it for several minutes.

She was tired, mentally, emotionally, physically, but she doubted her ability to enjoy an easy night's sleep.

There were too many thoughts chasing contrarily

through her mind, and she endeavoured to dispense with them as she removed her clothes. Make-up came next, then she donned a nightshirt and slid in between the sheets.

She must have slept, for she was caught up in a dream so realistically vivid she was *there*, living the fight to save her baby from being taken away. She screamed at the nurse to bring him back, but no sound came out, and she screamed again, louder this time, forcing her voice in a bid to be heard. But the nurse kept walking, and Tasha tried to get out of bed to go after her, only she was hooked up to various machines, drips, and she began pulling at the tubes, swearing at her seeming inability to disconnect them as she sought to free herself.

Then there was a familiar voice, hands whose soothing touch provided a calming influence, and although she heard the words, none of them seemed to register. The scene switched to another, one where the baby was now a young toddler, laughing as he played with toys on the lawn out back of a beautiful home, and she was there, watching with maternal pride.

Dreams, fantasy, wishful thinking. Perhaps a little of each. When she woke she retained a vivid recollection, and there was an awareness of the dawn filtering through the shutters, followed by the knowledge this wasn't the spare bedroom, nor was she alone.

Had she cried through the night? Or had Jared—?

'You called my name.' He'd hit the floor running

at the first scream, and arrived to pull her into his arms as the next scream emerged from her throat.

The tortured voice had chilled him to the bone, and he'd pulled her close, soothing until she quietened, then he'd brought her into his bed, gathered her in and held her through the night.

Was she aware she'd clung to him in her sleep? Whimpered indistinctly whenever he sought to ease her into a more comfortable position?

Tasha felt the strong, steady beat of his heart beneath her cheek, sensed the warmth and slight muskiness of his skin, and experienced a familiar sensation unfurling deep within. The quickened pulsebeat, the sensitised pores, and an electrifying awareness that curled through her body, rendering it boneless, *his,* anticipating the drift of his fingers, the touch of his lips.

It was an achingly familiar pattern most mornings as they indulged in a slow lovemaking. Soft sighs, lingering kisses, and the sweet sorcery of seduction.

Then they'd slip from this large bed, share a leisurely shower before dressing for the day ahead, eat breakfast together and take the lift down to the basement car park.

This morning was different. So much had changed in the past forty-eight hours. Gone was the easy camaraderie, the sanctuary of unreserved loving. Now there were barriers, doubts, reservations.

Insecurities and unresolved resentment, she added silently, aware that every second she remained quiescent related to an invitation she was reluctant to offer.

Two years of unrestrained loving, yet at this moment she felt as nervous as she had the first time they'd shared sex.

'I must get up.'

Jared's hand slid from her ribcage to her stomach. 'Stay.'

The breath caught in her throat, and she tamped down the need. If she stayed, there could only be one end, and although she craved the wild, primitive pleasure his touch would provide, she'd only despise herself afterwards for giving in.

'I can't.'

There was a lost, almost forlorn edge to her voice that tore at him more than the words she uttered.

'Stay,' he repeated gently. 'With me.'

Did he have any idea how hard it was for her to refuse? Or how easy it would be to give in? But what price a love that wasn't equal? Self-survival had to be her ultimate goal. And she couldn't, wouldn't settle for anything less than his total commitment. Willingly given, not out of duty.

Right now she needed to get out of this bed and put some distance between them, for if he kissed her she'd be lost.

'I need to go into the office early this morning.' Even as she uttered the words she was easing away from him, smooth, deliberate movements he made no effort to still as she slid from the bed and crossed to the door. If she chose to shower in the adjacent *en suite* he might see it as an invitation to join her, and the resulting intimacy would be more than she could bear.

Half an hour later she'd showered and utilised the hair-drier. All her clothes, she qualified with a faint grimace, were in the master bedroom, along with her lingerie, hose, shoes.

With luck, Jared would be in the shower and she could retrieve what she needed without him being aware she was there.

Chance would be a fine thing, she acknowledged on re-entering the bedroom. He was in the process of dressing, a pair of black silk briefs sparing his tall muscular frame from nudity.

She caught a glimpse of broad shoulders, lightly tanned flesh and the fluid movement of muscle and sinew as he reached for a white cotton shirt, aware of the ease with which he closed the buttons before pulling on elegantly tailored trousers to his waist and deftly sliding the zip fastener closed.

There was nothing she could do to prevent the spiralling sensation curling through her body. Trying to stop it was akin to halting an incoming tide…impossible.

Part of her ached for the loss of their affectionate humour, the light-hearted teasing. A week ago she'd have crossed to his side, lifted her face to his and kissed him, exulting in the lingering afterglow of a fine loving.

She adored the sight and the feel of him, his male muskiness, the subtle aroma of his favoured Cerruti

THE PREGNANCY PROPOSAL

cologne. It felt so right to sink into him, so incredibly reassuring to have his arms close around her slender frame and pull her in.

His mouth… Dear heaven, just thinking about the erotic pleasure he could bestow heated her blood and sent it coursing through her veins.

Stop it. The self-admonition came as a silent scream.

Tasha drew in a deep breath, then systematically gathered what she needed and retreated to the spare bedroom.

It took determined effort to dress, fix her hair and apply make-up. Force of habit had her tidying the room, straightening bedcovers, then she collected her briefcase and walked out to the kitchen where the smell of freshly perked coffee teased her taste buds.

She'd have killed for a cup of hot black coffee, and bit her lip as she filled the electric kettle, slotted bread into the toaster, and settled for tea.

'Anything in particular on the day's agenda?' Jared queried as she took a seat at the breakfast bar. 'You expressed a need to go in to work early,' he added at her faintly startled glance.

He was adept at interpreting body language, and hers held a transparent quality lacking in artifice. Infectious wit, unerring courage and conviction, honesty, integrity. Add charm, and she'd shone like a beacon in a sea of multi-layered women whose true personality lay buried so deep he'd treated them as they regarded him…a pleasant social and sexual partner.

Until Tasha.

'A few things I need to catch up on,' she managed evenly. It was an extension of the truth, for all it entailed was checking a file, making a notation, and requesting one of the stenographers insert the correction and run another copy off ready for the client to sign.

Five minutes…ten, at the most. And the client's appointment was timed for nine-thirty.

She finished her toast, drank the last of her tea, then she stood to her feet and caught up her briefcase.

'I could be late tonight.'

Jared regarded her steadily. 'Same goes. Don't wait dinner.' He reached out a hand and caught hold of her arm. 'Aren't you forgetting something?'

He took advantage of her surprise to pull her close, slanting his mouth over hers before she had a chance to resist.

She possessed the sweetest lips, full and generously curved, and he savoured them gently, nibbling at the lower centre before deepening the kiss into something flagrantly sensual.

Tasha didn't want to respond, and for the space of a few seconds she succeeded, only to succumb to the witching magic of his touch.

When he lifted his head she barely resisted the temptation to pull his head down to hers and kiss him back.

Did he sense her indecision? Perhaps deliberately playing on it in the hope it might persuade her to cease looking for an apartment of her own?

All the more reason, she determined, to seek independence. *Soon.* For the longer she remained in Jared's apartment, the harder it would be not to succumb to temptation.

Jared was a master when it came to seduction technique, she acknowledged wryly. His brooding look with its element of heat and passion, the light tracery as his fingers sought the veins at her wrist, a sensuous curve to his mouth…it added up to a magnetic culmination of the senses, and she became lost, drawn to him as a moth to a flame.

She didn't want to crash and burn. She needed to survive.

Without a word she turned and walked through the lounge to the front door, closed it quietly behind her and summoned the lift.

It became a day where anything that could go wrong, did. Two stenographers called in sick, and redistributing their workload meant documentation which should have been ready for client signature wasn't available for scheduled appointments.

Tasha's immediate superior succumbed to a migraine mid-morning and took a cab home, leaving Tasha to reshuffle appointments.

Lunch was something she sent out for and ate at her desk while she put one call after another through to various real-estate agents in the hope one of them might at least have two suitable apartments on their books she could arrange to view. Preferably after work today.

The sooner she moved into an apartment of her own the better. It was one thing if her subconscious mind was intent on providing her with nightmarish dreams...but quite another if it led to her calling Jared's name in her sleep.

A tremor ran through her body. Waking in his arms put her far too close to the danger zone.

Did he have any conception just how vulnerable she was? Or how difficult it had been not to reach for him and slip easily into their customary early-morning loving?

She'd managed to escape this morning. But how long would it take for her to give in? Especially when Jared was intent on taking unfair advantage of every situation? A day, two, *three*? Then she'd be lost, her bid for independence a foolish quirk so easily overcome. Worse, it would be at variance with her own inestimable code regarding marriage.

A pain pierced her heart, and an incredible sadness clouded her eyes. Marriage to Jared would be heaven on earth. He was her love, the very air she breathed. But she didn't want a 'comfortable' union, one based on duty or convenience.

Nor could she bear to think he felt trapped into doing the *honourable* thing because of the existence of a child.

Others had maintained a live-in relationship and raised children without the benefit of wedlock. But it went against her principles to condone a lack of total commitment to the child.

If marriage born out of love wasn't on the agenda, then it was better to bring a child into the world where clear boundaries were in place. No false misconceptions or misunderstandings from the onset.

'You have?' Tasha queried with relief, and made a note of an address, satisfied she knew the area reasonably well. 'Shall we say six-thirty?'

She disconnected the call. Two agents, each with two apartments immediately available, one of which sounded promising.

It was after five when she left the office, and she met the first agent outside the designated address.

She'd been specific with her requirements, and this didn't come close. It was a walk-up, no lift, no garage facilities. The second apartment was little better.

Two down and two to go, Tasha concluded wryly as she pulled in to where she was to meet the second agent.

The location was fine, the apartment building multi-storeyed and modern. It looked promising, she decided as she walked towards the entrance.

Half an hour later she'd signed a lease, handed over a cheque, arranged to collect a key the next day and move in on Saturday.

It was, she assured silently as she entered the stream of traffic heading towards a bridge crossing the river, a sensible decision.

So why did she feel as if she was about to amputate a limb?

Life was all about adapting to change, she qualified. This latest change would work out. She'd make sure of it.

Tasha began making a mental list. Ring a carrier and organise a time for her furniture to be collected from the storage shed and delivered to her new address. She'd need to organise utilities, the phone and electricity, shopping…

It was a relief to see Jared's car absent from his parking bay, and she rode the lift, entered the apartment, and paused long enough to make a light meal, eat it, then she discarded the office suit, took a shower, donned a robe, then she settled down at the dining-room table with her laptop.

Organisational skills were a prerequisite in any professional arena, and Tasha had serious respect for her work and the firm's clientele. Her salary package was commensurate with her qualifications and experience. Diligent dedication was an innate quality she hoped would eventually elevate her to an associate position. A partnership offer would be the ultimate.

An achiever had been a commendable tag on her scholastic report cards, a compliment from law lecturers, her legal superiors.

Becoming a single mother and taking responsibility for the rearing and education of her child shouldn't alter her goal. A number of successful women managed to rear children and uphold a career...and so would she.

There were professional nannies, childcare centres, after-school care. Boarding-school was a possibility...but not before the age of twelve. She'd share the child with Jared at alternate weekends, and arrange to split her annual leave to coincide with school holidays.

It should, Tasha decided, all work out.

She placed a hand to her waist and rested it there. An instinctive movement as she pondered the sex of her child, its precise size...and made a note to buy a book on pregnancy.

Meanwhile, she had work, and she turned her attention back to the laptop screen.

It was there Jared found her, two law books open to one side, a yellow legal pad with filled pages folded over the spine, and her appointment diary. An empty teacup rested strategically on its saucer in the mix.

'Still at it?'

Tasha lifted her head long enough to spare him a glance, then continued keying in data. 'Yes.'

He crossed into the kitchen, took a carton of milk from the refrigerator, caught up a glass, filled it, then drank long and deep.

'Tough day?' She looked pale, and her eyes seemed too large and much too dark. He stifled the urge to cross to her side, press the *save* key, shut the laptop, then sweep her into his arms and carry her to their bed.

Two nights ago he would have done precisely that, stifled her protest with a kiss, removed his clothes, disrobed her, then indulged them both in a leisurely, evocative loving.

'You don't want to know,' Tasha conceded, without glancing in his direction. She didn't need to, for her concentration was shot to hell with his presence. Looking at him would only make things worse.

'You should be resting.'

Now she did lift her head to spare him a quick look. 'What century are you in...the nineteenth?'

He moved to where she sat, aware how the silk robe shaped her breasts, glimpsed the valley between each, the soft cleavage revealed by the loosened lapels, and controlled the urge to stand behind her and loosen the silken folds even further. He knew the feel of her breasts, their firmness, the way the rosy tips peaked and hardened at his slightest touch.

Instead, he contented himself with working the pins free from the twist of hair she'd secured half-heartedly on top of her head hours before. In serious danger of falling apart, wisps had already escaped and fell in soft curls at her temples, behind her ears, at her nape.

It was a beguiling picture, and one he was unable to resist.

'Don't—please,' she added on a slightly breathless note, hating the vulnerability evident in her voice.

He let his hands linger at the curve of her nape,

then he slowly slid them to curl over each shoulder, cupping them momentarily before letting his hands drop to his sides.

'It's late, Tasha.' His voice was quiet, with a hint of gentleness. 'Pack it in, and come to bed.'

With him? As if.

Should she tell him she wanted to work until she was bone weary so she'd fall into such a deep sleep no dreams would penetrate her subconscious mind?

'Five, maybe ten minutes, then I'll be done.'

Jared shrugged out of his jacket and hooked it over one shoulder. 'I'll take a shower.'

How long would it take him to come looking for her when she didn't show? Or would he bother?

There was no precedent, dammit. In two years they'd never let their differences last through until morning. Hell, apart from the few occasions Jared had been away on business, last night was the first time they'd slept in separate beds.

Surely he didn't—couldn't, think she'd choose to ignore their argument and change her mind about moving out? That all it would take was some time, patience and understanding on his part for her to come to her senses?

If so, he was in for a rude shock.

Tasha spared her watch a glance and saw it was after eleven. Enough, she decided, was enough. Tomorrow was another day.

Minutes later she'd bookmarked her notes, restored the law books to Jared's library, and was safely ensconced in the spare bedroom.

If he came looking for her... Well, she'd deal with it, she decided as she plumped the pillow and reached out to snap off the bedside lamp.

Sleep came quickly. So quickly she was unaware of the door opening, or the shaft of light illuminating part of the room.

Jared crossed to the bed and stood looking down at her, seeing the soft features in repose, the way her hair curled against one cheek and spilled onto the pillow. One hand lay tucked beneath its edge, and she bore the innocence of a child.

Something twisted inside his gut. *His.* His woman. Stubborn, independent, and proud. He wouldn't lose her. Damned if he would.

He wanted to slip in beside her and hold her close through the night. To wake her in the early dawn light and have her reach for him.

For a long time he stood watching her, and then he turned and walked quietly from the room.

CHAPTER FOUR

JARED left early for the city, preferring quiet, uninterrupted time his chambers provided to go over the transcripts, and direct his line of questioning. He left a note for Tasha propped against the toaster, penned in the black ink he preferred.

The trial was proving to be a long, arduous one, the witnesses many, and the prosecuting attorney an arch rival who loved to grandstand the jury. A show pony, Jared acknowledged, with few, if any, scruples, walking the fine edge of the law and invoking judicial warnings as he tried the presiding judge's patience to its limit.

Yesterday's session had presented a chink… granted, only small, and probably insignificant. But he wanted the opportunity to peruse every detail.

The city was quiet at this hour, the traffic minimal, and the sky was a clear azure, the air crisp with the promise of another fine early-summer day. The river resembled mirrored glass, reflecting the tall city towers of steel and glass.

The traffic lights were mostly in his favour, and he turned in to the private car park beneath his office block, inserted his security-coded card to gain access, then swept down to his allotted parking bay.

Allowing time for a consult with his client's so-licitor prior to leaving chambers, he had three hours before he needed to gown up and head off to court.

The lift transported him with electronic speed to a high floor, and he entered the large foyer with its empty secretarial station. He savoured the silence and the solitude as he crossed to his rooms and un-locked the door.

From that moment he assumed another persona, giving everything over to the case in hand, its nu-ances, flaws, the jury's perception of them, and how he could tailor his queries, his address, to maximum effect.

Any thoughts relating to his private life were put on hold. And that included Tasha.

Tonight he would focus on all matters of a per-sonal nature. He had the weekend, and he intended to convince Tasha to remain with him. Dammit, he'd make sure of it.

Meanwhile, the current brief and his appearance in court held prime importance.

Tasha cut the connection on her cell-phone, marked off another line on her list, and walked from her office to the reception area to greet her eleven-thirty appointment.

An hour later she made the third of six private calls, tended to some paperwork, then she took a short lunch-break and completed the remaining calls.

Tasha left the office early and reached the new

apartment minutes ahead of the removalist, who together with his assistant brought in and placed the furniture and variously marked crates.

The refrigerator hummed reassuringly at the flick of a switch, and she unpacked linen, consigned one set to the washing machine, then set to unpacking crockery, cutlery, pots and pans.

It was late when she finished, much later than she had anticipated. She was hungry, tired…but satisfied. All that remained for her to do tomorrow was transport all her clothes from Jared's apartment, then visit the supermarket.

An insistent peal penetrated, sounding loud in the silence of the room, and Tasha crossed to the table and retrieved her cell-phone from her bag.

'Where in hell are you?' Jared's voice held an icy anger she chose to ignore.

'I said not to wait dinner,' she managed equably, and sensed rather than heard his husky oath.

'Do you have any idea what the time is?'

She hadn't thought to look, and her eyes widened as she cast a glance at her watch. Eleven-fifteen.

'Sorry, I got carried away.' Wasn't that the truth!

'Where are you?'

There was no time like the present. 'Settling furniture into my apartment.'

The silence was so deafening it would have been possible to hear a pin drop.

'Would you care to run that by me again?' Jared queried in a tone that was silky smooth and dangerous.

'I don't believe you possess defective hearing.'

'Tasha,' he growled in warning.

'What part of "I'm moving out" didn't you understand?'

His silence was palpable, and she could sense the effort he made to retain control. 'Where are you?'

'I'll write down the address and give it to you tomorrow when I collect my clothes.' Cool, calm, *polite*. 'Goodnight.'

'You're not coming home?'

The decision was made, and she didn't intend to renege. 'I'll see you in the morning.' She ended the call before he had a chance to say another word.

She looked at the cell-phone as if it had suddenly become an alien object. Then slowly her gaze lifted and trailed the room. Dear heaven, what had she done?

Her stomach rumbled, a reminder she hadn't eaten since lunch, and she crossed to her briefcase, extracted a banana she'd bought earlier in the day, then she peeled and ate it.

Followed by a long glass of water, and she felt measurably better. She'd take a shower, make up the bed, then crawl into it and hopefully sleep.

The fact she did owed much to the events of the day, and she woke late, rose and dressed in the same clothes she'd worn the day before, then she took the lift down to basement-level and drove to a nearby bakery where she ordered croissants and tea.

The nerves inside her stomach moved from a slow

waltz to a heated tango as she used her key to enter Jared's apartment.

Part of her hoped he'd be out, but *hope* wasn't on her side, for he was there, waiting, looming large and faintly ominous, attired in black fitted jeans and a black polo top.

'If you don't mind, I'll go pack my clothes,' Tasha inclined politely, watching warily as if she expected him to pounce.

'And if I do mind?'

Her chin lifted fractionally, and she took a deep breath, then slowly released it. 'We already did this last night.' She moved towards the hallway, only to come to an abrupt halt as he moved to bar her way.

'You may have, but I'm far from done.'

'There's no point in repeating what has already been said,' she inclined politely, stepping around him as she moved a few paces to a storage cupboard and pulled down one suitcase and followed it with another, then she carried them down to the main bedroom.

Jared followed her and stood just inside the room, watching as she opened drawers and emptied their contents without any pretence at neatness.

He resembled a dark angel, tall, broad shoulders, lean hips, long legs, and the face of a brooding warrior. Control, he had it…but for how long?

She'd never had reason to test it before, and she wasn't sure she wanted to begin now.

'There's nothing I can do or say to change your mind?'

The words held a dangerous edge she chose to ignore. 'No.' It sounded final...too final. Pain shafted through her body, and her breath caught at its intensity.

Get a grip, she mentally chastised. You've made your decision, so just...get on with it.

She crossed to the walk-in wardrobe and began sliding clothes from hangers. Two suitcases weren't going to do it, she perceived. If she piled her work suits on the back seat of the car and stowed the suitcases in the boot she should be able to make one trip.

'You perceive our relationship as being over?'

The silkiness in his voice slithered like ice down the length of her spine, and each word pierced her emotional heart.

Tasha carried out an armful of garments and placed them carefully on the bed, then she turned to look at him...and almost wished she hadn't.

There was something evident in his features she'd never seen before. A hardness, a distancing that tore at her in a way that made her want to retract her words.

'I think we both need to take some time out,' she said carefully.

'And you moving to another apartment will work?'

She held his gaze. 'I don't know.'

'You're carrying my child.'

Dear heaven, what was she *doing*? 'Please,' she

begged, aware of the ache of unshed tears. 'Don't make this more difficult than it is.'

He could verbally tear her to shreds, and it said much he resisted the temptation to do so. 'You expect me to stand here and not fight to keep you?'

Her eyes filled, and she barely held on to her composure. 'I'm not walking out of your life.'

'Just out of my apartment.'

She wasn't able to utter a word for the lump that had risen in her throat. 'Yes,' she managed at last.

'The object of the exercise is to acquire independence and some space?' He didn't like the idea, but he could handle it.

She stood motionless for a few seconds. 'Yes.' Civility, politeness, even gratitude. She could do that. Without a further word she turned and walked back to the walk-in wardrobe to collect the remaining clothes.

When it was done, Jared collected his keys and carried the cases out to the lift.

'I can manage them.'

He swept her a brief, hard look. 'I'll follow you in my car.'

'That's not—'

'Shut up.' The command was silk-soft and deadly, and her mouth thinned as the lift doors swept open.

She didn't offer a word during the descent, nor did she comment when he slung her luggage into the boot of his car.

Instead she slid behind the wheel of her BMW and drove to street-level, then took the route to her apartment, all too aware of Jared's Jaguar following close behind.

Would he approve where she'd chosen to live? She told herself she didn't care. It was her choice, her decision, and she'd be damned if she'd seek his comment.

Which was just as well, as he refrained from offering any as he followed her in and deposited the cases in the main bedroom...easy to find, as it was the only one.

Jared emerged into the lounge. 'Thanks.' Oh, hell, this was awkward.

At that moment the doorbell pealed, and Jared opened the door.

'Hi,' a pleasant male voice greeted. 'I'm Damian, from across the hall. And you are?'

'Tasha's partner,' Jared drawled, which drew raised eyebrows in response.

'Yet she's moving in alone.'

'Not by my choice.'

Tasha drew level with the doorway and incurred a soft, appreciative whistle from a young man who resembled a graduate fresh out of university, tall, lean and...well, fresh, she perceived as she offered a musing smile. 'Tasha.'

'Ah. So I can look, but not touch?' Damian's grin was infectious. 'Pity.' He offered Tasha a devilish wink. 'Anything you need, just call.' He turned and sauntered back to his own apartment.

Jared closed the door and swung round to face her. 'Interesting character.'

'Yes, isn't he?' She moved back a step and spared him a level look. 'Thanks for your help with the luggage. I'd offer you tea or coffee, but I haven't had a chance to get to the supermarket.'

He wanted to say something, but he bit back the words. Instead, he leant forward and laid his mouth over hers in a brief, hard kiss, then he straightened. 'Any problems, call me.'

She wasn't capable of uttering a sound, and she watched as he opened the door, then closed it quietly behind him.

She was alone. That was what she wanted…wasn't it?

Oh, dammit, this wasn't the time to stand around brooding. She needed to go shopping, she needed to unpack.

Tasha spent the weekend getting everything straight.

Jared rang each evening, and they both resorted to conversation that was courteous, but brief.

There was something to be said for having her own space, Tasha reflected as she consigned fresh fruit and milk to the refrigerator. The only person she had to please was herself. No one she was obligated to phone and say she'd be late, or unable to make dinner.

Living alone was her own decision. So why the slight twist in her stomach each time she entered her empty apartment? After three days in residence, it wasn't getting any easier.

Stop it, she silently admonished. You wanted this, you've got it…so live with it.

The alternative…let's not go there.

She moved through to the bedroom, caught up fresh underwear and made for the bathroom, where she discarded her clothes, then stepped beneath the shower.

A dinner invitation, Jared had reminded when he rang, issued by the Haight-Smythes a fortnight ago and one he felt obliged to keep.

Tasha's first thought was to refuse. Any soirée hosted by Jonathon and Emily Haight-Smythe was an *occasion* attended by the cream of the city's social echelon.

It meant dressing to kill, air-kisses and indulging in scintillating conversation. None of which particularly appealed.

A challenge, she assured as she applied make-up and styled her hair. Her first choice was a black figure-hugging gown, all but strapless except for tiny lace cap sleeves. Except even with blusher and a deep rose lip-colour she looked far too pale and wan.

Red, she decided, with its bias-cut panels, clever frills and side-split.

Matching shoes and evening bag made it a heart-stopping ensemble, and she swept her hair high, added ear-studs, a pendant.

She entered the lounge as the intercom buzzed. Jared, right on time.

'I'm on my way down.'

He was waiting in the lobby, a tall, dark angel

whose height and breadth of shoulder were emphasised by an immaculate dinner suit, dark blue shirt and matching silk tie.

His facial features were achingly familiar, and all her sensory impulses came alive in primitive recognition.

How was it possible for one man to invade her senses to this degree? To be so attuned to him, mentally, emotionally, spiritually, it seemed as if her heart, her soul meshed with his to become one.

Even now, she had to physically restrain herself from seeking his embrace, linking her hands together at his nape as she pulled his head down to hers.

She wanted, needed his touch, his taste as his tongue mated with her own in a sensuous dance that was a prelude to how the evening would end.

Anticipation. The light teasing, a musing smile, a tantalising promise.

'Hi.' As a greeting it was carelessly casual, as she meant it to be.

'Tasha,' Jared acknowledged. 'How are you?' He moved forward and brushed his lips to her temple.

It wasn't enough, and it left her feeling more disturbed than she was prepared to admit.

'Fine.' And she was, physically. In fact she felt disgustingly healthy. 'Shall we leave?'

The Haight-Smythe residence nestled across the river against the curve of a hill in suburban Ascot, where stately homes merged with imposing modern structures. Old and new money meshed with graceful style, the streets rimmed by leafy trees and neat grass verges.

Emily and Jonathon's home had been built at the beginning of the twentieth century, and faithfully renovated, restored and maintained to closely resemble the original. Ornate pressed ceilings with elaborately designed cornices, highly polished parquet floors covered in part with lush oriental rugs. Expensive curtains, antique furniture, magnificent original works of art graced the walls.

Elegance personified, Tasha accorded as she accepted orange juice from a proffered tray and allowed her gaze to drift idly around the room.

Most of their fellow guests were known to her, and it was remarkably easy to mingle at Jared's side, exchange a few pleasantries, smile and converse as if everything in her world was exactly the same as it had been a week ago.

Except it wasn't, and she was supremely aware of the difference.

Body language could be more revealing than one expected, and, although she failed to detect any artificiality in Jared's attitude towards her, she felt as if her body was a tightly coiled spring.

Was her smile a little too bright? Her tone tinged with something indefinable? Did her usual warmth and spontaneity seem too contrived?

'Relax,' Jared drawled, watchful of the slightest change in her expression. Did she know he could define the direction of her thoughts?

Right now she'd prefer to be anywhere else but

here. It would have been easy for her to opt out of tonight's invitation, plead a headache or any minor ailment as a suitable excuse. Except she hadn't. Sheer stubborn-mindedness, or the challenge of playing the social game?

'What makes you think I'm not?'

He picked up her hand and lightly traced the veins inside her wrist. The pulse beat fast there, and he soothed it, stilling her effort to pull free.

'Jared.'

The well-modulated feminine voice was familiar, and Tasha turned slightly to face Soleil Emile, the daughter and third-generation Emile of the prestigious legal firm, Emile and Associates.

Tall, slender, with long, lustrous auburn hair, Soleil resembled a model playing at the legal role of solicitor. Her mode of attire was European designer label, her footwear hand-tooled from the finest shoemakers in Italy and France.

It irked that Soleil excelled at her job, and proved a minor irritation when the glamorous Soleil frequently managed to be the solicitor at Jared's side in the courtroom.

Had they enjoyed an affair? Jared, when Tasha asked, had uttered an amused denial. Soleil, however, liked to infer the friendship was something more than professional.

Why query it now? Tasha demanded silently. Because if Soleil caught so much as a whisper Jared and Tasha were no longer an item, Soleil would zoom in for the kill.

The mere thought acted like an arrow piercing her heart. 'Soleil,' she managed with admirable politeness.

It was all terribly civil, Tasha reflected as they indulged in social pleasantries. Talking 'shop' in general terms was permissible. Openly discussing a case or a client was not.

'You won't mind if I steal Jared for a short while later in the evening?' Soleil didn't wait for an answer as she turned towards Jared. 'I'll confirm the information via email, but I'd like the opportunity to put you in the picture.'

Who did she think she was kidding? The only picture Soleil was interested in had everything to do with Jared North, the man.

How could Jared be so blind to imagine Soleil had only his current legal brief in mind?

Or was he aware of Soleil's guise, and skilfully kept the relationship on a strictly professional basis?

For heaven's sake, get a grip, Tasha chided silently. Soleil has been a part of Jared's professional life for as long as you've known him. Why choose to agonise about it now?

'If you'll excuse me?'

Tasha detected the sensual purr beneath the polite veneer, and barely restrained a retaliatory feline growl as Soleil glided gracefully away.

Dinner was announced a short while later, and it proved to be a culinary triumph served with sophisticated flair.

Jared was attentive, more so than usual, and at

one stage she leaned in close, offered him a sweet smile and said quietly, 'You're verging close to overkill.'

'Think so?'

His voice was low, husky, and far too intimate for her peace of mind. Did he have any idea of the effect he had on her?

Without doubt. They shared a history together, the memory of which was hauntingly vivid. His mouth, the touch of his hands, the way he used both to drive her wild. Beyond reason, where intense passion ruled, transcending anything she'd known or imagined possible.

And you're giving this up? a tiny voice taunted mercilessly. *Are you mad?*

Was it expecting too much to want it all? Were her expectations too high, too impossible to achieve?

In all honesty she had to admit she'd considered marriage to Jared a possibility...correction, probability. She'd been reasonably positive their relationship held a relative permanency when they chose to live together.

Yet he hadn't mentioned marriage, and she mentally questioned if he observed the axiom 'if it ain't broke, don't fix it'?

'Want to share?'

Tasha returned to the present in a second, and she managed a faint smile. 'Not particularly.' At least, not now, not here.

She glimpsed something in his dark gaze, fleeting

and indefinable, then it was gone. Surprise widened her eyes as he caught her hand and lifted it to his lips, and for a few seconds she became lost in the evocative warmth his gesture generated.

How could she do that when she was at odds with him? It irked unbearably the pull of the senses was stronger than her capacity to control them...even briefly.

Was he aware of it? Deliberately instigating a public gesture as a reminder?

He lowered their hands to rest on his thigh, and his fingers tightened as she made a furtive effort to pull free.

Dessert was a delightful concoction, and Tasha used a dessert fork in one hand whilst conducting a silent battle with the other.

Did anyone notice? Somehow she doubted it, for the conversation flowed, as did the wine, and there was a sense of relief as the dessert plates were removed and guests were invited to sample a variety of cheeses from a well-stocked platter.

Eventually the meal came to a close and Emily encouraged her guests to adjourn to the lounge for coffee.

Tasha was aware of Jared's hand against the small of her back as they vacated the dining-room. 'Must you?' she demanded quietly beneath the veneer of a soft smile, and met his hooded appraisal.

She was behaving out of character, and it didn't sit well. An apology hovered on her lips, yet it remained unuttered as a fellow guest claimed his attention.

She requested tea, accepted the delicate china cup and saucer from their hostess, and moved a few paces to join Jonathan Haight-Smythe.

A supreme-court judge, he'd witnessed every aspect of human nature, mediated, adjudicated, and directed the course of justice. Inside the courtroom he was known to be a stickler for protocol, intolerant of grandstanding, and unsympathetic to anyone who attempted to pervert judicial action.

'Tasha, how nice you were able to join us tonight.'

'A lovely meal and delightful company,' she complimented with sincerity. 'Thank you for the invitation.'

'Our pleasure. One trusts the corporate world is treating you well?'

The mores and vagaries of the legal fraternity were complex, and Tasha managed a suitably innocuous response that earned a solemn smile.

Soleil, she noted idly, had managed to capture Jared's attention and the image of his head inclined towards hers remained as a photographic visualisation that continued to haunt during the evening.

Tasha was deep in conversation with the wife of a noted prosecuting attorney when she sensed Jared's presence at her side.

She possessed an internal antenna where he was concerned, almost a sixth sense that was as uncanny as it was surprising. A few weeks ago she would have viewed the feeling with benevolent affection, mentally waxing lyrical they might have known each other in another life...perhaps twin halves of a soul.

Now it was accompanied by an unaccustomed ache in the region of her heart that had little to do with anything she cared to name.

'You'll excuse us, Jonathon?'

Jared's voice was silk-smooth, polite with the merest edge. Tasha wondered at it, and the coil of tension emanating from his powerful body.

This close she could sense the faint drift of his exclusive cologne mingling with the scent of freshly laundered cotton, the elusive smell of expensive cloth used by the Italian tailor who'd fashioned his suit.

Old money, inherited through several generations, wisely invested to ensure wealth built and multiplied during the lifetimes of several highly professional men.

Jared, she knew, was pursued for his wealth and social standing. Beneath the sophisticated façade was an innate wariness, a cynicism prepared to deal with the social climbers and opportunists. An undetectable barrier only those very close to him were aware of.

It had amused him when she'd refused to accept his gifts, with the exception of birthdays and Christmas.

She could recall informing him with solemn dignity that, while she appreciated his intention, she believed the most important gift was beyond price…and he'd already gifted her that. Himself.

Now she wasn't so sure.

'You'll excuse us if we leave?' Jared inclined, reaching for her hand as he offered Jonathon a salutary compliment. 'There are a few aspects I need to clarify in my notes before tomorrow's session.'

Five minutes later Tasha buckled the seat belt as Jared slid in behind the wheel, fired the engine, then he eased the car down the driveway and onto the street.

A sudden shower swept in, lashing the windscreen with rain, only to ease to a light drizzle within minutes.

At this evening hour the traffic had slowed considerably, and Jared brought the car to a smooth halt in a parking bay adjacent to the main entrance to her apartment building, then cut the engine and doused the lights.

Tasha reached for the door clasp. 'Thanks for the ride.'

He rested a forearm on the steering wheel and leaned towards her. 'Why the hurry?'

Because if he touched her, she'd be lost. 'You expressed the need to go through your notes.'

'Concern for my welfare, Tasha?'

'Your client,' she corrected evenly, and her eyes widened as he captured her face.

'How considerate.' He lowered his head and brushed his mouth to hers in a slow, sweet kiss.

Dear heaven. It took all her strength not to respond to the light graze of his teeth, and a low groan rose and died in her throat as he took her deep in an evocative sensual onslaught that left her wanting more.

So much more, she despaired, aware just how easy it would be to succumb to his persuasive touch. There was a part of her that wanted to fist his shirt in one hand and drag him indoors, ride the lift to her apartment, and tear off his clothes as she pulled him into the bedroom.

She wanted his mouth at her breast, the feel of his arousal against her belly, his hands...and she wanted to touch him, savour the taste of his skin, absorb his male essence, in a no-holds-barred mating that took sexual hunger to a new dimension.

A faint whimper escaped from her throat as Jared eased back a little, and for a wild moment she clung to him, on the verge of beseeching him for more.

Oh, God. Words rose to the surface, and she held them back with difficulty. The blood drained from her face, leaving it pale in the reflected outdoor lighting, and her eyes were large from shock and unshed tears.

His fingers brushed her cheek, then settled at the edge of her mouth to linger and lightly trace the soft contours of her lips swollen from his kiss.

He wanted to make love with her. Hold her close, and never let her go. And he would...soon. For now, he had to give her the time and space she vowed she needed. But not for long.

'I left making out in cars behind with my teens,' he teased musingly.

She had to try for levity. Anything else would be a recipe for disaster...hers. 'Would that have been the BMW, Jag, four-wheel-drive? Or had you progressed to a Porsche?'

'I remember the occasion, but not the vehicle.' His response brought the reaction he coveted...a light-hearted laugh.

'And the girl?'

'Some were more memorable than others.' But none who came close to you, he added silently.

There was an awkward silence, one neither of them rushed to fill. Then Tasha drew apart from him and unlatched the door. 'Goodnight.'

He watched as she slid from the car. 'I'll call you.'

Jared waited as she used a coded key to open the outer door, then bypass the security system. She didn't look back as she stepped towards the bank of lifts, and he only fired the engine when the lift doors closed behind her.

CHAPTER FIVE

IN a way it was a relief to absorb the extra workload distribution incurred by an associate absent due to emergency family leave, for it kept Tasha busy with little time to think or brood on personal issues.

Or at least that was what she told herself.

In reality Jared's image was *there*, so frequently to the forefront of her mind she had to school herself to focus on the work in hand.

Mistakes were inexcusable, and she went to painstaking lengths to ensure none was made. 'Autopilot' mode wasn't an option.

Just as she thought she had a handle on things there was a call from Reception.

'There's a special delivery for you,' Amanda informed.

Tasha checked her watch and verified she had five minutes before a client appointment. 'I'll be right out.'

She was expecting a contract via courier service, a document she needed to peruse and compile an overview of before presenting it to an associate colleague the next day. Legalese presented a multi-faceted minefield which could prove hazardous to the unwary. Each clause required close examination to ensure there were no loopholes and locked in a client's express needs.

Except it wasn't a slim courier package on Amanda's reception desk. Instead, a large bouquet of red roses bound in Cellophane reposed there, and her stomach lurched at the thought of who had sent them.

'Special occasion, or something?'

Tasha managed a smile. 'Or something.'

'I'll organise a vase,' Amanda declared with friendly efficiency.

'Thanks.' She caught up the bouquet and waited until she was in her office before extracting the card.

'Love, Jared'.

Love? That was a joke. Did he even comprehend the true meaning of the word?

His interpretation didn't match her own. And if he thought a bouquet of roses would soften her resolve, then he was way off base.

In the privacy of her office she took a few seconds to admire the perfect velvet-petalled buds, and she inhaled their scent, remembering other occasions when Jared had gifted her roses.

Don't go there.

There was a tap on her door, and she hurriedly composed herself as she bade entry.

'Vase with water,' Amanda said cheerfully as she deposited it on a credenza. 'Want some help? Your client is waiting in Reception.'

Tasha offered a warm smile. 'Thanks. Give me a minute, then show her in.'

The courier duly delivered the contract, which she perused over lunch sent out for and eaten at her desk. She noted down queries, points of reference, then she dealt with what the afternoon threw at her, staying back an hour before driving home.

Although *home* was a misnomer, and there was a teeth-gnashing moment when she automatically entered a familiar traffic lane on exiting her office block...only to discover at the next intersection it would lead her over the river *en route* to Jared's apartment. A muttered imprecation at her absent-mindedness was followed by something more explicit when no one would allow her to switch lanes...which meant she was trapped into following a route she didn't want.

It was several minutes before she could divert and backtrack, and she ignored the insistent peal of her cell-phone, choosing to let the call go to message-bank.

Jared. He could wait, she decided, until she'd had something to eat and taken time to relax and unwind a little from a hectic day. One that was far from done, for she needed to go through her notes, check references, and compile a suitable précis. An early night wasn't going to be an option.

First she needed to slip out of her stiletto heels and exchange her formal suit for casual attire, then she'd unpin her hair from its smooth twist and cleanse off her make-up.

A chicken salad sufficed as dinner, and she added

some fruit, then she took bottled water from the refrigerator and set up her laptop at the kitchen table.

She was on to the third reference analysis when the doorbell pealed, and she stilled momentarily, curious when the only person to her knowledge who knew her new address was Jared. Given the building's security, he'd have had to buzz her first before gaining entry.

Cautious, she checked the peephole, identified her immediate neighbour, and unlocked the door.

'Damian.' His infectious grin brought forth a faint smile. 'Is this a social call? I'm kind of busy right now.'

'Social. I'm meeting up with a few friends at a downtown café, and thought you might like to join us.'

'Thanks, but—'

'No, thanks?' he interceded with a quizzical lift of one eyebrow.

'Another time, perhaps?'

The insistent peal of her cell-phone proved an interruption, and she lifted both hands in an apologetic gesture. 'I'd better take that.'

She closed the door, then picked up on the call.

'Rough day?'

Her toes curled at the sound of Jared's deep drawl, and she closed her eyes in self-directed exasperation at the effect he had on her nervous system.

'You could say that,' she managed politely, then memory and good manners rose to the surface.

'Thanks for the roses.' She'd left them at the office. In the morning she intended to shift them out to Reception for the firm's clientele to enjoy.

'My pleasure.'

Just thinking what his *pleasure* could involve sent her pulse into overdrive. 'Is there a particular reason for your call?'

'Other than to say *hello*?'

She bit back an expressive sigh. 'I've brought work home, I have at least three hours ahead of me, and I'm—'

'Have you eaten?'

Her fingers tightened round the cell-phone. 'What is this? Check-up time?'

'A simple *yes* or *no* will suffice.'

'Yes.'

'Shall we start over?' He sounded vaguely amused.

'As in?'

'I was going to suggest we go somewhere for coffee.'

'I'm not dressed to go anywhere.'

'We don't necessarily have to go out.'

Staying in held implications she didn't care to pursue. 'I don't think that's a good idea.'

Sometimes it was necessary to lose a battle in order to win the war. 'Not if you need to work late. Goodnight, Tasha. Sleep well.'

Who did he think he was, keeping tabs on her? She felt inclined to call him back and tell him just what she thought of him!

She was about to dial his number when the cellphone rang.

She activated the call and recited her personalised series of digits, then uttered a curt, 'Yes?'

'Is this a bad time?'

'Eloise.' She took a deep breath and released it. 'Hi.'

'Lunch, tomorrow? That lovely place upstairs in the gallery of the Brisbane arcade? One o'clock?'

'Love to. Shall I ring and book a table?'

'I'll take care of it. Are you OK?'

'I'm fine,' she assured, and knew she lied. 'Just a bad day, staff away, a work overload. You know how it goes.'

'We'll talk tomorrow.'

Tasha arrived late through no fault of her own, gave her order, and prepared for a barrage of questions.

Eloise didn't disappoint, and after requesting a detailed description of the apartment, the move, work…the next subject was Jared.

'We speak on the phone,' Tasha admitted and caught a speculative gleam as Eloise queried,

'Have you been out together?'

'Not exactly.'

'Sweetheart, either you have or you haven't.'

She shrugged. 'Dinner on Monday in response to an invitation issued a couple of weeks ago.'

'And?'

'There is no *and*,' she refuted firmly.

'Like, it was a *date*? Jared picked you up and dropped you home again? No—'

'No,' Tasha interrupted firmly.

'I'm impressed.' Eloise offered an infectious smile. 'Anything else?'

'You're unconscionable.'

'I'm also your very best friend.'

A friendship that extended way back to junior-grade school. They'd shared teenage years, been there for each other during the bad times. Eloise's parents' divorce was one of them. Tasha's father's succession of failed marriages numbered five at the last count, and the last she'd heard he was courting a wealthy Texan widow. Tasha had no sooner become used to one stepmother when there was another lined up waiting to take her place.

It hadn't made for a stable upbringing, and boarding-school had become a haven, together with a resolve to get a law degree and succeed.

Tasha covered Eloise's hand with her own. 'I know.' She worried her bottom lip with the edge of her teeth. 'He sent me roses.'

'The man adores you,' Eloise said with certainty.

'He enjoyed what we had,' she amended. 'A comfortable lifestyle, commitment to each other, no strings. At least not the ties that bind.'

'And you want those ties?'

Her eyes darkened and she dug fingernails into her palm. 'For the right reasons.' She picked up her teacup and was surprised to discover her hand was trembling. 'Do you blame me? My father hasn't exactly provided a shining example of wedded bliss.'

'It doesn't mean you'll follow the same pattern,' Eloise said gently.

Tasha replaced the cup and checked her watch. 'I have to get back. You don't need to leave. Stay and finish your coffee. I'm taking care of the tab.'

'No, you're not.'

'Humour me. You can pick up on the next one.'

Tasha woke next morning at the sound of the alarm, stretched, then made a dash for the bathroom.

Dear heaven, if this was morning sickness, she didn't want it!

Hot sweet tea and toast. It had worked yesterday. It had better work today, she vowed grimly as she stepped into the kitchen. The shower could wait…everything could wait until her stomach settled.

Some pregnant women, she'd read in the pregnancy bible, suffered sickness symptoms morning, noon and night. For the entire nine months.

She placed a hand over her stomach. 'Baby,' she admonished huskily, 'if you do the morning, noon and night thing to me, Mama is going to utter words your tender ears should never hear!'

Within half an hour she felt relatively human, and she hurriedly showered, dressed, and left for the city.

As days went, hers was a doozy.

It was bad enough she was running late, a situation made worse when her car refused to start. No mechanic, she nevertheless checked the rudimentary possibilities, then switched on the ignition. Nothing.

Hell and damnation.

'Trouble?' a voice queried, and she turned, recognised Damian, and threw her hands up in the air.

'It won't start.'

He popped the hood and fiddled, then slid in behind the wheel, twisted the key in the ignition, then pursed his lips. 'Battery. Dead as a dodo.'

As she saw it, she had two choices. Organise a replacement and be late in to the office. Or call a taxi.

'Leave your car key with Management,' Damian suggested. 'I'll drop you into the city, and you can use your cell-phone to arrange with a mobile battery service to instal a replacement and bill you.'

Constructive help was a godsend, and she told him so. 'I owe you one.'

Nevertheless she was late, a fact that earned a terse reprimand from an important client who made it evident he didn't appreciate cooling his heels for any reason.

From there on in, things got worse. A meeting ran over time, the secretarial pool was diminished by two absent on sick leave, resulting in documents only ranking high on priority were prepared, and lunch was something she missed entirely.

Mid-afternoon her inter-office line buzzed, and she frowned as she reached for the phone. Her next appointment wasn't due for another half-hour.

'Delivery for you,' Amanda informed with bright efficiency.

'I'll come get it.'

A single red rose in a Cellophane cylinder reposed in Reception, and Tasha met the receptionist's dreamy smile.

'Jared North is such a romantic hunk.'

Two weeks ago she would have given a delighted laugh, agreed, and become a little misty-eyed herself. Now she simply smiled and said, 'Yes, isn't he?'

When she returned to her office she retrieved her cell-phone, checked with the management office and had it confirmed a battery had been fitted in her BMW.

It was almost six when she walked out of the office building and joined a queue waiting for a taxi.

She was tired, hungry, and felt faintly incongruous holding on to a long-stemmed rose in one hand, a bulging briefcase in the other while balancing her shoulder bag.

The sound of a car horn was just one of many, and Tasha merely cast a cursory glance at the vehicle which swooped to a halt at the kerb.

The window slid down kerb-side and the male driver leaned sideways. 'Tasha. Hop in and I'll give you a lift home.'

She took a closer look, recognised Damian, hesitated, gave the lengthy queue a glance, and slid into the front passenger seat. 'Thanks.'

'No problem.' He shifted gears and sent the car

into the stream of traffic, eased into the lane that would eventually lead to Kangaroo Point, and sent her a friendly grin as he paused at the next set of lights.

'I'm going to stop for Chinese takeaway. What say I get enough for two and we share?'

It beat having to cook. 'OK, but I'm buying.'

'Will you argue if I refuse?'

'Consider it thanks for helping out this morning.'

'Your place or mine?' Damian queried half an hour later as they emerged onto their floor from the lift.

Tasha effected a light shrug. 'Doesn't matter. Yours.' she decided.

He unlocked the door and ushered her in to what was ostensibly a typical bachelor pad, huge TV screen, expensive stereo equipment, black leather sofa and chairs.

Damian placed the take-out sack on the dining-room table, collected two cans of beer from the refrigerator, and indicated they eat.

'Not for me. I don't drink.' A new dictum, and one that would be in force for the remainder of her pregnancy.

'Cola, soda, water?'

She settled for the latter, broke open the containers, and used chopsticks with practical dexterity.

'So, why does a gorgeous young thing like you choose to live alone?'

Tasha shot him a direct look. 'Is this ''getting to know you'' or the third degree?'

'Both.'

'With a view to…?'

'Asking for a date.' He took time to scoop up another mouthful of noodles, and swallowed them down. 'That is, if the partner is no longer a partner.' He tried for boyish helplessness, and failed miserably. 'And you'd consider going out with me.'

It was time for total honesty. 'I'm pregnant to the partner,' she said quietly. 'Who feels obligated to offer marriage.'

His expression was a study. 'Got it.'

She doubted he had. 'I hope we can still be friends.'

'I'm good with kids. Uncle to five nephews and three nieces.' He offered a wicked grin. 'Dab hand with the diaper thing.'

'Someone I can call on in a crisis.'

The grin was still in evidence. 'Don't see any reason why we can't go to a movie some time, or share a take-out.'

He was nice. 'No reason at all.' She finished the last mouthful, and reached for the glass of water just as her cell-phone rang.

Jared. 'Can I call you back?' she began without preamble.

'Of course.'

She cut the connection and slid the unit back into her bag.

'Let me guess,' Damian interposed. 'The partner?'

'You got it in one.'

'So, should you go running back to your apartment, or can you take time for tea or coffee?'

'Tea would be lovely.'

'Not going to run to his bidding, huh?' he teased. 'I admire that in a woman.' He rose to his feet and crossed into the kitchen, where he filled and plugged in the electric kettle.

Tasha took her time drinking the tea. Damian was easy to talk to, interesting, and pleasant company.

Consequently it was almost an hour later when she bade Damian 'goodnight' and crossed the hall to let herself into her apartment.

With automatic movements she dropped her briefcase, then she undid the Cellophane cylinder and deposited the rose in water. Next she turned on the television, then crossed into the bedroom, undressed, and took a leisurely shower.

Towelled dry, she pulled on a nightshirt, added a robe, then she picked up the phone and dialled Jared's number.

'It's unnecessary for you to ring me every day,' Tasha said coolly when he picked up.

'Get used to it.' There was an edge to his voice she chose to ignore.

'You have no right—'

'Don't even go there,' he warned. 'Shall we start over, and enquire about each other's day?'

'You want to play *polite*?'

'You want to argue?'

No, dammit, she didn't. 'So—how was your day?'

'Challenging.' It had been all of that and more. 'And you?'

'You mean, apart from the flat battery, an irate client?'

'You should have called me.'

'For what, specifically?'

'The flat battery.'

'Damian came to the rescue, and drove me into the city.'

'Did he, indeed?' Jared drawled. 'Kind of him.'

'We shared a Chinese take-out.'

'Perhaps you'd care to fill me in?'

Was there an edge to his voice? She couldn't be sure. 'He happened to drive past while I was waiting for a taxi, so he offered me a lift, and we stopped by for take-out.'

'Which you ate together where?'

She wasn't sure she liked the way this was heading. 'His apartment.'

There was a moment's silence. 'Would you like to run that by me again?'

She took a deep breath, then released it. 'Not particularly.'

'You allowed a man you'd met once, briefly, drive you into the city, willingly stepped into his car again in the evening, and you spent hours in his apartment?'

'Dammit, Jared,' she vented. 'He lives across the hall from me!'

'And that makes it all right?'

'I owed him for helping out. Sharing a take-out

meal with him was no big deal. Besides,' she added, on a roll, 'you have no right to dictate what I do, where I go, or who I spend time with!'

'That's a matter of opinion.'

Her fingers tightened until her knuckles showed white. 'I'm going to end this conversation. Goodnight.' She cut the connection and switched off the phone.

Damn him. How dared he?

Yet he has a point, a small voice taunted as she lay in bed on the edge of sleep.

Another thought occurred…and the possibility he might be jealous gave her momentary satisfaction.

CHAPTER SIX

THE phone rang just after eight, and Tasha checked the ID screen, saw the caller was Jared, and almost didn't pick up.

'I really don't want to speak to you.'

'Nothing to say, Tasha?' His voice was a musing drawl, and she mentally counted to ten.

'Don't tempt me,' she said darkly, and was maddened by his husky chuckle. 'There's a reason why you rang?' The demand was cool and incredibly polite.

'Monica is flying in tomorrow for a visit.'

His widowed mother. An extremely pleasant woman for whom Tasha held an affection. 'Oh.' Had he told her they were no longer living together?

'I thought we'd take her out to dinner and perhaps book theatre tickets for Saturday evening. She leaves Sunday for a few days on the Coast before flying home.'

'And if I say *no*?'

'She'll be incredibly disappointed at not seeing you.'

It was nothing less than the truth, and she felt truly torn. 'Dinner,' she agreed, compromising.

'I'll get back to you with details.'

So much for gaining some time and space for herself, Tasha reflected as she fought city traffic half an hour later.

It had been almost a week since she'd moved out of his apartment, yet he'd phoned every day, they'd dined out together and he'd sent flowers...red roses.

Now Monica was due in town.

Next week, who or what would it be necessitating their joint presence?

As a separation, theirs was becoming a farce.

And whose fault was that?

Tasha gained the underground car park beneath her office building, rode the lift, and became caught up with the day, only to return to her apartment that evening wondering if a 'glowing pregnancy' was merely a myth. General lassitude and mild nauseousness through the day had left her feeling anything but 'glowing'.

Now all she wanted was a shower, something to eat, then she'd curl up in a chair with a good book.

She'd just settled into the chair when the phone rang, and she gave a grateful sigh on discovering it was Eloise on the line.

'Lunch, tomorrow? One o'clock? The usual place in the Brisbane arcade? I'll ring and book a table, shall I?'

'Sounds good to me.'

'How are you feeling?'

Tasha grimaced. 'You don't really want to know.'

'Like that, is it?' Eloise said cheerfully. 'Should I ask about Jared?'

'Don't.'

'Tomorrow, Tasha. Sleep well.'

That was something she had no trouble with, and she woke next morning feeling refreshed and ready to face the day. For all of five minutes, before junior began to rock and roll and she had to make a quick dash to the bathroom.

The office was harmoniously efficient with a full complement of secretarial staff. Hence a backlog of work began to show up on her desk, and she spent time checking documentation and organising appointments.

Eloise was already seated when Tasha arrived.

'Hi, have you been waiting long?' She leant forward and bestowed an affectionate hug before slipping into the seat opposite.

Eloise's smile was warm. 'I arrived early. Now, what are you going to have?'

Tasha ordered tea, then checked the menu and made her selection.

'I didn't want to give you the news over the phone,' Eloise began as soon as a waitress served their food.

'Do I get to guess, or are you going to tell me?' she teased, for her friend was brimming over with withheld excitement.

'Simon has been offered a position in New York. We talked about it, he's accepted.' She paused for breath. 'He flies out in a fortnight, and I'll follow two weeks after him.'

'That's wonderful,' Tasha said with genuine enthusiasm. 'I'll miss you dreadfully.' And knew it to be true. One had many acquaintances, but very few really good friends.

'Hey,' Eloise chided. 'We'll email each other constantly, and I've already told Simon I'm flying back for the birth of your babe.'

'You'll do that?'

'Wouldn't miss it for the world. Besides,' she chided with mock severity, 'that little person you're carrying is going to be my godchild.'

'The honour was always going to be yours.' She glimpsed Eloise's slight frown, and queried, 'What's wrong?'

'Jared has just entered the balcony with Soleil in tow.'

Tasha felt every muscle in her body tense. 'They're headed this way?'

'Looks like it.'

'Soleil is the solicitor on Jared's case.' Couldn't be a lunch break, she rationalised. Court was already back in session for the afternoon.

'Jared has just sighted us,' Eloise enlightened. 'Soleil is trying hard not to look displeased.'

'The woman is a consummate actress.'

'Should be interesting,' Eloise said quietly an instant before her mouth curved into a warm smile. 'Jared, how nice to see you.' She inclined her head towards the woman at his side. 'Soleil.'

'Tasha.' His hand curved over her shoulder as he leaned down and brushed his lips to her cheek. 'The case adjourned until tomorrow. Soleil suggested lunch on the way back to chambers.'

I just bet she did. And of all the restaurants and café's along the mall stretch, she took a punt and chose one which, if I happened to be lunching out, I'd most likely frequent.

'Why don't you join us?' Eloise suggested sweetly, blandly ignoring Tasha's dark glance.

'We wouldn't want to interrupt your girl-talk,' Soleil declared. 'Besides, Jared and I have certain aspects of the case which require discussion.'

Tasha elected to play along. 'Confidential, naturally.' She deliberately scanned the room. 'I doubt you'll find a table. Eloise and I are just about done. You can have ours.'

'There's no need to hurry off,' Jared drawled.

Was he blind to the existing undercurrents? Somehow she doubted it. However, she had no intention of watching Soleil's attempt at one-upmanship. 'I need to get back to the office.' A bald-faced fabrication, but only she knew that. 'Eloise, this is my treat.' She stood to her feet, and, loyal ally that Eloise was, she followed suit. 'Bye, Jared. Soleil.'

'Just what do you think you're doing?' Eloise demanded *sotto voce* the instant they were out of earshot.

'Removing myself from the scene before I lapsed into impoliteness.'

'Thereby allowing Soleil to score one against you.'

'Quite frankly, I don't give a damn.'

'Yes, you do.'

They entered the main thoroughfare, and Eloise gave her a quick hug. 'Thanks for lunch. It was supposed to be my turn. Ring me.'

They turned and began walking in opposite directions, and Tasha spent the afternoon concentrating on the job in hand in the hope of dispelling an image of Jared and Soleil sharing lunch.

It was, she told herself, exactly how Jared described it. Something they'd probably done several times in the past. It didn't mean a thing. Heavens, she'd lunched and dined with colleagues on a strictly business basis.

So why did Soleil bother her so much?

Because she's a merciless schemer who'll stop at nothing to get what she wants.

Someone who didn't hesitate to press any advantage home, she determined when Amanda announced Soleil Emile was on line two.

Tasha glanced at her watch as she picked up. Four o'clock. She hadn't wasted much time.

'Soleil,' she acknowledged coolly. 'What can I do for you?'

'Just a friendly warning. I intend to make my move now you and Jared are no longer a couple.'

'Really?' She tried to sound uninterested, and didn't quite make it. 'And you deduced that news—how?'

'Does the *how* matter?'

'What took you so long?'

'To make a play for Jared?' A tinkling laugh sounded down the line. 'I do possess some scruples.'

And pigs fly, Tasha accorded in silent derision. 'Am I supposed to wish you "good luck"?'

Soleil's tinkling laugh sent Tasha's blood pressure up at least ten points. 'I make it a practice never to rely on luck.'

'Is that it, Soleil? I have a client waiting.' She didn't, but Soleil wasn't to know that.

'I think so.'

Tasha ended the call, and resisted the temptation to throw something.

The aggravation remained as she battled traffic *en route* to her apartment, so much so she muttered something reprehensible when another driver cut her up.

Damian was waiting at the lift well when she parked her car, and he held the lift.

'Wow, I hope it's not me you're mad at.' He pressed the appropriate button on the instrument panel. 'The partner?' he hazarded as the lift sped rapidly upward. 'Work?'

'Take your pick.'

'Well, now, I have just the remedy.' He offered her a cheeky grin as the lift slid to a halt and they emerged into the lobby. 'Go get rid of your brief-case, change out of the corporate gear, and we'll go grab something to eat and take in a movie.'

Why not? 'You don't have anything better to do?'

'Not a thing.' He took out his keys and inserted one into the door lock. 'Ten minutes OK with you?'

They went in his car, had hamburgers and fries, then chose a comedy at the nearest cinema-plex.

The movie was a riot, and there had to be some truth in laughter being the best medicine, for she emerged feeling in a great mood.

Until she caught sight of an auburn-haired, green-eyed witch of a woman who saw her at the same moment and was bent on making her presence felt.

'Well, this is a coincidence,' Soleil all but purred as she drew level. She looked pointedly at Damian and lifted an enquiring eyebrow. 'Aren't you going to introduce me?'

Tasha opened her mouth, but Damian spoke first. 'Damian. One of Tasha's friends.'

'Really? A business acquaintance?'

'No.'

Soleil shifted her gaze to Tasha. 'I must tell Jared we met.'

'Do that, Soleil,' Tasha encouraged, and tucked her hand through Damian's arm. 'You'll excuse us?'

He caught on quick, and led the way out of the auditorium. 'I gather she's not one of your favourite people?'

'How did you guess?'

'Oh, just the fact you could cut the air with a knife, and you were on the verge of challenging pistols at dawn.' He wriggled his eyebrows with comical amusement. 'Little things like that.'

'You're good.'

'I can do better. She has her eye on the partner?'

'His name is Jared.'

'I take it she doesn't know about your pregnancy?'

'In a word—no.'

'Doesn't matter.' They reached the car, which he unlocked, and she slid into the passenger seat.

'Within a week or two Jared is going to sweep you back into his apartment, his life, and Soleil won't exist…if she ever did.'

'What planet are you from?' she teased, and he lifted his hands in the air.

'The man is no fool. He might be cutting you some slack now, but soon he's going to reel you in.'

She looked at him as he fired the ignition. 'What if I don't want to be reeled in?'

He shot her a piercing glance. 'Don't you?'

Oh, hell. She wasn't sure she was ready for such in-depth perception.

They completed the distance to Kangaroo Point in silence, and as they emerged from the lift Tasha touched a light hand to his arm.

'Thanks. It was a great evening. I'd like to do it again some time if it's OK with you.'

His smile lit up his pleasant features. 'All you need to do is say the word.' He paused, then added, 'Call if you need me.'

She entered her apartment, secured the lock, then stepped into her room, shed her clothes and slid in between the bedcovers.

Sharing dinner with Jared's mother had always been a pleasant experience, and Tasha liked to think that two years' acquaintance had promoted a warm friendship between them.

Did Monica assume Tasha's live-in relationship with Jared would eventually lead to something permanent? Such as marriage? Children? Was that something she hoped for?

Infinitely tactful, Monica had been careful not to allude to anything, and, as no engagement had been announced, the woman could be forgiven for wondering how her son regarded the relationship.

Consequently, Tasha viewed the evening with a degree of mild trepidation.

In the need to dredge up her reserves of confidence, she selected an elegant trouser suit in a brilliant red, stepped into stilettos, kept her make-up to a minimum except for matching lipstick, gloss, and paid attention to her eyes.

Jared had indicated six, and she left her apartment at five fifty-five, took the lift down to the main lobby, and emerged just as Jared's Jaguar drew to a halt at the front entrance.

For a brief moment she wondered what Jared had told his mother about his and Tasha's separate living arrangements. Would there be silent reproof or disappointment evident in Monica's greeting?

As to the pregnancy…had he mentioned anything in advance of this evening, or did he intend dropping the news like a bombshell over dinner?

How did she greet him? A simple 'hello' seemed inadequate, yet—

Jared took the decision out of her hands by lowering his head and closing his mouth over hers in a brief but evocative tongue-tangling kiss that suc-

ceeded in bringing alive each and every separate
nerve-end.

It wasn't fair, *he* wasn't playing fair, and if it
hadn't been for his mother's presence she would
have torn strips off him.

'Tasha.' Monica stepped forward and took hold
of her hands. 'It's so good to see you again.'

'Likewise,' she agreed warmly. 'I believe you're
heading down to the Coast for a few days.'

They moved to the car, and Jared opened both
front and rear passenger doors.

'You sit in front, my dear,' Monica indicated, and
shook her head as Tasha voiced a refusal. 'I insist.'

Deliberately coupling her with Jared, she acknowledged as he eased the car out onto the road.

The restaurant he'd chosen was one of the city's
finest, well known for its superb cuisine. The *maître
d'* greeted Jared with great deference and led them
to a coveted table.

'You must tell me all your news,' Monica invited
as they waited for the wine steward to deliver their
drinks.

Here was the moment she'd been unconsciously
waiting for. Should she go with truth or fiction? She
decided to hedge her bets. 'You mean, apart from
moving into my own apartment?'

'I'm sure you had a very good reason.'

Tasha met Jared's inscrutable gaze, and was unable to discern anything from his expression.

The arrival of the wine steward brought the conversation to a halt, and Jared waited until the waiter was out of earshot.

'The floor is all yours.' His indolent drawl held a tinge of silk, and she threw him a killing glare.

'You're so good with words.' Let him take the hot seat! 'I think you should tell Monica.'

His soft laughter almost undid her. 'I assure you she'll be delighted to hear she's going to be a grandmother.'

'You're having a baby?' Surprised joy lit her attractive features. 'Oh, I'm so happy for you both.' She pressed her hands together and leaned forward. 'My dear, are you keeping well?'

'The mornings aren't so good,' Jared drawled. 'And yes,' he added to what he anticipated would be Monica's next question, 'I've asked Tasha to marry me.'

'My dear, if I can help with wedding plans, please let me know.'

And now came the difficult part. 'There isn't going to be a wedding,' she said gently. 'The pregnancy was unplanned.'

Monica turned towards her son. 'Jared?'

'I'm working on it,' he assured.

Was he, indeed?

It was as well the waiter presented their starters, and Tasha had to admire Monica for keeping the conversational ball rolling.

Jared's mother was active with various charity committees, and led a busy social existence. She had many amusing anecdotes to relay, and Tasha began to relax a little.

'There was a terribly embarrassing moment at the close of the summer-collection showing last month when one of the models refused to part with jewellery lent for the occasion. It took some diplomatic soothing of ruffled feathers, a quiet but official word from the head of security before she graciously conceded to a misunderstanding.'

'Tricky,' Tasha ventured, and Monica chuckled at the memory.

'Very.' She shook her head as Jared indicated if she wanted more wine. 'I'm really looking forward to the theatre production. I have great respect for David Williamson's work.'

The food was divine, and Tasha spared an envious glance at Jared's plate. He'd ordered a prawn dish and they looked plump and succulent.

He cast her a warm smile and speared one with his fork. 'Try this.' He lifted it to her mouth, and she bit into the delicate white flesh, tasted the sauce accompanying it, and almost sighed with enjoyment.

He speared another and fed it to her, and she was supremely conscious of the intimacy of the gesture. She became caught up in the spell of it, the primitive alchemy that existed between them, and for a moment she wished she could turn back the clock to a time when everything was right between them.

Could it be again?

Possibly, she qualified. Except the doubt would always be there. She didn't want a marriage built on a shaky foundation. Nor could she bear entering a marriage based on the premise that if it didn't work out, divorce was an easy answer. As her father had. Without thought to how the consequences of his actions might affect the children of those subsequent marriages. Did he know what it was like to hold back from getting too close to any one of four stepmothers because they never stayed around very long? Or not to become fond of any young stepsiblings, because their mothers took them away?

She'd become isolated and self-sufficient, aware survival of self was of prime importance.

'Where did you go?' Jared queried quietly, observing her fleeting expression, the shadows. He wanted to gather her in, override her fears, and keep her close. So close, she'd never have reason to doubt anything again.

Tasha summoned a faint smile. 'Nowhere special.' She no longer felt hungry, and she replaced her cutlery and pushed her plate forward. 'I'm sorry.'

'No need to apologise, my dear,' Monica said gently.

Tasha declined dessert and opted for tea.

It was after ten when Jared settled the bill, and as they walked from the restaurant he caught hold of her hand and linked his fingers through her own.

His touch was warm and strong, and she didn't pull away until they reached the car.

The theatre lobby was filled with mingling patrons attired in glamorous evening attire.

Tasha recognised a few acquaintances, two clients, and offered a smile in acknowledgement as she stood with Jared and Monica.

Conversation was difficult, given the noise of muted social chatter vying with piped music.

Jared stood at her side, much too close for her peace of mind, for she could sense the strength emanating from his powerful frame, aware to a startling degree of the shape and size of him beneath the trappings of fine clothes.

She had the strangest urge to lean in against his side, have his arm circle her waist, and feel the brush of his lips against her hair.

All she had to do was shift her stance a little. Just a fraction, and the curve of her shoulder would nudge against his chest.

Think, she cautioned silently, of the consequences of such an action. She didn't play games, and pretending someone had jostled her simply wouldn't wash.

An electronic buzzer sounded, and she heard Monica's voiced relief.

'It'll be nice to take our seats. It's become a little crowded here, hasn't it?'

Tasha murmured an appropriate response as Jared moved between them as the patrons began to move towards the main entrance.

The play was a modern parody with flashes of insight and humour, the acting superb, making it an extremely pleasurable few hours that captured and entranced the audience.

Monica rhapsodised eloquently as they emerged into the foyer following the final act, and Jared chuckled a little as he brought her hand to his lips.

'I'm glad you enjoyed it.'

Tasha felt his arm along the back of her waist, the splay of his hand over her hip bone, and wondered if he knew the effect he had on her equilibrium.

A month ago she would have lifted her face and met his dark gaze with the veiled promise of how the evening would end. Smiled, even teased him a little. And relished in the anticipation, the slow building of heat until they both burned with it.

Abstinence was a bad bedfellow, and she longed for his touch, the feel of his skin beneath her lips, the silkiness as it stretched over taut muscle and sinew. His scent was an erotic aphrodisiac, one she wanted to feast with ravishing hunger.

He had the skill to turn her into a weak-willed wanton, savouring every pleasure he chose to bestow, then return it tenfold until the breath hissed between his teeth as he sought control…and lost it, taking her with him as they scaled the heights.

'Jared.'

Tasha turned slightly at the sound of that familiar feminine purr, and felt her edge of her teeth dig into the soft underside of her lip.

Soleil. Partnered by a legal associate whose name she failed to recollect.

'Amazing first night,' Soleil enthused as she

trailed perfectly manicured nails down the sleeve of Jared's jacket.

Her gaze shifted to Tasha, who gained a perfunctory acknowledgement, before taking in the older woman at Jared's side.

'Monica.'

It was a definite gush, Tasha conceded. Not overdone, but lacking in sincerity.

'How wonderful to see you again. I take it you're enjoying your visit?'

'Very much so.'

'Robert and I are going to Michael's for coffee. We'd be delighted to have you join us. It would give me the opportunity to catch up with Monica. We have a common interest in charity fundraisers.'

Oh, my. Was Jared going to buy that? The only person Soleil wanted to catch up with was *him*…and she was prepared to stretch the bounds of their professional relationship to achieve it. Her interest in charity fundraisers only extended to attending society functions in the latest designer gear and ensuring her photo with appropriate caption appeared in the glossy magazines, whereas Monica was actively involved behind the scenes, tirelessly giving her time within the various organisations.

'Thank you,' Jared inclined. 'We've made other arrangements.'

They had?

Soleil masked her disappointment with a smile that didn't reach her eyes. 'Another time, perhaps?'

'Perhaps.'

They moved with the crowd, then separated as they reached the pavement, and Monica turned towards her son.

'Thank you.'

Humour lifted the edge of his mouth. 'For what, specifically?'

'Dinner, the theatre, and excusing me from enduring Soleil Emile's company.'

'Think nothing of it.'

'I knew her mother. Nice woman. Pity her daughter didn't inherit her mother's demeanour.'

'She's very good at her job.'

His mother sent him a searching look. 'She must be, if you concede to liaise with her professionally.'

They walked the short distance to where Jared had parked the car, said their goodbyes and, although the drive to Tasha's apartment building wasn't a silent one, afterwards she had little recollection of their conversation.

'There's no need to get out,' she said quietly as Jared brought the car to a halt outside the main entrance. Except he did, anyway, walking her to the outer door and waiting as she inserted her security key.

She opened her mouth to thank him, only to have his finger press her lips closed.

'Shut up.'

It was a husky admonition as he drew her close and closed his mouth over hers with a thoroughness that staked a claim.

'I'll call you tomorrow.'

She wasn't capable of saying a word, and she stepped into the outer foyer, keyed in her code, then walked through to the bank of lifts.

The doors of one slid open immediately, and she pressed the button for her floor, then glanced towards the entrance as the doors slid closed.

Jared had moved to the car, waiting until she was out of sight.

Tasha rose early Sunday morning, and after breakfast she tidied the apartment, then, dressed casually in jeans and a loose cotton-knit top, she collected her sunglasses, keys, and rode the lift down to the basement car park.

The day beckoned, the sun shone, and the late-spring weather was warm and balmy as she drove through the city to Southbank.

She wanted to explore the markets, visit the various attractions, eat lunch at one of the outdoor cafés, and afterwards she'd stop by one of two city department stores. There were a few things she needed, and she intended to browse without the constraints of a minimum business lunch hour.

The sun was setting in a glorious blaze of orange and rose streaks in a paling sky when she drove beneath her apartment building. Her purchases reposed on the back seat, and there was a bag of Chinese take-out breathing a redolent aroma on the seat beside her.

Tasha planned nothing more vigorous than sinking into a chair, watching television as she ate, then she intended to shower and slip into bed with a good book.

The phone rang at eight, only seconds after she'd emerged from the shower, and she hurriedly grabbed a towel, then raced into the bedroom to pick up the extension.

'Tasha.'

The sound of Jared's voice sent goose-bumps scudding over the surface of her skin, and she tightened the towel she'd wound round her slender form. A gesture of self-defence?

'Jared,' she responded politely, and heard his husky chuckle. 'How are you?'

'Buried beneath a pile of law books, referencing information into the laptop. And you?'

'About to hit the bed with a good book.'

'I could offer something much more interesting.'

Her pulse quickened and began to race. 'I'm sure you could.' Just the thought of how *interesting* had heat pooling deep within. 'But you won't.' She composed herself, and kept her voice level. 'I presume there's a reason for your call?'

'I have tickets to a fundraiser at the Hilton Hotel on Tuesday evening. Valuable estate items have been donated to charity, and the executors have collaborated to hold an auction.'

Playing dress-up and indulging in the social niceties for several hours—

'It's a worthy charity.' He named it, adding, 'The catalogue lists genuine art, porcelain and jewellery.'

The 'porcelain' clinched it, as he knew it would.

'I assume you're inviting me to attend?'

He wanted to kiss and shake her, not necessarily in that order. 'Your assumption is correct.'

'In that case, yes.'

'Be ready at six-thirty. The invitation states seven, for champagne and canapés prior to the auction scheduled for eight.'

'Yessir.'

There was a measurable pause. '*Sassy* is safe over the phone, darling. Will you be so brave in person?' It was the voice he used in the night...gentle, velvet-soft, with a silky hint of promised retribution.

'You know better.' She told herself there was no quaver evident in her tone, but she had a terrible feeling she was fooling herself.

'Tuesday, Tasha. Goodnight.'

CHAPTER SEVEN

MONDAY brought the delivery of a single red rose in Reception for her, and was followed by another on Tuesday.

Tasha added each one to the vase where the others reposed, aware someone, presumably the night-time cleaners, religiously changed the water and tended to the stems, discarding a bloom only when its petals began to fall.

Choosing what to wear to the charity auction took some deliberation, and she eventually settled for a long black fitted skirt with a conventional split, a black top with silver thread, and she draped a long silk evening scarf in varying shades of silver, grey and black round her neck. Stiletto-heeled pumps completed the outfit, and she took care with her make-up, sweeping the length of her hair into a careless knot atop her head.

Jared buzzed her apartment on time, and she picked up the in-house phone. 'I'm on my way down.'

There was no doubt he looked sensational in an evening suit, white pin-tucked shirt and black bow-tie. Definitely *wow* territory, she conceded as she moved forward to greet him.

The warm gleam in those dark eyes gave her a pleasurable kick.

'If I say you look beautiful, will you hold it against me?'

'Why would I do that?'

Jared seated her in the car, then crossed round to slide in behind the wheel.

Valet parking at the Hilton made for a timely arrival, and they stepped into the main lobby, then rode the lift to the ballroom, where guests gathered in the foyer sipping champagne.

An eclectic group, Tasha noted as Jared ordered orange juice and took champagne from a proffered tray.

At seven-thirty the ballroom doors opened to allow the guests an opportunity to view the various items on display.

Security was tight, and Jared remained at her side as she headed towards the porcelain exhibits. Exquisite, delicately hand-painted pieces, some she recognised, with others she referred to the catalogue. There were crystal pieces, Baccarat and Lalique, figurines.

'See anything you particularly like?'

'It might be easier to state the ones that don't appeal.' Tasha turned towards him. 'Is there anything you'd like to view?'

Art was his preference, and it came as no surprise that he'd marked the catalogue in advance.

The Haight-Smythes were fellow guests, and they paused to exchange a few pleasantries before moving on. There would be time at the auction's conclusion to mix and mingle.

'Jared, I thought you'd attend tonight's soirée.'

Tasha turned slowly, met Soleil's deliberately musing gaze, recognised Soleil's father, and forced a polite greeting. She even managed what she hoped was a warm smile.

'We'll catch you later. Father wants to examine the jewellery.'

Had Jared known Soleil would be here tonight?

'No,' Jared said quietly, reading her mind.

Running into Soleil on every social occasion was becoming tiresome.

'I agree.'

'You possess telepathic capabilities?'

His smile reached down and plucked her heartstrings. 'You're an easy read.'

'Oh, great.'

'It has certain advantages.'

'Such as?'

He ran a finger lightly over her lower lip. 'It's kept me sane.'

'I see.'

'I'm not sure you do.'

It was as well the charity chairman took the podium and gave an inspiring speech before introducing the auctioneer, who announced the basic rules of auction, indicated the first item, then declared the bidding would begin.

It was an intriguing few hours, with a minimum

number of items passed in for failing to meet the set reserve, and the money raised by evening's end surpassed even the charity chairman's wildest expectations.

Tasha hadn't bid, but Jared did, securing a magnificent oil painting, an exquisite Lladro porcelain, and a Lalique crystal sculpture.

When financial details had been settled, guests were invited into the foyer, where champagne was offered, together with canapés, petit fours, together with coffee and tea.

It was there Soleil and her father sought Jared out, and Soleil was so incredibly *sweet* it almost made Tasha sick.

Was she trying to impress Jared or her father...or both? Whatever, she was a consummate actress. So much so, Tasha found it almost impossible not to respond in kind.

'It would appear we share a similar taste in social activities,' Tasha noted, and saw Soleil's eyes narrow.

'Brisbane's social élite frequently attend the same functions.' A light, amused laugh escaped her perfectly painted mouth. 'Let's face it, this is hardly New York.'

'I have a feeling that, even if it were, you'd still manage to hunt down your prey.'

'Oh, nasty, darling. But I'm glad you recognise my intention.' She took a moment to examine her nails before fixing Tasha with a veiled look. 'It makes it so much easier.'

'Do you think so?'

'Definitely.'

At that moment Jared took hold of her hand and lifted it to his lips. 'Ready, darling?'

'Definitely,' Tasha copied, and inclined her head towards Soleil, then her father. 'Goodnight.' She almost added 'It's been a pleasure', but decided against it. Fabrication wasn't her forte.

'Would you care to explain what that was all about?' Jared queried as they threaded their way towards the lift.

'Not really.'

'Soleil is—'

'Very good at her job,' Tasha finished as they stepped into the lift.

'Over-zealous when it comes to pursuit of men.' He punched the button that would take them down to the lobby.

'Ah, you noticed.'

They reached their destination, and Jared strolled towards the concierge, who promptly arranged for his car to be brought up from parking.

'It's an integral part of my nature.'

The Jaguar slid into sight, and the porter opened the passenger door, saw her seated, then discreetly accepted his tip.

'I'm impressed,' Tasha declared, and caught the faint cynical twist to his answering smile.

'A compliment, Tasha?' He ignited the engine.

'Perhaps,' she conceded as he eased the car forward, gained the side-road, and began negotiating inner-city one-way traffic.

It didn't take long to reach her apartment building, and she released the seat-belt and reached for the door-clasp as soon as he drew the car to a halt outside the main entrance.

'It was an interesting evening. Thank you,' Tasha added, wanting to escape, yet conversely wanting to stay.

There was a part of her that craved his mouth on hers, the intimacy of sensual contact. Except it wouldn't be enough. She'd want more, much more, and therein lay the danger.

It would be so easy to invite him into her apartment. But if she did it could only have one ending, and, while the sex would be incredible, it wouldn't solve or resolve anything.

'Goodnight.' Oh, lord, she had to get out of here before she said or did something foolish.

'You forgot something,' Jared said quietly.

He caught her startled gaze an instant before he captured her face between his hands, and kissed her. Thoroughly, with such shameless eroticism it became a total ravishment of the senses.

When he lifted his head she wasn't capable of uttering a word, and he brushed his lips to hers in a gentle gesture.

'If you don't want me to share your bed tonight, I suggest you get out of the car now.'

His husky warning was all she needed, and she slid quickly from her seat, then stepped towards the entrance, decoded the inner door, and walked through to the banks of lifts without a backwards glance.

Jared drummed fingers against his desk and admitted he'd never felt so helpless in his life. Or afraid.

In a matter of days his personal world had turned upside-down. Moved from emotional contentment and satisfaction to a place he neither liked nor coveted.

The apartment seemed empty and horribly silent. There was no light, laughing voice to greet him, no eager arms reaching for him in the night. Dear heaven, no joy without the warmth of her sweet body curled close against his own.

His control was such he could focus in the courtroom. Out of it, he merely went through the motions. Work, he buried himself in it, putting in long hours in his chambers, taking work home to labour over late into the night.

There was a part of him that found it difficult to accept Tasha's actions. *Two years*...and now suddenly it appeared as if those two years had evaporated in a puff of smoke.

Or had they?

Dammit, he'd asked her to marry him. Wasn't that enough?

Apparently not.

At first, he'd been angry. Sure in his mind she wouldn't go through with her plan to move out, and when she had, he'd been convinced it would last only a few days...a week at most.

She took his calls, answered his messages, and was so exceedingly polite it took strength of will not to shake her.

He wanted her back…in his arms, his apartment, his life. Dammit, he *needed* her.

Jared tugged fingers through his hair, ruffling its customary groomed look. He sank back in his chair and cast the neat pile of files on his desk a cursory glance, then he turned towards the plate-glass window and gazed contemplatively beyond the cityscape.

For days and far into the night he'd considered his options, presenting arguments for and against with each and every one, and had reluctantly come to the conclusion he was powerless to implement any of them.

He did, however, have an advantage in Tasha's acquiescence to continue their social obligations together.

He picked up a pen and tapped it idly against the leather-bound blotter on his desk.

She didn't seem averse to going out with him. He picked her up and dropped her back to her apartment. And she didn't ask him in.

His gaze narrowed and a soft oath escaped his throat.

They'd regressed from live-in lovers to dating. It was ridiculous.

Yet with all his legal expertise, his ability to tie his opponents into verbal knots, he had little or no power with Tasha.

Except one. Call it chemistry, sexual compatibility, shared sensuality, passion…hell, call it *love*. Whatever, the mesmeric primeval emotion existent between them was an ecstasy he'd never experienced in this lifetime. And knew deep in his gut he never would with anyone else.

Was it the same for Tasha? The answer was an unequivocal *yes*. No woman was capable of losing control to the extent she did, or becoming so wild, so totally abandoned… There were times when he'd driven her so far, so high, she'd become incandescent in his arms. *His*, only his.

Yet it was more than sex. Much more. She was his light, his heart, the very air he breathed. His reason for being.

He was damned if he'd lose her. Reduced to being a father by remote control, allowed visiting rights…and seeing another man take his place in her bed.

His hand clenched at the mere thought, and he barely controlled an animalistic snarl as the phone buzzed on his desk.

'There's a delivery for you in Reception.'

Tasha put a marker on the file she was accessing. 'I'll be right out.'

It was a boxed *something*, she saw at once, and she met Amanda's interested expression as she signed for it. 'Thanks.'

'You do intend opening it before you take it home?'

'I'll buzz you when I do.'

'Ah, hoped you might.'

'You can bring the McCormick file in at the same time.'

'Shall do.' One of the many incoming lines beeped, requiring Amanda's attention, and Tasha returned to her office.

There was a card tucked into the wrapping, and she plucked it out, opened and read the words, 'Thought this would suit your office. Jared.'

He hadn't, had he? Her fingers removed the Sellotape, the wrapping, polystyrene chips providing protective packaging for the exquisite Lladro figurine Jared had successfully bid for at auction on Tuesday night.

She touched it reverently, admiring the perfection, and carefully placed it on the mahogany credenza.

Tasha reached for her cell-phone, keyed in a text message, and sent it to him.

There was a tap on her door, and Amanda entered with the requested file.

'What do you think?' She indicated the figurine, and glimpsed the receptionist's admiration.

'It's gorgeous. Jared, of course.' Amanda placed the file down on the desk, then indicated the box and wrapping. 'Want me to take these for you?'

'Thanks.'

Tasha rang him soon after reaching her apartment, and he picked up on the fifth ring.

'Thank you,' she said with genuine sincerity. 'It's beautiful.'

'My pleasure. I enjoy gifting you things.'

A *double entendre*, if ever there was one. Tasha controlled the quivery sensation invading her body at the husky, almost sensuous tone in his voice.

'I intended calling you tonight,' Jared continued. 'You haven't forgotten we have tickets for the show at Conrad-Jupiter's Casino?'

Tasha closed her eyes, then opened them again. It had temporarily slipped her mind. Excusable, given events of the past week.

Dammit, she really wanted to see the spectacular extravaganza, had been excited when it was first advertised, delighted when Jared suggested they combine the show with a weekend at the Gold Coast. He owned an apartment in an exclusive block with beach access at Main Beach, and she adored the time they spent there.

She should refuse. 'I'd prefer not to stay over.' It was capitulation with conditions, and didn't fool him in the slightest.

'The apartment has two bedrooms.'

And that was meant to be reassurance? 'Jared—'

'Be ready at midday, Tasha.'

He ended the call before she had a chance to voice a qualifying refusal.

CHAPTER EIGHT

IT WAS insane to consider spending a weekend on the Coast with Jared. So why was she seated in the passenger seat of his car listening idly to music emitting from his CD player while attempting to focus on the passing scenery as they travelled the M1?

No matter how she justified wanting to see the live show featured at the Coast's casino, nothing changed the fact she was dicing with danger in agreeing to share his apartment overnight.

More than once she'd picked up her cell-phone to ring and cancel, only to put it off until later. Except *later* somehow never eventuated, as every time she started to dial his number she became angry with herself for wimping out.

She needed to prove she could resist him on every level, except that of *friend*. They had a future together by virtue of the child she was carrying. A friendship based on affection was better than one with acrimonious undertones.

She could play friend, and she *would*, even if it nearly killed her!

'It's a beautiful day.' Had she actually spoken those words? They sounded so banal, so...dammit, like excruciatingly polite conversation. Crazy, when she'd shared every intimacy imaginable with this man.

Just thinking about *intimacy* brought forth visions she didn't want to consider right now. Or any other time, she assured silently. That part of their relationship was over.

She adored the Gold Coast, with its shopping complexes, theme parks, waterways. All the advantages of a city without the many disadvantages. Essentially a tourist Mecca, it had a holiday atmosphere all year round.

That first glimpse of the tall high-rise buildings dotting the curved foreshore and the sparkling blue waters of the broadwater held a magic all its own.

Jared took the Main Beach turn-off and minutes later eased the Jaguar down into an underground carpark.

'We'll offload our overnight bags, then wander through to Tedder Avenue for lunch.'

'Sounds good to me,' she offered lightly as they made their way to the lift.

Tedder Avenue was a trendy area where several of the social élite chose to catch up with friends over a meal or any one of several types of coffee. For some it was brunch at Bahia, a series of lattes at Mustang Sally, then home to spend a few hours getting ready to hit one of the top restaurants in town.

Not a life Tasha would willingly choose on a permanent basis, but to indulge over a weekend offered light-hearted enjoyment.

Jared's apartment had a wealth of floor-to-ceiling

glass, open-plan living with luxurious furnishings and fittings in muted colours.

A great place to relax and unwind, Tasha accorded as she took her overnight bag into the spare bedroom and quickly extracted the outfit she intended to wear that evening and placed it on a hanger, then she caught up her shoulder bag and went out to the lounge.

Jared was standing observing the view, and he turned as she entered the room.

She was unprepared for the curling sensation deep inside, or the way her pulse seemed to pick up and race to a thudding beat.

He had it all, she perceived. The height and physique most men would envy. Sculptured bone structure and facial features made for a rugged attractiveness. Add innate sensuality, and it became one hell of a package.

Yet there was a depth to him, a development of character that included intelligence and sophisticated charm. Existent also was something indefinable, hidden deep beneath the surface. A ruthless, primitive element that boded ill for any adversary, almost lethal. A man you'd covet as friend and ally, and run far and fast if he ever became an enemy.

'Ready?'

'Yes. Let's go find some food.' The need to eat little and often had manifested itself over the past week, and although there were no visible physical changes to her body as yet, there were a few differences she'd begun to notice.

A five-minute walk brought them into the heart
of Tedder Avenue, where they selected a café, chose
a table and perused the menu.

'Is there anything you'd particularly like to do this
afternoon?' Jared queried when they'd given their
order.

A host of choices presented itself, yet she veered
towards the simplistic. 'A walk along the beach, a
swim.'

'No trawling the boutiques?' Jared drawled.

'There's nothing I need.' With one exception, and
it couldn't be bought.

It was after three when they finished their meal,
and they wandered towards the beach, then followed
the sandy foreshore towards the Sheraton Mirage
Hotel, where they entered the lounge bar and had a
cool drink before taking the footbridge across the
road to the adjacent shopping complex.

Around five they strolled back to the apartment,
showered and changed ready to dine and take in the
show.

Tasha had chosen to wear a black, figure-hugging
dress that owed everything to its cut and design.
Diamond ear-studs, a diamond pendant on a slender
gold chain comprised her only jewellery, and she
took care with her make-up, swept her hair into a
carefree knot, teased a few tendrils free to curl at
her ears, then she slid her feet into stiletto pumps
and caught up an evening purse.

Jared surprised her by heading towards the Spit,

and eased the car into the entrance of the Palazzo Versace Hotel.

Upmarket, six-star and exclusive.

The concierge came forward, offered valet parking, and swiftly opened the passenger door.

Jared cast her a level glance as they entered the luxurious foyer. 'This numbers high among your favourite places.'

'Yes, it does.' She remembered the first time he'd brought her here soon after the Palazzo's official opening. Her appreciative enthusiasm for the elegant interior with its marble floors and pillars, the internal beach-pool, exquisite lighting, and the view across the broadwater encompassing the sweep of high-rise apartment buildings lining the curved foreshore.

'Thank you,' she said quietly.

'My pleasure.'

She smiled in response, chilling out from placing too much meaning on those two words, for they held connotations she didn't want to explore.

Just go with the flow, she bade silently as the *mâitre 'd* seated them.

Dusk was settling in, and soon darkness would fall, giving the night-scape a different dimension.

The service was excellent, the food superb, and they lingered as long as they dared before leaving for the Casino, sited a few kilometres south.

Throughout the day Tasha had become increasingly conscious of the man at her side. The light touch of his hand at the back of her waist, briefly resting on her shoulder, as he threaded his fingers through her own.

It was impossible to ignore the warmth in his gaze, or the way he affected her.

Was he aware of her increased heart-beat? The way all of her nerve-ends curled at his slightest touch?

She'd have given anything to lean in against him and lift her face for his kiss…and almost did on one occasion as a sort of reflex action so familiar it became an unconscious movement she only just checked at the last second.

The Casino was a hive of activity with people mingling everywhere, and Jared caught hold of her hand as they made their way down to the auditorium.

Spectacular, incredible…were only two of the accolades Tasha summoned to describe the live show, for the music, costumes, theme were magnificent, and she said as much during the interval.

Jared wondered if she knew how beautiful she was, not only visually, but on the inside, where it mattered. There was no artifice, no game-playing. She'd entered his life like a breath of fresh air, and had stayed.

Somehow he'd not given much thought to if or when she might leave, and if it had crossed his mind he imagined it would be *he* who did the leaving. Not the other way round.

'I wouldn't have missed this for the world,' Tasha

declared, meeting his dark, gleaming gaze. 'Isn't it fantastic?'

'Indeed. Shall we go get something to drink?'

'OK.'

They gained the foyer, and she slipped off to the powder-room while Jared fronted the bar.

When she returned he was deep in conversation with Soleil. Coincidence, Tasha wondered, or design? It seemed a little too convenient for Soleil to have booked tickets for a live show at the Coast on the same night.

A part of her registered they presented an attractive couple. Soleil's rich auburn hair was a stunning attribute. Add a faultless figure, expensive clothes, perfect facial features, and it all added up to *gorgeous*.

Jared slid an arm around her waist as she reached his side, and his smile was something else.

'Soleil.' The acknowledgement held polite warmth, a quality that was somewhat lacking in the solicitor's response.

At that moment the buzzer sounded, indicating patrons should return to the auditorium.

'Shall we say upstairs in the Atrium bar after the show?'

'Tasha?'

The last thing she wanted to do was spend social time with Soleil. Yet she fixed Jared with a brilliant smile. 'Why not?'

The remaining half of the show was equally breathtaking, the finale amazing, and there was a sense of disappointment as the curtain came down for the last time.

She was tempted to make the excuse she was tired, or nursing a headache…anything to give meeting Soleil a miss.

It would be easy enough to do, except she was loath to provide Soleil with a victory, no matter how minor it might be.

How hard had Soleil lobbied to act as Jared's solicitor? The fact she'd used unfair influence to persuade her father's recommendation was a given.

Soleil was waiting for them, and she was alone. Jared found a table, and placed an order with the waitress, then he settled well back in his chair and steered the conversation to the show.

'If you'll excuse me for a few minutes?' Tasha offered a polite smile and rose to her feet. Another change she'd discovered over the past week was the frequent need to visit a powder-room.

'I'll come with you.'

Oh, *great*. If Soleil had a girlie *tête-à-tête* in mind, she could go jump in the lake.

If Soleil made use of the facilities, she did so in record time, for she was refreshing her make-up when Tasha emerged.

'Is there any substance to the rumour you've moved out of Jared's apartment?'

Oh, my, she didn't bandy words, just aimed straight for the jugular. 'Does it look as if Jared and I are estranged?'

Soleil's mouth tightened, and her eyes took on a

hardness that was vaguely chilling. 'Answer the question, darling.'

'I'm not on a witness stand, nor am I obliged to discuss my personal life.'

'If it weren't true, you'd have issued a vehement denial.' The other woman's vividly painted mouth curved into a satisfied smile. 'Just a little warning...Jared's mine.'

'Good luck.'

'I never rely on luck.'

Tasha closed her evening purse and walked towards the door, where she turned and offered a parting shot. 'Merely manipulative engineering.'

There was something exhilarating about having the last word, although she had a dire feeling it wouldn't last long.

She arrived back at their table ahead of Soleil, and met Jared's speculative gaze with a brilliant smile.

'Should I ask?' His husky drawl held a tinge of humour.

'Don't,' she advised a few seconds ahead of Soleil's reappearance.

'Are you driving back to Brisbane tonight?' she queried as Soleil sipped her coffee.

'No. I've booked a suite at Royal Pines. I thought I might have an early round of golf.' She paused, then said smoothly as if the idea had just occurred, 'Perhaps you'd care to join me?'

To his credit Jared took his time and infused just the right degree of regret in his tone. 'Thanks for the invitation, but Tasha and I have already made plans for the day.'

None that she was aware of. 'We have?'

He offered a lazy smile. 'Yes.'

She glanced at Soleil and effected a light shrug. 'It doesn't appear golf is on his agenda.'

He drained his coffee, then fixed the bill. 'If you're ready?'

Tasha caught up her evening purse and stood to her feet. 'Enjoy your weekend, Soleil. I'm sure we'll catch up again soon.' Unfortunately.

She didn't utter so much as a word as they took the lift down to the level where Jared had parked the car.

'Would you care to tell me what that was all about?'

Tasha didn't shift her gaze, and instead she watched the tall, brightly lit apartment buildings lining the highway as they travelled the few kilometres to Main Beach.

'Soleil chose to warn me if the rumour I've moved out of your apartment is true, she intends moving in for the kill,' she relayed without preamble.

'And your response was?'

'I wished her ''good luck''.'

They reached the Main Beach turn-off, and within minutes Jared eased the car down into the underground car park of his apartment building.

They rode the lift and exited at their designated floor. 'Soleil bothers you?' Jared unlocked the apartment door, then tossed the keys down onto a side-table.

'She has a *thing* for you.' She moved into the lounge, stepped out of stiletto-heeled pumps, and removed her ear-studs.

'Should I be flattered?'

'Oh, for heaven's sake,' Tasha said with exasperation. 'All women between sixteen and sixty have a thing for you!' She resisted the temptation to throw something at him. 'You'd have to be blind Freddy not to notice.'

He was the antithesis of *blind*. Observing and interpreting body language was an integral part of his job. So, too, was the analysis of the human psyche.

She was all too aware he could read her like a book, and she wasn't particularly inclined to bandy words with him tonight.

She gathered up her shoes and her evening purse. 'Thanks for dinner and the show. I enjoyed both.'

'Soleil being the exception.'

Honesty forbade anything but the truth. 'Yes.' She turned and walked the few steps to the spare bedroom, entered it and quietly closed the door.

Within minutes she shed her clothes, cleansed her face of make-up, tugged on a cotton nightshirt, then she slid into bed, determinedly discarding any thought of Jared's glamorous solicitor.

She must have slept, for she woke in the dark, disoriented for a few seconds, until the need for a drink had her padding out to the kitchen.

Moonlight filtered in through the glass doors of

the lounge, and she extracted a glass, filled it with filtered water, then drank it down.

For some unknown reason she felt too restless to return to bed just yet, and she crossed through the dining area to stand gazing out at the night-scape.

The sky was a deep indigo, and she glimpsed the faint pinprick of stars high in the galaxy. Soon they'd begin to fade in a prelude to the encroaching dawn.

Something moved at the peripheral edge of her vision, and she focused on the light, identifying it as a small jet plane *en route* to Coolangatta Airport some thirty kilometres south.

Apartment high-rise buildings stood like tall sentinels, mostly unlit, apart from the occasional window. Street-lights illuminated the main thoroughfare leading to and from central Surfer's Paradise, and there was an occasional glimpse of bright red and green neon.

Traffic was minimal at this hour, and she watched as one crazy motorist raced another on the main road, only to be pursued by a police car with its red and blue lights flashing and siren wailing.

Young hoons risking a drag race, caught up in the adrenalin rush...only to incur a massive fine, loss of licence, and a police record.

'Unable to sleep?'

She'd been so engrossed in the scene below she hadn't heard or sensed his presence. 'I woke up thirsty and came out to get a drink. Did I disturb you?'

More than you know, Jared allowed silently. 'I was awake.'

Tasha didn't say anything for several seconds, then she offered, 'It's so peaceful at this hour.'

He was close, much too close, and she wanted to move away...except her limbs refused to obey the dictates of her brain.

She was aware of him, the faint muskiness lingering from his cologne, his body heat, and his potent masculinity. He slept naked, and she had no trouble envisaging his image, the powerful musculature, his arousal.

Her body swayed a little, almost as if it had a mind of its own, acutely sensitised and receptive to the primitive energy existent between them.

Please, she begged silently. Turn and walk away. I don't think I could bear for you to stay.

She was like a finely tuned instrument, waiting for a master's touch to release the music of her soul. To mesh with his and become something so bewitchingly magical it had the power to rob her of breath, sanity.

She felt the touch of his hands as they cupped her shoulders, and her body sighed, then began to respond.

The fine hairs on her skin lifted, seeking his caress, and emotion curled round her nerve-ends, tugging them into vibrant life.

Jared didn't move, and neither did she. It was almost as if they were teetering on the brink, each afraid to say or do anything to break the spell.

Tasha felt his breath stir the hair at her temples, followed by the fleeting touch of his lips.

His fingers lightly brushed aside a swathe of hair, baring her nape, and sensation spiralled deep within as he pressed his mouth to the curve of her neck, then trailed a light path to tease an earlobe.

She should tell him to stop; and she should take the few steps to move away from him.

Except she stayed, held by a primeval alchemy she found impossible to resist.

A kiss, she told herself. Just…one kiss.

He turned her gently to face him and slid his hands to cup her face, then his mouth closed over hers in a tender supplication that brought a lump to her throat.

His tongue stroked hers, then curved to tease its edge from stem to tip in a persuasive dance, and she felt her bones begin to melt.

The tips of her fingers brushed his shoulders in a light tactile exploration, only to withdraw as if afraid of the heat as his mouth began an evocative exploration…taking, giving, until she was helpless. *His.*

It wasn't enough. It would never be enough, and she groaned as his hand slid down to caress her hip, then slipped to her thigh to skim the bare skin as he pushed up the hem of her nightshirt.

He adored the silky feel of her skin, it was so firm and smooth, and warm to his touch. Sensitive, just inside her hip bone, the indentation at the edge of her waist. He felt the slight tremor run through her body as his hand trailed low and teased the curls at the apex of her thighs. A husky moan escaped her lips when he explored the moistness, the satin cleft, and she sank in against him as he stroked the swollen clitoris.

With one careful movement he pulled the nightshirt over her head and let it fall on the carpet, then he closed his mouth over hers in passionate possession.

When he released her she could only look at him, lost in a sea of emotions so deep, so incredibly complex, it was all she could do not to cry out.

With deliberate intent Jared cupped her bottom, then spread her thighs as he lifted her up against him.

'I don't think—'

'Don't,' he bade huskily, *'think.'* He buried his mouth in the sweet curve of her neck, savoured the sensitive pulse beating there, then he trailed a hand up her spine to cup her nape and caressed her mouth with evocative slowness.

It was a flagrant seduction, and she told herself she didn't care. She wanted this, needed to be swept away by the magic of his lovemaking.

One night, just this one night. Was it so bad to want him so much?

His mouth lifted, and she buried her face in the hollow at the edge of his neck, afraid of what he might see as he walked towards the bedroom.

His bedroom, where moonlight streamed through the non-reflective glass, outlining the furniture, the large bed where he carefully laid her down before joining her there.

'Jared—'

He pressed a finger to the centre of her lower lip, then traced its soft fullness.

'I want to pleasure you,' he said gently, and her mouth quivered as his mouth trailed a path to her breast, savouring the tender peak before rendering a similar treatment to its twin.

Heat arced through her body as he moved lower, and her eyes shimmered with unshed tears as he pressed a series of open-mouthed kisses at her waist, her stomach, before moving low, intent on bestowing the most intimate kiss of all.

At the first stroke of his tongue she went up in flames, spiralling high again and again, until she shattered as ecstasy overwhelmed her.

Her skin was damp, heated as she reached for him, pushing his hands aside as she began a tasting feast that had the breath hissing through his teeth.

There was only one way this could end, and she took him to the brink, then exulted in his possession, the long, slow thrusts as he took her on an evocative ride that was electrifying, mesmeric.

Magical, she added dreamily a long time later as she lay held close in his arms, their limbs entwined, on the edge of sleep.

The room was lighter as night turned into day with a new dawn. Soon the sun would rise above the horizon, gently flooding everything with light and colour as the city woke and came alive.

Tasha's eyelids swept down as she buried her head against Jared's shoulder and slept.

It was late when she woke. Ten, at least, she decided, too lazy to roll over and check the digital clock.

She stretched a little, a purely feline movement, and brushed her foot against a hard, muscular leg. She froze for a second, then memory kicked in, and she turned her head to meet Jared's gleaming gaze.

CHAPTER NINE

'YOU slept well.'

Tasha opened her mouth to say she always slept well after sex, then she closed it again.

He lifted a hand and brushed gentle fingers down her cheek. His mouth curved into a warm smile that was wholly sensual. 'What we shared was beautiful.'

She swallowed the sudden lump in her throat. 'Great sex,' she managed to accord lightly, and saw his eyes darken.

'More than that. Much more.'

She wanted to agree with him, but the words wouldn't emerge. 'I'll go shower.' She had to return to the prosaic, otherwise she'd say something stupid. 'Do you want to eat breakfast in, or shall we go out?'

It didn't work. The pulse beating rapidly at the edge of her throat was a give-away, and her breathing was uneven at best.

This close he was too much. Way too much. Her recollection of last night was hauntingly vivid, and she could still *feel* the effects of his possession.

And worse, there was a part of her that wanted him again. Madness, she derided silently. Total insanity.

141

He'd seen her naked a thousand times…more, if she was counting. So why was she suddenly reticent about slipping from the bed and walking into the *en suite*?

Oh, damn self-consciousness, she cursed, and did it anyway.

She turned the water dial in the shower to warm, then stood beneath the spray, gradually increasing the temperature before reaching for the soap.

Only to give a surprised yelp as Jared stepped into the cubicle and took the soap from her hand.

'Go away,' she spat fiercely as he began smoothing the soap down the length of her arm.

'Not a chance.'

She put the palm of each hand on his chest and pushed…except it made not the slightest difference. He was immovable.

'Jared—' Her voice became momentarily locked in her throat as he ran the soap over her breast, and his eyes sharpened at her involuntary flinch.

'I hurt you?'

'I…' Oh, hell. She closed her eyes, then opened them again. 'They've become extra-sensitive.'

He held a vivid memory of suckling there, teasing the tender peaks with the edge of his teeth as he took her to the brink between pleasure and pain.

His husky curse was barely audible as he fastened his mouth on hers in a brief, hard kiss before continuing his ministrations.

'Don't.' Tasha curled one hand into a fist and

aimed it at his shoulder as he reached the juncture between her thighs.

He paused, then straightened and met her troubled gaze.

'Last night...' Dammit. 'Just because we had sex, it doesn't mean anything has been resolved.'

Jared stilled, and his expression became an enigmatic mask. 'You call what we shared just...*sex*?'

It was more than that, much more. 'I'd prefer not to discuss it.'

'Avoiding the issue won't make it go away,' Jared warned, and her chin tilted as she held his gaze.

'Any more than you'll allow me to forget it.'

A muscle bunched at the edge of his jaw. 'Take that as a given.'

Tasha turned away from him. 'If you don't mind, I'd prefer to shower alone.'

Hands curved over her shoulders and he brought her round to face him. 'And if I do mind?'

Anger lent her eyes a fiery sparkle. 'Tough.'

His mouth covered hers, hard and possessively demanding as he tore her initial resistance to shreds.

She balled one hand into a fist and took aim, uncaring where she connected, only to cry out as he took hold of her hand and clamped it behind her back, then brought the other to join it in a movement that succeeded in bringing her up against him.

He held her easily, quelling any struggle she attempted as he slid his other hand to her nape, and he angled his head, using the strength of his jaw to force open her mouth.

She made a sound deep in her throat that was part groan, part entreaty, and after a few timeless seconds he wrenched his mouth from hers.

Tasha wasn't capable of saying a word. Her lips, her tongue felt numb from his invasion, and he released her with a sound of self-disgust.

Tears rose to the surface, shimmered there, and she blinked in an effort to prevent their spill.

Firm fingers caught hold of her chin, lifting it so she had no recourse but to look at him, and she swiftly lowered her lashes in an effort to hide the pain of his violation.

His husky oath was indistinguishable, and she stiffened as he traced a gentle finger over the swollen contours of her mouth.

'Go,' Jared adjured quietly. 'Before I do or say something totally regrettable.'

She didn't need second bidding, and she stepped out of the shower stall, caught up a towel, wrapped it round her slender curves and escaped into the bedroom, where, towelled dry, she donned fresh underwear, stepped into jeans and pulled on a cotton-knit top.

Jared emerged into the bedroom, a towel tucked low over his hips, and Tasha felt the impact of his analytical appraisal. At that precise moment she hated him, so much so it brought on a wave of nauseousness.

She must have paled, for she heard his sharpened demand. 'Tasha?'

Seconds later she made a running dive for the *en suite* and was horribly, violently ill.

He was there, holding her shaking shoulders, stroking the hair back from her face, then when it was over he caught up a face cloth and cleansed her face.

'OK?' he queried gently.

Oh, God. 'I think so.' Morning sickness had reared its head again. With a vengeance, she accorded wryly, and wretched timing.

'Stay here. I'll go make some tea and toast.'

Her stomach roiled at the thought of food. Yet the pregnant mother's manual was big on tea and something light to ease the symptoms.

'I don't think I'm quite done,' she managed a few seconds ahead of a repeat performance.

Jared held her, then cleansed her face again, swearing softly as he caught sight of the tears welling in her eyes.

'Don't.'

It was just reaction, and she told him so as he lightly kissed the moisture from beneath each eye.

'I'll be OK. Just...get me that tea,' she said shakily.

While he was gone she cleaned her teeth, brushed her hair and tied it back, then when Jared returned she sank into a chair and sipped the hot, sweet tea. The slice of toast helped, and by the time she'd finished both tea and toast she felt almost human again.

'Thanks.'

He took the empty cup and plate and placed them on the bedside pedestal.

'How long have you been suffering morning sickness?'

'About a week.'

He stroked gentle fingers down her cheek. 'Do you feel up to a walk along the beach, then breakfast at Tedder Avenue?'

The thought of fresh air and sunshine was a welcome one. 'Yes.'

'Give me five minutes to shave and dress.'

Tasha slid her feet into trainers, fixed the laces, then she collected the cup and plate and took them out to the kitchen.

Jared joined her there, and together they rode the lift down to the lobby, then stepped out onto the expanse of sand.

He caught hold of her hand and threaded his fingers through her own. She wanted to remain angry with him for that punishing kiss in the shower. Except somehow his caring for her afterwards negated any feeling of animosity.

It was a lovely morning, the sun's warmth caressed her skin as a soft ocean breeze teased a few loose tendrils of her hair. The smell of the sea was subtle, just a drift in the air, and Tasha lifted her face to catch it as they wandered towards Narrow Neck, then turned and retraced their steps.

Breakfast became brunch, and afterwards they returned to the apartment to pick up their overnight bags, then Jared headed the car towards the mountains, taking the steep, winding gradient up to Mount Tamborine, where they stopped at one of several roadside cafés for tea and scones before browsing the crafts and wares.

Tasha bought some homemade jam and a cute little pottery cat, then they took the road through Canungra and onto the northern motorway, reaching Brisbane just before dark.

'Shall we settle for pizza or Chinese?' Jared queried as the Brisbane river came into view.

'Pizza.'

'Take-out, or eat in?'

'You're giving me a choice?'

'Of course.'

She thought of red-checked tablecloths, empty Chianti bottles with lit candles, the redolent aroma of spices and garlic bread, and didn't hesitate in naming an upmarket pizzeria in suburban Milton.

It was a very pleasant way to end the day, and she selected her favoured capriccioso while Jared settled for one loaded with salami, olives and sun-dried tomatoes.

Heaven, Tasha decided as she finished one slice and reached for another.

'You're due to appear in court tomorrow.' A well-publicised rape case which promised to be a media circus. 'Are you happy with the jury selection?' Something that was often a long and arduous process before the defence and prosecuting legal representatives were satisfied.

'Yes.'

It was a definitive answer, and she knew only too well the long hours he'd devoted to the case, the research involved. 'Who is the presiding judge?'

Jared named him, and her eyebrows rose a little. Well-respected, the judge was nevertheless known in legal circles for his tough stance on certain issues, and rape was one of them.

The facts were indisputable, the evidence weighted very strongly in favour of the victim. However, she was aware one of Jared's highly skilled colleagues had been engaged as defence.

'A clash of the titans,' she observed lightly. It was an unnecessary question, but she asked it anyway. 'Soleil is in on the case?'

'Her father offered me the brief,' Jared drawled, and she inclined her head.

'Of course,' she acknowledged wryly.

'Cynicism doesn't suit you.'

'She wants you,' she posed with pseudo-sweetness.

'While I see her only as an associate.'

'Albeit a very attractive one.'

He regarded her quizzically. 'You want me to deny that?'

'And lie to me?'

A husky chuckle emerged from his throat. 'Are you going to finish that pizza?'

'Don't change the subject.'

The exchange of light banter brought forth memories of other occasions when they'd stopped off for pizza after a lazy Sunday. Except then when the meal was over they'd drive home, share the spa and indulge in a glass of wine, before making love long into the night.

Tonight, however, would have a different ending, and she experienced a twinge of sadness as Jared drew the car to a halt outside the entrance to her Kangaroo Point apartment.

'If I ask you to collect a few changes of clothes and come back with me,' Jared posed quietly, 'will you refuse?'

Did he know just how much she wanted to do that? To go back to where they were ten days ago? But there was the thing…you couldn't turn back the clock. You could only go forward.

'I—don't think that's a good idea.'

'Because you don't want to? Or you can't?'

'Both.'

'You know I won't leave it there?'

She chose not to answer as she released her seat belt and opened the door. 'I'll just collect my bag.'

He doused the lights and switched off the engine.

'There's no need to get out.'

'Don't be ridiculous.' He reached into the back seat and retrieved her overnight bag.

'Thanks,' Tasha said seconds later as they reached the entrance. She used her key to open the outer door and took hold of her bag. 'Goodnight.'

CHAPTER TEN

JARED rang just before eight as she was finishing her second cup of tea.

'How did you fare this morning?'

Tasha endeavoured to ignore the way her pulse leapt at the sound of Jared's voice. 'A repeat of yesterday.'

'That bad, huh?'

She wanted to say *yes*, and it's all your fault. Except it wasn't his fault any more than it was hers.

'I'll be fine.' She'd be even better if she wasn't bent on doing this alone.

'I'll call you tonight.'

Tasha disconnected the call, then headed for the shower.

The following few days were hectic, with work consuming most of Tasha's waking hours. She went in to the office early, and took paperwork home, often not closing her laptop until late. Only to repeat the procedure all over again.

Jared was similarly caught up with the current case in hand, and he phoned each day, usually in the morning from his chambers before she left for the city.

It came as no surprise when he rang Wednesday

morning just as she was putting the finishing touches
to her make-up, and she kept her tone brisk.

'I'm about to walk out the door.'

'So keep it brief?'

'Please.'

'I have to fly down to Melbourne tomorrow morning for a mediation meeting.'

'Is Soleil going with you?'

'Yes.'

Wonderful. 'Have fun,' she managed lightly, and
heard the mild exasperation in his voice as he said,
'I'll ring when I get back.'

'There's no need,' she said stiffly. She'd tried for
'nice' and failed. Soleil had that effect on her.

It didn't sit well Soleil was accompanying him to
Melbourne, no matter how she qualified it was busi-
ness and they'd be on the evening flight back to
Brisbane.

Instinct did much to assure Soleil's innuendo was
based on wishful thinking. Yet there were sufficient
facts woven in with the lies to cast doubt.

Strong feelings, even stronger emotions had
roused her temper, and it wasn't done yet.

'Have a good trip, a successful day.' The words
held little more than formal politeness. Angry with
herself, *him,* she cut the call.

It was as well the day was a hectic one, for there
was little or no time to think. A lunch break became
something she sacrificed in lieu of a sandwich
snatched between seeing clients, supplemented by
fruit, ditto.

She stayed late, took work home, and retired later than she should have, only to wake at dawn unable to get back to sleep.

It didn't help to have Jared's image rise up and taunt her, or for the way her mind seemed bent on reflection.

Her doubt had centred around his perspective, his long-term commitment, and not wanting to force the issue of marriage if he hadn't wanted the legality of it.

Yet in the past few weeks nothing had changed, except the changes she herself had made.

At what point would he relinquish the relationship and resign himself to being a single father?

Worse, move on to another relationship?

It wasn't as if there weren't any number of women only too willing to step into her shoes! Soleil was merely one of many.

The thought she might lose him filled her with fear.

Dammit, she couldn't just lie here and stew. She'd go make some tea, nibble a slice of toast, boot up her laptop and work until it was time to shower and dress, and go into the office.

Tonight, she'd call Jared and suggest they meet and attempt to reconcile their differences. There really wasn't any other way…for her. And she clung to the hope it was the same for him.

The day became a replica of the preceding one, with a staff shortfall and urgent work redistributed.

It proved a welcome distraction, and she entered

her apartment at six, fixed a healthy chicken salad and ate it as she browsed through the day's newspaper.

When she finished she dealt with the dishes, filled a glass with chilled water, then she crossed to the lounge and switched on the television.

The news was running, and she stood engrossed in an update on a worsening crisis in the Middle East. The picture disappeared, the newsreader picked up an updated bulletin and began reading as the tele-monitor ran a newsflash across the lower edge of the screen.

Bomb explosion at Melbourne's Tullamarine Airport. Seven dead, several injured. Domestic terminal evacuated and all flights cancelled until further notice.

Did stomachs plummet? Hearts stop? Tasha felt as if she experienced both in succession.

Jared. Ohmigod, *Jared*. She felt as if she couldn't breathe, and she fought against the terror as she raced to the phone.

If he was OK, he'd have rung from his cell-phone. Somehow the fact he hadn't only heightened her fear.

Except she had his number on speed dial, and she tried it first. Just in case. Only to receive the 'out of range' signal. Maybe he'd switched it off prior to boarding. She sent an SMS text message, and waited anxiously for a response, but none came.

There had to be an emergency number set up for direct enquiries. The television station would screen it, and she flicked from channel to channel before she discovered the newsflash, then began dialling.

There was no indication of the passage of time as her call was dealt with, particulars patiently taken, a seemingly interminable wait while the operator checked available details.

'We have no one of that name listed among the injured,' the operator confirmed, then offered quietly, 'Please check back in an hour.'

Tasha knew she'd go mad if she had to wait an hour, but she had no recourse other than to sit by the phone as she watched newsflash updates via television.

Jared has to be alive. He has to be OK.

The words kept echoing through her brain like a mantra. After a while she began doing deals with the deity.

One clear fact emerged. Life without Jared would be no life at all.

It was something she'd known all along, yet she had stupidly clung to principles…principles which now meant nothing.

Tasha gazed sightlessly at images on the television screen, and only jerked into full alert when the latest newsflash showed.

Five minutes before the hour was up she redialled the emergency number, only to wait in line until her call could be answered by an operative.

Ten minutes later she was told Jared's name did not appear on their growing list of identified injured.

There was an overriding need to board a flight and go there in person. As if that would do any good. But at least she'd be *there*.

Oh, dear God. If anything happened to him, she'd die.

The sudden peal of her cell-phone didn't register for a millisecond, then she snatched it up with shaking fingers and activated the call.

'Tasha.'

The sound of Jared's voice sent her into a tailspin, and she clutched the phone unit so hard her fingers went numb. 'Are you OK?' She hardly recognised her own voice; it was so choked the words were almost indistinguishable.

'A scratch or two from flying debris.' He wouldn't reveal how luck had played a part, or just how close he'd come to serious injury. 'The medics insisted we all be transported to hospital. My cell-phone died. This is the first chance I had to get to a phone. We'll be accommodated overnight, flights are being rescheduled from another airport. I'll phone as soon as I have further details.' He paused fractionally, then added quietly, 'I love you.'

Tasha swallowed the lump in her throat, and wanted to weep as the connection was cut.

How could he say that, then hang up? Leave her literally gasping for air at a time when she'd just come out of a ragged few hours when she imagined he could be severely injured or worse?

Restless, too much so to *sit*, she sought physical activity in the form of house-cleaning. Not that the apartment needed much, but she directed her energies into removing every speck of dust and buffing everything to a gleaming shine.

It was after ten when she finished, and she opted for a shower, then bed. Would Jared ring again tonight? Unlikely, given Melbourne was on summer daylight-saving time and an hour ahead of Brisbane.

Sleep didn't come easily, and she twisted and turned in bed, punched her pillow countless times, then gave up in disgust and padded out to the lounge to sit curled up in a chair watching late-night television.

It was dawn when she stirred, and she crept into bed to sleep until the alarm woke her. She checked her cell-phone, but there were no text messages, and she showered, ate cereal and fruit for breakfast and washed it down with tea, then she dressed ready for work.

Her emotions were in an ambivalent state, swinging from nervous anticipation to excitement, then dipping to doubt as the morning progressed.

At ten her cell-phone buzzed with an incoming text message, and she counted off the seconds until the message registered before hurriedly accessing it.

'Returning late-afternoon flight. Be ready 7 pm. We'll dine out'.

Tasha quickly text messaged back 'OK'.

Thank heavens. Relief washed through her body, followed by slow, tingling warmth.

With conscious effort she focused on the day's work, took and kept appointments, and willed the hours to pass.

During her lunch break she visited a nearby florist and purchased a single red rose.

At five she shut her laptop, collected her brief-case, and walked out to the bank of lifts. Given peak-hour traffic, she should reach her apartment within half an hour.

She made it in less, and headed straight for the shower, washed and blow-dried her hair, then dressed with care, choosing an elegant black lace dress with a scooped neckline, elbow-length sleeves and a hemline halting an inch above the knee. Black stilettos, minimum jewellery, and skilled use of make-up completed the outfit, then she caught up an evening purse, the long-stemmed rose, and exited the apartment.

Jared's image was a constant, and the nerves in-side her stomach went from a slow waltz to an en-ergetic tango as she took the lift down to the lobby.

It was precisely seven when she emerged on the ground floor, and she saw Jared standing beside his car waiting for her.

Within seconds she reached his side, her gaze rak-ing his features for any visible sign of injury.

'Where are you hurt?' It was the most pressing question she had, and surpassed 'hello' by a mile.

He tunnelled his fingers through her hair and low-ered his head to hers to take possession of her mouth in a kiss that was hard, hot and hungry. Then he eased off and went back for more, this time with a gentleness that melted her bones.

Tasha felt the need to touch him, to hold on and never let go, and she sank in against him, loving the physical feel of him, knowing he was flesh and blood, *alive*.

'Are you really OK?'

His lips brushed her cheek, then settled at the edge of her mouth. 'A couple of scratches, a few bruises. I was one of the lucky ones.'

'Thank God,' she said with undue reverence, and saw his mouth curve into a warm, musing smile.

'My sentiments, exactly.'

She had to ask. 'Soleil?'

'A broken arm, several fractured ribs. She's staying in Melbourne until she feels sufficiently comfortable to travel.'

She touched the hard planes of his face, lingered there, then traced the curve of his mouth, and caught her breath as he pressed a warm kiss to her palm.

'I take it you want to eat?'

His teasing query brought forth a smile. 'I am hungry.' For food, as well as you, she added silently. But the waiting wouldn't go amiss, and anticipation was good for the soul.

He threaded his fingers through her own, then moved to open the passenger door, waiting until she was seated before crossing round to slide in behind the wheel.

The restaurant was situated in the suburbs, distant

from the trendy boutique restaurants populated by the city's café society.

Tasha doubted she'd ever been quite so nervous, and she wondered if Jared was aware her pulse was racing at a rapid beat.

Her heart felt as if it was thundering against her ribcage as they entered the softly lit interior. The *maitre d'* greeted them, she gave her name, and then preceded Jared to their table.

She set the rose down, then slid into the seat the waiter held out for her.

Jared indicated the delicate red bud on the table-cloth. 'I assume this has some special significance?'

'Yes.'

Did her hands shake as she perused the menu? She hoped not. Cool, calm, collected, she reminded silently.

Her gaze strayed to his elegant suit, and saw the male frame beneath it. The powerful musculature in those broad shoulders, the taut midriff, trim waist, lean hips, and...better not go there, she decided shakily. She was in such an emotionally fragile state any thought of his sexual prowess would bring her undone.

She was way too nervous to eat, and she ordered a small salad as a starter and followed it with an entrée-size main.

'Was the mediation meeting successful?'

Jared cast her a piercing look. 'I'm pleased with the way it went.'

Polite, she was being way too polite. Oh, what in

hell was the matter with her? Confidence had subtly changed to doubt, she acknowledged silently.

Yet the same stubborn resolve which had been responsible for her moving out of his apartment had motivated her to pose a question.

Sure, she mentally derided as she refused dessert and ordered tea. But would he say *yes*?

Except she'd come this far, and she wasn't about to wimp out.

Now, do it now, an inner voice commanded.

It took only seconds to retrieve the carefully written card from her evening bag. She met Jared's gaze with deliberate equanimity as she transferred the rose onto the table beside his plate and added the card.

'A gift,' she offered in explanation. For him, only him. The gift of herself and their unborn child.

Would he accept? Dear lord, she hoped so. A cold hand clutched hold of her heart, and squeezed.

Even thinking of rejection sent her tumbling into a downward spiral towards emotional despair.

There was nothing evident in his expression to indicate his reaction. She'd expected quizzical amusement, maybe a few bantering words in response.

She knew the words by heart. She'd used up a few cards getting the words right.

You are the love of my life. Will you marry me?

She waited, the breath locked in her throat. How long did it take for him to read the words? Assimilate...*answer* them?

It seemed forever before he lifted his head and met her gaze. 'Is there anything you want to add?'

Tasha swallowed painfully. 'This isn't because of the child. It's about *you*.' She gathered courage, and tried to ignore the way her fingers worked the linen napkin on her lap, pleating and re-pleating it in sheer nervousness. 'About not being trapped into something you didn't want,' she said quietly.

'Am I to surmise you don't think that any more?'

How could she? When the lovemaking had been so exquisite, so soul-shattering it had been all she could do not to splinter into a thousand pieces. 'Yes.'

Was she aware of the impact such a simple word had on him? How he'd suffered these past few weeks, wanting, needing, *aching* for her? Unable, helpless to do anything about it?

He hadn't had a decent night's sleep since she moved out of his apartment. The world, as he knew it, had turned upside-down and become a place he didn't want to be if she wasn't there with him.

He looked at her, saw the woman she was, what she'd become...her strengths, values, her integrity. And knew that he'd never take her for granted again. Love was a gift, given from the heart.

'Are you going to tell me what changed your mind?'

So many things, but she revealed the most important of all. 'You could have walked away, but you didn't,' she continued simply. Was that her voice? It sounded impossibly husky.

Something shifted in his eyes, a momentary darkness she couldn't define. 'Not entirely alone.'

She retained a vivid memory of their night together at the Gold Coast when passion had overcome them both.

Tasha managed a slight musing smile. 'No.'

He hadn't given her an answer. Was he stalling? Putting off the moment when he would regretfully decline?

Dear heaven. He couldn't...wouldn't...*No*. The word was a silent scream of despair. The ache of unshed tears filled her eyes, dimming her vision.

'I love you.' Her mouth shook a little, and she sought for control. 'Only you.' Oh, God, she was going to lose it completely. 'When news of the bomb blast broke...the thought you might have died...' She couldn't continue for a few seconds, then she took a deep breath and released it. 'My life would be worth nothing without you.'

Something sighed deep within, effecting a subtle shift in his emotional heart as everything fell into place. The blood coursed through his veins, sang a little.

He'd almost lost her. Thought for a while that he had. Yet he'd fought back, aware nothing came with any guarantees...not even love.

The most precious gift of all, beyond price.

He leant forward and trailed his fingers along the curve of her cheek. 'Yes.'

Yes? Did he mean—?

'I accept your proposal.'

Relief, elation were only two of the immediate emotions she experienced, and he watched as her expressive features lit with a joy so intense it made his heart ache.

'Soon,' Jared added softly. 'Very soon.' He wanted his ring on her finger, not as proof of his ownership, but as visible evidence they belonged to each other.

The waiter appeared at their table and laid a red rose on the tablecloth. 'For you, ma'am.' He cast Jared a smile. 'From your gentleman.'

She was so touched by the gesture she had to fight to hold back the shimmer of tears, and she picked up the rose and admired the soft velvet-like petals curving protectively layer upon layer in perfect symmetry.

'Two minds,' Jared said gently, indicating the rose she'd placed on the table earlier. 'In perfect accord.'

'It's beautiful,' she murmured, and absently stroked the bud with a forefinger. The delicate perfume was much sought-after by the world's top perfumeries, and she could understand why.

Jared summoned immense will-power in order to prevent himself from hauling her into his arms. 'Let's get out of here.'

Her gaze shifted to lock with his, and her eyes darkened at what she saw reflected in those mesmerising depths. 'You haven't finished your coffee.'

He summoned the waiter, settled the bill, then led Tasha out to the car.

She threaded her fingers through his own, and didn't relinquish them as they reached the Jaguar. There was just one last thing she wanted to say, and the words came easily as she met his dark enquiring gaze.

'You let me go. Allowed me time and space alone. I want to thank you for that.'

'It was the hardest thing I've ever had to do.'

But worth it, he assured silently, to have what they now shared…no doubts, no shadows. Just everything he'd hoped, prayed for—and prayer wasn't one of his strong points, except he'd been so desperate he'd have resorted to anything that might give him an edge.

He held her close, and adored the way she sank in against him. They were so completely in tune, so much a part of each other, he could only reflect with regret how he'd loved and cherished her, but had been so far entrenched in a comfort zone he'd neglected to provide the reassurance she needed.

'Your place, or mine?' It was one or the other.

She spared him a musing look as he opened the car door for her. 'Your choice.'

'Mine,' Jared said with satisfaction as the car sped towards the city. 'It's where you belong.'

And where she'd stay. He'd make sure of it. Not that it was the *where* that mattered, as long as she was with him for the rest of his life.

Jared drove with controlled care, the image of her sharing his bed…beneath him, her moist heat, the way her eyes went blank the moment she climaxed. It was enough to almost suspend his breathing.

He reached the underground car park and felt a measure of satisfaction at the faint squeal of rubber on concrete as he eased the Jaguar into its allotted space.

They both slid out at the same time, and joined hands *en route* to the lift. He lifted her hand to his lips during the rapid ascent, and almost drowned in the liquid warmth evident…her soft smile, the almost tremulous quiver of her mouth. A mouth he intended to take with his own the instant they were inside his apartment.

They barely made it. Tasha wanted the feel of skin on skin, the warmth, the heat and heart of him, and she wanted it now.

She slid her hands inside his jacket and pushed it over his shoulders, then her fingers tore at the buttons on his shirt, pulled it free from his trousers, and went for snap, the zip fastener.

Oh, dear heaven, his clean scent was heady like potent wine, and she savoured it with her lips, her tongue, running from shoulder to chest, where she teased the hair curling there, then laved a male nipple before sliding lower.

Jared hauled her up against him, and she wound her legs around his waist, then angled her mouth against his and took him deep, plundering until he held fast her head and savaged her mouth in a hard, hungry kiss that was nowhere near enough to slake their need.

It became his turn to dispense with her clothes, and he did so with economy of movement, then feasted on her breast, suckling, using the edge of his teeth to take her to the brink between pleasure and pain.

The bedroom. The bed. He wanted both, and he made his way there, tumbling her onto the mattress and following her down.

The rest of their clothes were tossed onto the carpet, and his fingers sought the moist heart of her, stroked, then dug deep and felt her go up and over as she groaned his name.

'Please. Now.'

He entered her slowly, relished her slick heat, and the breath husked from his throat as she enclosed him, moved with him as he set the rhythm, urging a pace he consciously controlled to a lesser degree.

It was good. Dear heaven, it was better than *good*.

Afterwards he supported his body above her own, and trailed his lips across her forehead, lingered at one temple, then began the slow slide down her cheek, paused at the edge of her mouth, traced its curve, and settled in a slow, erotic open-mouthed kiss that almost made her weep.

'Not fair,' Tasha murmured, and pushed him to lie on his back as she straddled him.

'Want to play, huh?'

His eyes gleamed as she bent low and nipped at the curve between his neck and shoulder.

'My turn.' She wanted to taste him, absorb his

essence…most of all, she wanted to drive him wild. With want, need, and desire for her. Only her.

She succeeded, with each indrawn breath, each hiss between clenched teeth, a husky groan adding to her euphoria.

There was a tremendous sense of power in pleasuring a man. Taking him to a place where he was no longer in control and completely at her mercy.

The ultimate in surrender. Absolute trust. Man at his most vulnerable.

She loved the way his stomach quivered at her touch, the clench of muscles as her lips teased and tantalised.

It became a glorious sensual feast from which they both emerged satisfied, sated, and emotionally spent.

They slept for a while, then woke through the night and sought each other again. And again.

It wasn't enough, would never be enough, and as the sun rose above the horizon Jared carried her into the *en suite*, ran the shower, then stepped into the large cubicle and picked up the soap.

Tasha simply closed her eyes and went with the intimate luxury of having him administer to her.

He was so incredibly gentle it almost made her weep, and she swayed slightly as his hand splayed over her stomach and lingered there.

When he was done, she took the soap from him and returned the favour, her eyes narrowing as she glimpsed bruises forming over his ribs, the edge of one shoulder, on the curve of his hip.

'Turn around.' When he didn't budge, she stepped round behind him and examined his back, found evidence of more bruising, and gritted her teeth. 'You should have told me.' A soft curse fell from her lips. 'Dammit, Jared. You should have been more careful when we—'

'I didn't feel a thing at the time.'

His voice held humour, and she lightly slapped his butt. 'I love it when you get physical.' He reached out and closed the water dial, then his eyes darkened as he felt the press of her lips against one bruise, and he stood still as she gently caressed each bruise in turn.

When she reached the last, he hauled her close and kissed her with infinite tenderness. Then he caught up a towel and gently dried her before applying the towel to himself.

He carried her back to bed, curled her in close, and pulled up the covers.

CHAPTER ELEVEN

THEY rose late, dressed, and went into the kitchen to cook breakfast. Jared took care of the eggs, bacon and hash-browns, while Tasha tended to the toast, tea and coffee.

There was no rush, and they took their time, sampling toast, offering each other a succulent piece of bacon, then lingered over tea and coffee.

Together they cleared the table, rinsed dishes and stacked them in the dishwasher.

'There's something I want to show you.'

Tasha closed the dishwasher and turned towards him. Attired in jeans and a black T-shirt, he looked ruggedly attractive and vaguely piratical. Absent was the formality of a barrister at law, and her stomach executed a slow somersault at the way the T-shirt emphasised his muscular breadth of shoulder.

She had a vivid memory of how she'd clung to him through the night, over and over again, in a sensual dance that had been without equal.

Jared crossed to her side, caught hold of her hand and threaded his fingers through her own. 'Let's go.'

She lifted her face to his, saw the purposeful gleam apparent, and offered a warm laugh. 'Do I get to ask *where*?'

He bestowed a brief, hard kiss to her mouth, then softened it with a slow sweep of his tongue. 'No.' He led her into the lounge, collected his keys and slid them into his pocket. 'I want it to be a surprise.'

'OK.'

He slanted her a musing smile. 'Just *OK*?'

'You want I should argue?'

His mouth curved, deepening the faint vertical grooves slashing each cheek. 'Sassy, huh?'

She lifted their linked hands to her mouth and brushed his knuckles with her lips. 'Happy,' she declared quietly. 'And so in love with you.'

Jared paused in reaching for the door, and drew her into his arms. His lips touched her temple, then trailed to the edge of her mouth, savoured the sensual curve and absorbed the sound of his name as it rose from her throat.

A hand slid beneath her hair, cupping her nape, angling her head as he embarked on an evocative tasting that left her weak-willed and yearning.

He released her slowly, and his eyes darkened as she ran the edge of her tongue over her lower lip.

'If we don't get out of here, I doubt we'll make it at all,' Tasha opined shakily.

Without a word Jared reached out and opened the door, and they crossed the foyer to the bank of lifts, where one took them down to the basement carpark.

Jared set the Jaguar across the bridge spanning the river, and drove through the city to suburban Ascot.

Late spring saw many gardens bursting with flowers, their colours varying from a wild, unplanned mix to sculptured colour-co-ordinated beds carefully tended by an expert's hand. Neat mown lawns, symmetrical topiary, and clipped shrubbery.

A delightful suburb, with beautiful tree-lined avenues, spacious older homes, some of which were set in their original grounds and occupied by second- and third-generation families.

There were also the newer residences, built of brick and stone, cement-rendered, modern, with floor-to-ceiling glass the better to view the river and inner harbour.

Tasha was intrigued when Jared turned off the main road circling the river and began an ascending gradient that took them high onto the hill.

'I'm not exactly dressed for visiting anyone,' she began cautiously, aware of her jeans and top, and he offered a warm smile.

'You're fine as you are,' he assured as he accessed an avenue, drove a hundred metres, then turned into a curved driveway.

The house stood well back in large, spacious grounds, and it was all she could do not to breathe an appreciative sigh as she admired its gracious lines, the verandas framing the east and west sides. French doors, shutters…a beautiful blend of stunning architecture.

The only thing blotting such perfection was a cavernous hole in the grounds, and a mound of builders' supplies which indicated interior renovations together with the addition of a swimming pool.

The view was fantastic, and would hold an even wider scope from any of the upstairs windows. Although she doubted she'd have the opportunity to see it.

Jared drew the car to a halt and released his seat belt. 'Let's go in, shall we?'

Tasha followed suit and slid to her feet. There was a gentle breeze, the air crisp and clean, and she caught the drift of scented roses from a manicured rose-bed near by.

'Are we expected?' It was Saturday, mid-morning. The owners could be out, or perhaps ferrying children to a sports activity.

At that moment the double front door opened and a middle-aged couple stood framed in the aperture.

'Mr North.'

Mr North seemed formal, unless they were clients. Which hardly made sense, when this was supposedly a social call.

'Amy and Joe Falconer. Tasha Peterson.' Jared performed the introduction. 'Amy and Joe are live-in caretakers until the renovations are completed.'

Disbelief was replaced by incredulity as she searched his features. 'This is your house?' Pleasure lent a sparkle to her eyes. 'You bought it?'

'Yes. Let's go indoors and explore.' He placed a hand on her shoulder. 'You can tell me if you like it.'

Large rooms, polished floors, high ceilings... She moved from room to room, loving the open fireplace, the spaciousness, the wide curved staircase leading to the upper floor.

'What's not to like?'

Delight was evident in her expression, and he curved an arm around her shoulders as they ascended the stairs.

Tasha listened to his plans as he led her along a wide central hallway. 'The bedroom next to the master bedroom is being turned into a nursery,' he outlined, indicating the partly finished structural changes. 'And the two rooms on this side will become a study and law library.'

There were three remaining bedrooms, two of which connected to an *en suite*, and a larger room with its own *en suite*.

'What do you think?'

'It's beautiful,' she said with heartfelt sincerity.

'The decorators are due to start the week after next. I want you to have an input in the colour scheme. Then there's furniture and furnishings.'

He had everything in hand, and that took some planning. 'When did you buy the house?' She told herself it didn't matter, that knowing was merely a curiosity factor.

'I've had my eye on it for some time.'

'That doesn't answer the question.'

He grasped both her hands, then slid his own up her arms to close over each shoulder. 'I clinched the deal within days of you telling me you were pregnant.'

'You were that sure of me?'

'I was sure of my own feelings,' he said gently. 'Certain I wanted to be with you for the rest of my life.' He cupped her face, tilted it. 'I just needed to prove it to you.'

She wasn't capable of saying a word.

'There are a couple more things.' He released her and reached into the pocket of his jeans. 'This.' He caught hold of her left hand and slid a ring onto her finger.

This was an exquisitely cut pear-shaped diamond which tore the breath from her throat.

'We have a date with a minister two weeks from today.'

'Two *weeks*?' She could feel her head begin to spin. 'You're joking...aren't you?' She couldn't possibly organise a dress—

'No,' Jared refuted, watching the play of emotions on her expressive features. 'And yes, you can,' he added gently, reading her mind. 'I'll arrange the reception venue, caterers. Just family and close friends. All you need to do is take care of yourself.'

And he did. Calling in favours, arranging everything down to the finest detail.

Tasha enlisted Eloise as her matron of honour, and her life became a whirlwind as they did the bridal boutiques, the couture houses, added lingerie to the list, indulged in a facial, massage, and bought make-up.

'Shop till you drop' was Eloise's favoured *modus operandi*. Add a full work schedule, and each day seemed more hectic than the last. At night Tasha fell asleep in Jared's arms, then rose to repeat the previous day all over again.

'You'll stay with us the night before the wedding,' Eloise declared, only to have Jared issue a rebuttal.

'The hell you will.'

'Don't want to let me out of your sight, huh?'

'Got it in one. Besides, Eloise will keep you up all night talking "girl-talk".'

That was entirely possible, and she offered him a wicked smile. 'I'll tell her to be here at ten.'

'The groom isn't supposed to see the bride on her wedding day until she walks down the aisle,' Eloise protested fiercely when Tasha relayed she'd be leaving for the church from Jared's apartment. 'Don't you *dare* imagine you're riding in the same car to the church.'

'Separate times, different cars,' Tasha vouched.

'That's OK, then. Now,' Eloise continued with unquenchable enthusiasm. 'Let's go through our list again.'

With only one day to go, 'the list' had diminished to a few last-minute essentials. Thank heavens. There had been times when elopement seemed an enviable option.

It was late when she slid into bed, and she sighed as Jared drew her close.

'Relax,' he bade quietly. 'And enjoy.'

He began with her feet, massaging gently, easing out the kinks in her calves, thighs, and she closed her eyes. It was heaven, all of it. A lover's touch.

There was nothing to surpass the blissful release of emotions.

When her breathing became deep and even, he carefully pulled up the bedcovers and settled down beside her, content in the knowledge of what the next day would bring.

Saturday dawned with a sprinkle of rain which cleared by mid-morning, followed by warm sunshine and azure skies.

It was a perfect day for a wedding. Although Tasha wouldn't have cared if the heavens opened and provided a deluge of rain. It was the occasion that held importance, not the weather.

'Nervous?'

She stood still as Eloise fixed the coronet of miniature roses in place.

'No.' There were no doubts, no hidden insecurities. Just a feeling of everything being right.

Eloise pressed the last hairclip in place, then stepped back to admire her handiwork. 'Beautiful,' she complimented gently and met Tasha's smile via mirrored reflection.

'Thanks.'

She'd chosen simplicity over froth and frills for her gown, and the fitted bodice with its scooped neckline, capped sleeves and gently billowing skirt complimented her slender figure.

A single pearl on a delicate gold chain and matching ear-studs completed the image, and her make-up was skilfully minimal.

'OK, sweetheart,' Eloise declared with impish affection. 'Let's get this show on the road.'

Family and close friends were already gathered inside the small stone church when the hired limousine deposited Tasha and Eloise immediately adjacent to the main doors.

Monica stood inside the vestibule, and she stepped forward to give Tasha a reassuring hug. 'I love you.'

Tears shimmered in the woman's eyes, and Tasha felt her own fill with moisture. 'Ditto,' she responded quietly.

'Cool it,' Eloise admonished succinctly. 'Smile now, cry later. Think *happy*.'

'We are,' Tasha and her prospective mother-in-law assured in unison.

'Jared's waiting.'

And he was, standing tall with his back to the altar as he watched his bride step down the aisle.

Tasha saw only him, and her gaze became trapped in his as the congregation faded from her vision. It was as if they were the only two people in the world, and her mouth trembled at the depth of emotion evident in those dark eyes. For her.

Her breath caught in her throat, and she was prepared to swear her heart stopped beating for a few seconds as sheer joy became an overwhelming entity.

She reached him as no other woman ever had, or ever would. Truly beautiful where beauty really mattered…in the heart and soul. It was something he'd never hold back from telling her.

Just as he had no intention of holding back now. To hell with convention and protocol.

Jared lifted his hands and captured her face, then he lowered his head and kissed her…with such lingering thoroughness it almost melted her bones.

'If the bride and groom are ready, perhaps we can begin?'

There was a ripple of amused laughter from the guests, and Tasha whispered, 'This is a serious occasion.'

'I've never been more serious in my life,' Jared reiterated, and brushed his lips to hers for good measure.

The ceremony held a special significance, as did the solemn words binding them together, and afterwards their shared happiness was something to behold, bringing a catch to many a female throat as the evening progressed.

It was almost ten when they took their leave, and used a chauffeured limousine to drive them to Jared's apartment, where they changed into casual clothes, collected overnight bags and took the limousine down to the Gold Coast.

Constraints of work and his appearance in court meant they only had the weekend, and they'd opted for the Main Beach apartment rather than a hotel.

Jared switched on the lights and locked the door as Tasha crossed the lounge and stood looking out at the view through floor-to-ceiling glass.

Tall apartment buildings with various lit windows outlined against an indigo sky. A steady stream of cars traversing the highway with their twin beams of light. The inky blackness of the river flowing out into the open sea.

'Looking at something in particular?' Jared drawled from behind.

She'd sensed rather than heard him cross the room, and she leaned back against him as his arms circled her waist.

'It's beautiful,' she said simply, indicating the night-scape. 'I don't think you could ever get tired of looking at it.'

He rested his chin on top of her head. 'Did I tell you how much I love you?'

She smiled, a warm, generous curve widening her mouth. 'Not in the last few hours.'

'Or how beautiful you are?'

'A girl could get a swelled head,' she teased lightly, and felt his lips shift to nuzzle at the edge of her neck. Sensation shimmered through her body, heating her blood with need.

'I want to hold you, touch you,' he said gently as he swept an arm beneath her knees and lifted her against his chest. 'And never let you go.'

Heaven, she breathed with a sigh, was right here with him. Deep in her heart she knew it always would be.

'Sweet-talking me into bed, huh?' She linked her hands at his nape and pressed a string of kisses to the edge of his jaw.

'Do I need to?'

He reached the bedroom and gently released her to her feet.

'I'm yours,' Tasha vowed softly, pulling his head down to hers. 'Always.'

The kiss became an erotic, evocative imitation of the sexual act itself, satisfying to a degree, but not enough.

Her hands tugged the shirt free from his trousers as he reached for the hem of her top, and seconds later they caressed warm, silk-smooth skin, the touch of lips, hands brought forth a telling sigh, a husky groan in the prelude to a long, sweet loving lasting far into the night.

They rarely made it out of the apartment during their stay, and only left the bed to shower and eat.

Monday morning they rose soon after the dawn, showered, dressed, drove to Tedder Avenue, where they ate breakfast at one of several pavement cafés, then they joined the stream of traffic traversing the highway to Brisbane.

Jared drew the car into the pavement outside her office building and pressed a brief, hard kiss to her mouth.

'Have a good day.' His smile was something else, and she could have drowned in the wealth of emotion in his dark eyes. 'Take care.'

She trailed gentle fingers down his cheek. 'You too.'

His hand closed round her wrist and brought her

fingers to his lips, touching them to the ring he'd placed there only two days ago. 'Until tonight.'

She wanted to laugh and cry at the same time. 'Count on it.' Then she slid from the seat, closed the door, and stood watching as he eased the car into the traffic.

Life, she accorded in silent bemusement, didn't get any better than this.

EPILOGUE

SIOBHAN MARIE NORTH made her appearance into the world three days early via an emergency Caesarean section, and proved with ear-splitting velocity there was nothing wrong with her lungs...or anything else, thank you very much.

Her father was utterly captivated at first sight, treating her as something so infinitely precious he intended to fiercely defend with his dying breath.

Dark hair, delicate features, she resembled her mother in miniature, with an impatience to feed that hinted at a strong mind.

'Stubborn,' Jared teased gently.

'Determined,' Tasha corrected, and felt her heart melt at the depth of love evident as he watched mother and child.

His gaze lifted to meet hers, and the heat in it seared right through to her soul. 'How soon before you can come home?'

Her smile held a mischievous sparkle. 'Five or six days.'

They took Siobhan home on the sixth day to be greeted by a doting grandmother. Monica revelled in the role, and organised meals, household chores for a few weeks, and returned for the christening.

A year to the day when Tasha had first discovered

her pregnancy. The date had been a coincidental choice, and she wondered if Jared realised its significance.

Their daughter had been changed and fed, and was on the verge of sleep as her parents stood close by, arms entwined round each other's waist.

The nursery light had been dimmed, the baby intercom system switched on, and a sense of peace reigned.

'No regrets?' Tasha queried quietly.

'Not one.'

His incredulity meant more than the words.

'I'm glad.'

'Independence is a fine thing in a woman,' Jared said gently, lowering his head to brush his lips to hers. 'But you didn't stand a chance of it being anything other than temporary.'

A matter of weeks, she mused in retrospect, her flight from his apartment and their separation a vivid memory.

'She's asleep,' he confirmed softly, easing his wife from the room.

The christening had gone well, Siobhan was a model babe, and the small celebration for family and close friends had been a success.

Now Jared had a few plans of his own.

'I should go downstairs and—'

'No.'

'No?'

'I have something else in mind.'

'Such as?'

'The way I figure it, we have three hours before our daughter is due to wake.'

An impish bubble of laughter escaped her throat. 'And in those three hours you hope to achieve...?'

His hand slid down to cup her bottom, then traced her spine to settle at her nape. 'A leisurely love-making with my wife.'

'I think that could be arranged.'

'A little persuasion might help?'

Tasha turned in to him and pulled his head down to hers. 'Try me.'

He did. With such care, his degree of *tendresse* made her want to cry.

'I love you.' Words eloquently spoken in the aftermath of passion.

Words they both knew they'd repeat again and again in the years to follow as they travelled life's journey together. And beyond.